"Phaedra, y
further

"You don't want me to touch you, just tell me. I just want to see you. Just let me look at you." He released the straps of her dress, letting them dangle down her back, yet the dress remained in place, hugging tightly to her curves. Bastien didn't lower the dress, but waited for Phaedra to show him the boundaries of where he could go.

Phaedra reached for Bastien's linen shirt and tugged upward. He shrugged out of it, draping it over the shower wall, and she splayed her hands across his chest, feeling the heat emanating from his skin. Bastien's unique scent wafted to her—smelling like all the best things of summer.

Phaedra couldn't resist. She had to know if Bastien tasted as good as he smelled, as delicious as he looked. She stood on tiptoe, wrapped her arms around his neck for leverage, and touched the tip of her tongue to his bottom lip. As she rose on her toes, the dress fell away, pooling at her feet.

GERI GUILLAUME

is the pseudonym for Krystal Williams Livingston. Mrs. Livingston was born in Jackson, Mississippi, in 1965. She received her undergraduate degree from Rice University in Houston, Texas, where she double-majored in English and legal studies. She is currently a full-time project manager for a documentation, training and marketing communications firm, as well as the mother of two wonderful children. Between her project management duties, volunteer work at church, her family and creative writing, Mrs. Livingston still holds firmly to her motto, "Too many words; not enough paper. Thank God there's e-mail!" This rallying cry has helped her publish several contemporary romance novels, a play for her alma mater and a family reunion planning guide. Mrs. Livingston currently makes her home in Houston, Texas.

Kiss Me Twice

Twice

GERI GUILLAUME

If you purchased this book without a cover you should be aware
that this book is stolen property. It was reported as "unsold and
destroyed" to the publisher, and neither the author nor the
publisher has received any payment for this "stripped book."

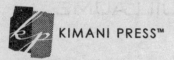

KIMANI PRESS™

ISBN-13: 978-0-373-86142-2

Recycling programs
for this product may
not exist in your area.

KISS ME TWICE

Copyright © 2009 by Krystal Williams

All rights reserved. The reproduction, transmission or utilization
of this work in whole or in part in any form by any electronic, mechanical
or other means, now known or hereafter invented, including xerography,
photocopying and recording, or in any information storage or retrieval
system, is forbidden without written permission. For permission please
contact Kimani Press, Editorial Office, 233 Broadway, New York, NY
10279 U.S.A.

This is a work of fiction. Names, characters, places and incidents are
either the product of the author's imagination or are used fictitiously,
and any resemblance to actual persons, living or dead, business establishments,
events or locales is entirely coincidental.

® and TM are trademarks. Trademarks indicated with ® are registered in
the United States Patent and Trademark Office, the Canadian Trade Marks
Office and/or other countries.

www.kimanipress.com

Printed in U.S.A.

Dear Reader,

It's been several years since I put the story of Jacie and Chas from *A Perfect Pair* and their experiences in the grain-inspection world to paper. Jacie began that story in dire straits—jobless, close to eviction, not knowing where her next dollar would come from. For *Kiss Me Twice,* I wanted to take a different approach. I wanted to pay homage to all of the hardworking women out there, all the women that I've ever had the pleasure of knowing personally or casually meeting, who've kept it together and were totally confident in their abilities. All of the women who'd ever mentored me, either directly or indirectly, became the model for my new heroine Phaedra.

Not to say that Phaedra's perfect. She has her own set of issues. But I'm hoping that you can take away a piece of her spirit—that spirit of uncompromising excellence, commitment to her chosen career, a heart for showing charity to others *and* a heart for her man. I hope you enjoy reading about Phaedra and Bastien's story as much as I've enjoyed writing it.

Until next time, dear reader!

Geri

Thank you, my precious family, for giving me the time—and the freedom—to continue my craft.

This novel is dedicated to my wonderful, supportive family. For my husband Robert, who provides the technical expertise for his ever-changing inspection industry. For my daughter RáVen, who has given me the great privilege of watching her blossom with confidence as she juggles church, career and her continuing education. And for my son William, whose quick wit and dry humor keeps me laughing even in the most stressful situations.

Chapter 1

The company van rolled by him. Yet Bastien Thibeadaux hardly recognized it. When his cousin Remy took it out of the garage yesterday, it looked nothing like it was looking now.

Remy, what in the world have you done now?

All Remy had to do was take the van out for a simple detailing job to prep it for a magazine ad photo shoot they'd scheduled. Wash and wax. Vacuum out the inside. Maybe touch up the plain white paint and the black stenciled letters bearing the company name and logo—CT Inspectorate. A simple job. Two hours tops. Now, nearly a day later, Remy was just getting back to the office. Just in time for quitting time. Typical Remy.

For maximum effect, Remy coasted by as if to make certain all eyes were on him. Bastien couldn't actually see his cousin behind the smoky, reflective tinted windows, but he could imagine Remy's *I'm all that* expression. Bastien caught his own scowling reflection in the window as Remy passed by him. He felt the vibrating thrum of the van's radio cranked high through the thick soles of his work boots as he stood out in the parking

lot along with some of his employees. He simmered as Remy
tried to maneuver the van into its parking spot. Hard to make
those tight turns, Bastien observed, now that Remy had replaced
the standard rims and tires with custom chrome rims and high-
profile tires.

"Are those twenty-twos?" Alonzo Benavidez, Bastien's first
shift crew chief, slid his sunglasses down onto the tip of his nose
and peered over the edge in admiration of Remy's new chrome
hubcaps. "*Dang!* That boy's rolling large."

"Those aren't twenty-twos. Those are thirty-inch rims…Gio-
vannas," Jayden Jeffers, Bastien's summer hire corrected.

"How would you know that?" Bastien asked. He knew the boy
was all about cars. His locker was jam-packed with trade magazines.

"I saw my brother searching on a rims Web site. My brother's
been saving up for three months for a set to put on his Hummer
H2."

"Here, let me get that for you." Melvin Weldon, the oldest
employee on Bastien's crew, peeled his sweat-drenched
bandanna off his head and made a motion as if to wipe the drool
from Jayden's mouth.

Jayden jerked his head back, distracted from Remy's grand
entrance by the sour smell of Melvin's sweat band. "Man, get
that funky rag out of my face." He turned back when Remy
revved the van's engine and stomped on the brakes to make the
van surge forward several times.

"Look at this fool here," Bastien muttered.

He immediately regretted that he'd said that out loud. He
should have kept his mouth shut. Remy wasn't only his cousin.
Like it or not, he was also his boss. And it just wasn't cool to
talk about your boss in front of the other employees.

Alonzo, Melvin and Jayden had all gathered in the parking
lot to firm up plans for hooking up later. Once a month Bastien
took his team away so they could talk openly, honestly—sometimes brutally honest—about what was going on around CT Inspectorate. Just as Remy pulled up, they'd decided to meet up

at Solly's Fast Lanz bowling alley and come up with solutions to their problems over a couple games and appetizers.

Bastien lifted his hand to call Remy over to them, but Remy ignored him and remained seated in the van with his eyes trained forward. One arm was draped across the steering wheel that he drummed while his head bobbed to the music. Remy looked over at Bastien's crew, acknowledging them with a lift of his chin and an implied "what's up?"

Bastien turned back to the group. "You guys go on ahead. I'll meet up with you at Solly's as soon as I finish up with Remy."

"You sure you don't want us to wait for you, boss? Maybe Remy will give us a ride to the bowling alley?" Jayden suggested.

Alonzo made a rude sound of dismissal. "You volunteering to ride in the company van? You were never that hot on riding in the van before."

"I think maybe Jayden is hoping that showing up at Fast Lanz in that will get him some action from the ladies," Melvin added. It was Monday night. Ladies' league night at Solly's.

"Nobody's riding in that clown car," Bastien said in disgust, gesturing at the newly applied vinyl decals. Trendy or not, Bastien thought the new decals were a hot mess. The tackiest custom detail job he'd ever seen. Orange flames shooting out of what was supposed to be a greenish-gray navy destroyer slicing through a swaying ocean of psychedelic purple wheat. A navy destroyer instead of a cargo vessel. What in the world was that supposed to convey in the magazine ad? That CT Inspectorate blew up its products *and* was color blind?

When Remy didn't get out right away, Bastien strode over to the van, planted his hands on the door and leaned in.

"Remy," he ground out his greeting through clenched teeth.

"I already know what you're going to say." Remy cut him off.

"No, I don't think you do. What is this supposed to be?"

"What? You don't like it?" Remy lifted an eyebrow in genuine surprise.

"Are you kidding me?"

"What are you so pissed off about?"

"Because G-Paw told me to prep the van for the magazine ad. Not pimp it."

Bastien wasn't looking forward to confessing to the owner of the company that he'd blown their entire advertising budget for the year with Remy's stunt. One magazine ad. That's all they were getting because of the money he must have put down for this. No more sixty-second television spots that Bastien had already lined up with a local basketball fan favorite to be their pitchman. No more traveling for trade shows where Bastien could get out and press the flesh of potential contracts. And they could forget sponsoring the local high school sports teams. Bastien would just have to call the athletic director and tell her that Inspectorate couldn't do it this year.

In his mind's eye, Bastien watched in frustration as the future growth of his division dried up and blew away on the wind like ashes from deliberately torched grain fields. All scorched by the withering glare of Charles Harrison Thibeadaux—the power behind CT Inspectorate. Everyone in the family called him G-Paw. Grandpa. In a normal family, that would have been a term of endearment. Nothing normal about his family, Bastien would be the first to admit. And nothing normal about the way that old man treated them either. The *G* might as well have stood for godforsaken. G-Paw was a tough old man—spawned, suckled and saved by Satan himself. G-Paw didn't have much love for his family. It was all poured into his grain inspection business. He knew how to handle his business and had not a whit of patience for those working with him who didn't have the same level of good business sense. A sentiment that he shared and pushed Remy, the number two man in the company, to enforce.

Too bad Remy didn't understand the spirit of what G-Paw was trying to do, Bastien commiserated.

Remy reminded Bastien of his perceived incompetence every day for the four years since Bastien transferred here from their Louisiana office. From the time he walked through the doors in the morning until the time Bastien clocked out, Remy was on his back. As far as Remy was concerned, Bastien was there at his indulgence, and either he would shape up to be a good little company man or he could ship out. Literally. Ship out with the next load of company-inspected grain heading for China, South America, Italy or any of the other international ports with which they did business.

"I told you that I'd take care of it." Remy's insistence brought Bastien out of his mental downward spiral of dejection.

"Take care of it, huh? You want to tell me how you got all of this accomplished on the shoestring budget I've been given."

"Don't you worry about it. I handled it."

"Remy," Bastien repeated.

"I said I handled it, okay? Now back up, Bastien!"

Bastien yanked on the door handle of the van, flinging it open, thinking that he was going to grab Remy by the scruff of his neck, toss him in the back of the van and beat the smug look off his face. "Get out of there, Remy," he ordered.

"Who do you think you're talking to?" Remy bristled.

Bastien modulated his tone. "Give me the keys. I'll put the van back into the garage."

Bastien thought if he could just get this monstrosity out of sight before anyone else saw it, he still might have time to clean up Remy's mess. Maybe he could call in a favor from a friend of his who owned a dealership. Borrow a similar looking van, rush to an overnight print shop and get a banner made with the company name and logo. Whatever he did, it would have to be fast and cheap.

"What for?"

So I can see what I can do to fix this hot, steaming mess you dropped in my lap, Bastien wanted to say. "Because it's going to rain," Bastien said reasonably. "You don't want your new detail job to be ruined by the rain, do you? Give me the keys and let me handle this."

He kept his voice low and looked back over his shoulder. His crew hadn't gone yet. They weren't exactly eavesdropping but they weren't making any moves to disperse, either. When Bastien looked back at them, Melvin shoved his hands in his coverall pockets and bent his head to examine his shoes, Jayden pretended to be scraping dirt from his fingernails with his pocketknife, and Alonzo suddenly seemed to be more interested in the clouds sailing overhead than in the brewing confrontation between Remy and Bastien.

"You don't have to handle anything," Remy said, stepping out of the van. He slapped at his chest with his open palm. "I told you. I've got this. The only thing you need to do is get me that work rotation schedule."

Bastien blinked, caught off guard by Remy's request. Bastien knew by Remy's tone that it wasn't a request. He was serious.

"The rotation schedule?"

"The new rotation schedule for the month. I need it on my desk before you leave tonight."

"It's due Fridays," Bastien reminded him. "By close of business." Bastien never failed to provide the shift schedule to Remy on time. It had been due every Friday since before he started working at CT Inspectorate. Why was Remy sweating him now for it?

"I'll be too busy to review it Friday. I need it now, Bastien, before you leave."

Bastien considered telling Remy what he could do with that rotation schedule. It was only Monday. Remy didn't need it now.

"Fine," Bastien conceded. "You'll have it on your desk when you get into the office in the morning."

"I don't think you heard me," Remy said. "I want it tonight. And I want it done right." Remy paused, giving Bastien a humorless smile by forcing up the corners of his mouth. "Whatcha eyeballing me for, cuz? It's not my fault we're a couple men short and have to jump through hoops to make up for lost time. Your screwup. You fix it."

Bastien couldn't argue with that. One of the reasons he was taking his crew off-site was to discuss a rash of accidents that had put one of his employees in the hospital, another on administrative leave. But he didn't need Remy throwing that fact in his face. Bastien was all too aware of the problems his workers had.

"Fine," Bastien repeated, turning his back on Remy. He called out to the group, still waiting for him, and waved them on.

"You boys go on and get the party started without me," he said. "I won't be long." He hustled inside and wondered if all his extra efforts could truly turn his accident-plagued division around.

Chapter 2

By the time Bastien pulled into the parking lot at the Fast Lanz bowling alley four hours later than he'd planned, it was almost closing time. The parking lot was close to empty with a scattering of vehicles that he didn't recognize. None of the cars that remained belonged to his employees. So he pulled into a spot near the side entrance, waving at Solly's son Samuel, who was hauling trash out to the Dumpster.

"They're all gone, Mr. T," Samuel said in greeting as he struggled to lift the heavy plastic lid on the huge, industrial Dumpster and toss in two overstuffed garbage bags.

"I figured that," Bastien said, grabbing a couple bags himself and flinging them into the bin. One by one, as each of his employees had left the bowling alley, they'd called while he was still in his office finishing Remy's schedule or left messages on his cell phone.

"Dad is still inside," Samuel said, pointing with his thumb back over his shoulder.

Bastien went inside and found his friend sitting at one of the tables across from the snack bar.

Solomon Greenwood looked up and pulled out a chair.

"You're late," he said in greeting. "The others waited as long as they could then had to cut out."

Bastien flopped down in a chair, a sudden weariness dragging his shoulders in a slump. "I know. I saw Samuel outside and he told me." Bastien paused and asked, "What did he do that you've got him on trash detail?"

Samuel was only five feet tall, small for a fifteen year old. He suffered from asthma and looked as though one of those trash bags would crush him if they fell on him. Solly usually kept him on light cleanup detail: straightening the shoe rack, wiping down the lane keypads with disinfectant wipes, restocking the restrooms.

"Sammy brought home a D in algebra," Solly growled. "Got his head twisted around by some little gal in his English class so he's lost his focus."

"Give him a break, Solly. Samuel's a good kid."

"And he needs good grades to get into a good college. I ain't playin' with that boy, Bastien. He's got two weeks to bring that D up or I swear I'm gonna kill him."

"You're not gonna hurt your only son," Bastien contradicted. He rose from his seat, walked around to the snack bar and started to help himself to whatever wasn't put away. He made himself a heaping tray of corn chips and drowned it with two ladles of melted cheese and chili sauce.

He pulled a bottled soda out of the cooler for himself and a beer for Solly, then rejoined him at the table.

"You missed out," Solly told Bastien. "Without you at the table tonight, it was all ragging and no resolutions. What are you going to do about the gripe this month?" Solly initiated the conversation. "The crew said no raises this year. Salaries are frozen. Is that right?"

"Not much I can do, now. My budget's busted. You know what that fool Remy did?"

Solly threw back his head, laughing so loud that it echoed through the entire bowling alley. "Yeah, I heard. You should have been here to hear Jayden scheming about how he was gonna take the keys from Remy. Remy had better watch his back. That young blood's got some creative ideas for jacking your cousin for that van."

"Oh, you think that's funny?" Bastien was not amused. "Thanks to Remy, my advertising budget is gone. No advertising, no new customers. No new customers, no contracts. No contracts, no bonus payouts."

"Yeah, I understand. Though I can't complain myself. This economy's kicking our tails, but my business is up fifteen percent." He shook a handful of receipts at Bastien. "Will you look at this? You know what they're calling staying close to home to have fun? Staycations! This is the best month I've had all year, and it's only May."

"Glad to hear business is good for you," Bastien said with a wry smile. "I've got G-Paw on my back about those lost time accidents. Folks that I hired on and I vouched for are messin' up—got Chas to convince G-Paw to pay for their transfer and moving expenses from the Louisiana office. Now they're all messing up! I've had one slip and fall. One serious cut on the hand. Sliced a nerve so that I don't know if he'll ever be back to work. One railcar loaded with the wrong product. I nearly lost us a major account by the time we figured that one out. And one fool nearly took a tumble off a walkway when I warned him, *warned* him, to keep his hands on the rails and to secure his tie line."

"I heard them talking about it. But I didn't know it was that bad for you, B. What have you done to take care of it?"

"Maybe you should ask what I haven't tried! I tried talking to my crew. I've tried yellin' at them and threatenin'—no promisin'—to dock their pay if they didn't straighten themselves out. I've tried random drug tests to make sure they weren't passin' something around. I've tried making extra meetings to talk about safety concerns. Nothing seems to work, Solly. I can't get those guys to follow a few simple rules. What am I supposed to do about that? If I don't get those lost time accidents under control…"

Bastien didn't have to finish the sentence. Solly already knew. That crusty old owner of CT Inspectorate was well into his nineties, but he could still swing a big stick. He made sure everybody around there knew it, too. He didn't let anything come between him and his ability to make money. That included his own family.

Solly leaned forward, clasped his hands in front of him, tapping his mouth in concentration.

"What kind of a budget do you have left?"

"Not much. I've got to go back and crunch the numbers. It's almost the end of the quarter. Nobody's spending any money. Nobody but Remy that is. I'm looking for creative ways to do more with less, and Remy's out there blowin' it as fast as I can bring it in."

"What's he doing with it? Besides tricking out your van, that is?"

Bastien shrugged. "I don't see most of the invoices for the company. But I heard through the grapevine that over half of my operations budget is being spent on entertainment. Remy's supposedly been wining and dining potential clients. Not much left for me to work with."

"Why does that old man let him get away with it?"

"I think the old man is slowing down. He's sick and he's tired. It's either that or Remy is drugging him to keep him out of his hair."

Solly grunted in agreement. He toyed with his beer bottle, peeling off the label in slow strips. He then set the bottle down on the table with a thump and said, "I might know somebody who could help you."

"Who?" Bastien didn't want to sound too hopeful. But he was running out of options and didn't know what else to try.

"A consultant."

"*Aw...hell, naw.* I know what that means." Bastien threw up his hands. He didn't trust consultants. Even after all of his research and verifying business references, the last consultant he dealt with back in New Orleans cashed the hefty check he'd written then filed for bankruptcy before he could finish the job. It was a hard lesson, one that Bastien took very personally. Maybe it skewed his perspective and made him overly suspicious of consultants, but overly suspicious meant more money kept in the company's bank account.

"You want me to throw away what little credibility I have left with the company on some pencil-pushing desk jockey who doesn't know the first thing about my business but will charge me out the behind to pretend that they do. Uh-uh. No way, Solly. Forget it."

"Wait a minute now, before you shoot me down. Just hear me out."

Bastien folded his arms across his chest, leaned back in the chair and set his face into a deep scowl. "Go on."

Solly took advantage of Bastien's distance from the table to reach for his chili cheese chips. He shoved a few into his mouth, crunched for a few minutes and wiped his hands on his already food-stained bowling shirt. "I know this lady. She's really sharp and classy."

"Who is she? And what's she got to do with the inspection business?"

"Her name's Phaedra Burke-Carter. Her cousin is Darryl Burke-Carter. Do you remember him?"

"Something about that name sounds familiar." Bastien snapped his fingers a couple of times, trying to remember.

"His family's big money here in Houston. They started the Burke-Carter Foundation."

Bastien drew his eyebrows together. His expression showed his ignorance.

"You know, the Burke-Carter foundation," Solly insisted as if repeating the words slowly would clear up the mystery for Bastien. "One of the largest independent, charitable foundations in west Texas. A clearinghouse for all kinds of grants. Education. Medical research. Community development. Promotion of the arts. Human rights welfare. If there's a worthy cause to be found, the Burke-Carters are champions of it."

"Hey, I'm not from here. I'm Louisiana bayou, born and bred."

"Don't you pull that Louisiana-bayou-born-and-bred routine with me. You only lay on that Creole accent thick as gumbo when you want to get to the ladies. You went to Prairie View A&M here in Texas, just like I did."

"But I finished up at LSU."

"But you brought your tail back and got your MBA from the

University of Houston. You've been here long enough to become a naturalized Texan."

"Naturalized my behind. I'll go back as soon as there's something to go back to."

"You ain't goin' anywhere," Solly predicted with certainty. "You've got too much invested here."

"All I've got here is trouble," Bastien muttered.

"I told you, I think I know the lady who can get you out of it. Burke-Carters are local philanthropists," Solly went on.

"This doesn't seem like the right solution for me." Bastien had heard enough and stood up as if to leave.

Solly reached out and grabbed Bastien's forearm. "I want you to ratchet down your pride for just a minute and listen to me, Bastien. I'm trying to tell you what the Burke-Carters are all about. Are you listening to me?"

"Yeah, I'm listening."

"Now sit your yellow butt down and keep on listening. Their great-grandfather made his first million before he was twenty. Everything they put their hands on turns to gold. They pass it on through their genes and through the generations."

"How can the Burke-Carters help me?"

"She's a well sought after health, safety and environmental consultant. Her specialty is the oil and gas industry. Rig safety. Refineries. Stuff like that. But I think she can help you, too."

"Is she expensive?"

"I suppose so," Solly said honestly. "She's in pretty high demand. She can charge a premium for her services if she wants to."

"I don't think Remy would authorize spending for that."

Solly felt badly about the pressure Bastien was under. Solly knew about the sacrifices Bastien had made in his personal life. He left his lady behind in New Orleans to chase after the job that G-Paw Thibeadaux offered him. It wasn't a topic that was open to discussion. Gabrielle wouldn't leave her family, couldn't pick up everything to move to Houston with him. Even if she had followed Bastien to Texas, he wouldn't have been able to give her the attention she needed. Not with Remy setting crazy hours for him. Tough job. Crazy boss. No social life. No wonder he was stressed out.

"Find out if this Burke-Carter woman would be willing to take on a pro bono client," Bastien suggested. "I can just see Remy blowing a gasket if I tell him that I want him to authorize spending out of my division."

Solly reached into his back pocket and pulled out his wallet. He withdrew a business card and held it, just out of Bastien's reach.

"Find out for yourself. I'm sure once you talk to her you'll have a lot more questions. Questions that I won't be able to answer for you. But don't take it if you're not serious, Bastien."

"I'm not convinced that I need to talk to her at all. I don't like spreading my business in the streets, Solly."

"Call the woman, Bastien. She won't spread your business around. She knows how to keep a confidence."

"How can you be so sure?"

"How come you aren't?"

"Why should I be? I've never heard of this woman before today."

Solly pinned Bastien with a hard stare. "Phaedra went to school with us, Bastien. You sure you don't remember her. Wound up at a couple of our frat parties. She would have been hard to miss. Big brown eyes. Thick black hair. Crazy thick. When she wore it down, it used to fly all around her head just like Diana Ross. She used to wear it in a long french braid. Five foot seven. Legs all the way up to her neck. Remember when she came to the homecoming Halloween party our senior year wearing only a leopard print bodysuit?"

"No, I don't remember that. How'd you happen to have this Phaedra Burke-Carter's card in your wallet?"

"I ran into her a couple weeks ago. Forgot I had the card until I listened to your boys talking tonight. So now I'm passing it on to you. You either use it or you don't. You ready to get yourself out of trouble?"

Solly extended his arm, holding the business card between his index and middle fingers.

Bastien hesitated for a moment "Give me the damn card," Bastien said before he snatched it out of Solly's hand.

"Now, is that any way to act toward someone who's planning your surprise birthday party?" Solly grinned at Bastien. He raised his beer to his lips, drained the last of it and set the bottle down on the table with a thump and a restrained belch.

Bastien ignored Solly, staring down at the business card as if a magic answer to his workplace problems would appear before him.

"Samuel told me about your surprise three weeks ago," Bastien said. "What time am I supposed to show up and try to look surprised?"

"Party starts at six on Saturday. You show up at seven and work on your surprise face and your attitude."

"What's wrong with my attitude?" Bastien asked, pretending to sound offended.

"What's right with it?" Solly countered. "Face it, Bastien. You tend to run roughshod over people when things are going too slow for you. You're more like that G-Paw Thibeadaux than you think you are. Don't go looking all surprised. You know it's true. So, when you call Phaedra, just remember to keep a civil tongue in your head. Don't you go talking crazy to her, Bastien. Remember, you need her help. She doesn't need you."

Bastien ran his finger along the business card's edges, thinking about what Solly had just said.

I need her. I need her?

Those three simple words galled him. How they ate at his gut. *I need her.* He didn't need anybody. He could handle his own problems. That was the CT Inspectorate motto. It was more than just a saying on a plaque. If you couldn't live up to it, you had no business there.

His impulse was to rip the card into pieces and throw it back into Solly's face, but Bastien didn't do that. He kept staring at it, waiting for it to magically solve all of his workplace woes. But it was just a standard business card. Strong block with raised print letters giving the woman's name, phone number and email, Web site and office addresses.

Plain. Simplistic. But elegant in its simplicity. The no-

nonsense effect of the business card contrasted with the image Solly painted in his head of the party girl from back in the day.

"So, you gonna do it or what?" Solly asked. "You gonna call her?"

"I don't know."

"Have your stuff together if you do. I got the impression that she's pretty tough."

"I can handle her," Bastien said confidently.

"So, you think you're going to call."

Bastien shoved the card into his jumper pocket. "I guess it doesn't cost anything to give the lady a call."

Chapter 3

"That'll be four seventy-nine."

The young man standing behind the register looked to Phaedra as if he could use a dose of his own product. Bleary-eyed and slow to move, he yawned as he accepted her money and squinted at the cash register, trying to find the button that would ring up the coffee purchase.

"Iced mocha. Iced…iced…iced…mocha latte. Iced mocha…" he repeated the order as if he were trying not to let himself forget.

"On the left."

When the clerk failed to locate the proper register key, Phaedra looked up from the PDA that she was scanning to review her next appointment and raised an eyebrow at him. She didn't have to say a word. The lift of her eyebrow told him everything. It spoke of impatience and intolerance with the lack of service that she'd gotten. *Where was Dana, the usual morning clerk?* Phaedra wondered. Dana knew what Phaedra liked without her even having to order. That's what Phaedra liked about coming here. The usual impeccable service.

"The left?" he echoed, shifting his entire body to the right as if the wires in his brain were misfiring.

"Third row from the bottom, second button from the left." Speaking in distinct, one-or-two syllable words, she enunciated clearly to make certain that he understood her.

"Oh. *Riiiiggghhhttt*... Now, I see it."

"Glad to hear it." She scooped up the extra large iced mocha latte.

"Hey, you must come here a lot," he remarked, indicating how well she seemed to know her way around the cash register.

"No," she added, and then muttered under her breath as she turned away. "Not anymore I won't."

Phaedra raised the white-lidded cup to her lips. She scanned the shop for a quiet place to sit. It was still early in the day. Not yet nine o'clock in the morning. Yet almost every couch, every booth, every table was occupied. She finally found one over in a corner near the window. Phaedra sat down in the deep cushioned club chair, set the coffee cup on the table beside her and opened her newspaper to the business section. It took her a moment to focus her thoughts as she lamented the early days of her favorite coffee shop's grand opening.

When the shop had opened a few months ago, she could usually count on a good hour or two of quiet contemplation before the shop filled up. She could take her purchases, browse through the newspaper or read through her notes in undisturbed silence. And everyone who'd come through that door was content to take their purchases, grab a seat and wrap themselves in their own solitude. They didn't bother her, and she didn't bother them. If anyone did get the idea that they could hit on her while she worked, a glare as scalding as the cappuccino machine steam was all it took to make them back off. This coffee shop was her second office, and she treated it with all the proper decorum it deserved. She'd even brought a client or two here and formed partnerships over cappuccino.

Phaedra checked her watch. Nearly an hour before her next appointment. Plenty of time to enjoy her coffee. Maybe she would send out a few e-mails. Surf the Internet looking for her next potential job before—

Phaedra's cell phone, set to vibrate, rattled in her purse.

So much for a quiet cup of coffee.

She checked the caller ID, slipped a Bluetooth wireless earpiece over her ear and spoke softly to keep her conversation as private as possible in the crowded coffeehouse.

"Hello. Phaedra Burke-Carter speaking."

"Ms. Burke-Carter?"

"Yes. Speaking," she repeated and pressed the earpiece closer to her ear. "Can you speak a little louder? I'm having trouble hearing you."

"Hold on a minute." A few seconds of muffled noise followed by the sound of a slamming door, but not before a disgruntled shout echoed in her ear. "Knock it off out there, will you! Can't you see that I'm on the phone?"

Wincing, Phaedra pulled the earpiece away. But then the voice came back again. Clearer this time. A man speaking with the slightest hint of a dialect that she couldn't quite place. Definitely Southern. A low, deep drawl, rich in timbre.

"Ms. Burke-Carter, my name's Bastien Thibeadaux."

Bastien Thibeadaux, she mentally repeated the name. Now the accent made sense to her. Definitely Southern. Mississippi. Georgia. With a name like Thibeadaux, most likely Louisiana.

Bastien Thibeadaux.

How did she know that name? From where? She closed her eyes, part of her listening to his end of the conversation that continued. The other part of her rooted through her memory, trying to dredge up a face with a name. Phaedra was usually pretty good at making and keeping connections like that. The face didn't immediately come to mind, so she stopped trying to remember and focused more on the caller. It would eventually come to her.

"I got your business card from a mutual friend from college. Solomon Greenwood."

"Solly! I just saw Solly a few weeks ago. How's he doing?"

Even though they both lived in Houston, it had been years since she'd seen Solly. Two weeks ago she'd run into him and his son at a sushi restaurant downtown. She was on her way to another appointment and didn't have time to talk. They'd exchanged information with the promise that they'd catch up on old times.

"He's doing fine. I'll tell him that you asked about him."

"How can I help you, Mr. Thibeadaux?"

"Ms. Burke-Carter, I'm not convinced you can. You're going to have to do some fast talking to sell me on your services."

The reply was frank to the point of bluntness. Phaedra didn't let it get to her. She was used to getting that tone. It was the kind of attitude she always received from men who were forced to seek the professional advice of a female. Maybe she was generalizing. All of her meetings didn't start off this way. Enough of them did, though. She knew what to do to keep the potential client talking, keep the conversation polite, but professional. The moment it strayed too far in a disrespectful direction, she was going to hang up. That's the way Phaedra maintained control.

"You called me. You must have some reason why, Mr. Thibeadaux."

"Because Solly told me to."

"I see."

"No, I don't think you do," he went on in a condescending tone.

"Then, if you can't make me understand why you called within the next fifteen seconds, I'm going to end this conversation. I have a very full schedule, Mr. Thibeadaux."

"What? You gonna hang up on me, now? Let me guess. In your rule book, time is money? I think maybe you wanna make time for me, *cher.*"

That southern dialect came out thick and strong then with his casual use of a term of endearment. *Cher.* Dear one. With it, he resurrected in Phaedra long-buried vestiges of a memory. Less than vestiges. Flashes. A jumbled mix of chaotic impressions. Images, though disjointed and out of sequence, that told Phaedra a story that she'd deliberately made herself forget.

Oh no!

Phaedra breathed the words so softly that she was certain no one could hear her. But anyone in the coffee shop watching her would see her distress. She picked up her newspaper and held it in front of her face while she composed herself.

Bastien Thibeadaux's voice took her back almost fifteen years. Like special effects from a science fiction show, she found herself no longer in the coffee shop but in a darkened room. A single light shone over in a far corner, casting shadows on the motions of a skinny young man in a baseball cap, tag still dangling from it, shifting back and forth between tables set up around him in a makeshift DJ's booth. He lifted old-school vinyl albums, inspecting yellow, white and red labels and making selections to keep the mood of the house party going.

As Phaedra sat shaking with a sudden anxiety attack at the coffee shop, her back stiffened in an instantaneous reflex as she remembered the feel of a solid wall against it and the rumble of bass turned up, squeaking treble turned low. The wall thrummed, vibrated up and down her spine, her bottom and her thighs. Wasn't too much separating the wall and her skin. A thin layer of leopard print spandex and nothing else. No bra. No panties. Just the leopard print catsuit, a headband with leopard ears and a mask covering her eyes and cheekbones.

Her back had been against the wall, but she hadn't planned to be a wallflower. Not *that* night.

Junior year. Combination homecoming and Halloween party on The Hill, a familiar name for her alma mater Prairie View A&M University. Enough booze and bodies to make her *want* to forget that she was at a party she shouldn't have gone to. Her back was against the wall, in the shadows, because Phaedra didn't want anyone else to see how she'd allowed—even encouraged—one or two or maybe three of the frat brothers who were throwing that party to approach her. She was playing all of them at the same time, using her anonymity and their arousal to her advantage.

She remembered that voice now. That soft, sexy voice that was finally able to convince her to move from the shadows. That voice. How could she have forgotten it? Southern and slowed from one too many whiskey shots. Half the night, she'd watched with horrified fascination and counted each one as he'd tossed the shot glasses back, draining each of the amber liquid. Party crowd chanting. Egging on. Applause. Cheers. And jeers when he got up from the table victorious, last man standing, and looking for someone to share in the celebration.

The glow of luminous hazel eyes, more green than brown, scanned the room, finally landing on her. Her of all people! Quiet, studious, oh-so-serious Phaedra Burke-Carter determined to be freed from her chrysalis and the voice, *his voice,* that offered her the key to that freedom. The voice that promised to take her to paradise if she consented to ditch the party and go with him to one of the rooms upstairs. Of all the young men who'd approached her that night, he was the only one who'd gotten close enough to make her consider his offer.

What was it about him? All swagger and confidence. Hardness, heat and hormones. He wasn't the typical Texas boy that she'd known. Something set him apart. Something about him that night caught and held her attention. The moment she'd laid eyes on him, something about him said, "That's the one."

Was this the same person? Phaedra was torn between wanting and *not* wanting to know for certain. Was this that Louisiana boy from her college days? Maybe it wasn't. He wasn't calling himself Bastien then, but some stupid football inspired nickname. And his friends were all calling him by an initial. B? T? She wasn't sure. Maybe she wasn't remembering correctly. He certainly didn't seem to remember her. Small wonder. It was fifteen years ago. Why would he remember her? It was only one party. She wasn't even giving her real name to any of those guys at the party, either. Or her right phone number. It was all a game back then. Play the boys before you got played.

Phaedra snapped back from her reverie to respond to Bastien Thibeadaux's question. Enough traipsing down memory lane; this was business. A potential client.

She set the newspaper aside, folding it carefully in half and placing it on the table next to her coffee.

"Time is money. Not necessarily. In my book, time isn't money. But my time is precious. So, tell me what you need from me, Mr. Thibeadaux, or cut the conversation short."

"Solly tells me that you get paid to keep people safe."

"That's a simplistic way of putting what I do. The same can be said for bodyguards, Mr. Thibeadaux. I'm not in the body-guarding business, if that's what you're looking for."

"Workplace safety," he clarified. "I've got some trouble at work. Some…let's say…behaviors…that I want to nip in the bud before somebody gets hurt. Really hurt. You know what I mean?" He paused.

"And…" she encouraged.

"And Solly seems to think you can help me solve them. Can you?"

"I have to be honest with you, Mr. Thibeadaux, I don't know. I need to…" She couldn't make an assessment without knowing more details about his situation, but he didn't give her the chance to finish her sentence.

"Then what am I doing wasting your time and mine?" he snapped.

"I didn't call you. You called me. I'm not in the habit of wasting time. So why don't I hang up and save us both contin-ued irritation?"

Phaedra noted the considerable pause. She listened carefully but could only hear his breathing. Rapid and shallow at first, then slowing as he clamped down on his anger. When he spoke again, it was with a more conciliatory tone.

"I think maybe, Ms. Burke-Carter, we got off to a shaky start."

"I agree. Shall we start again?"

"When can you come out to discuss my particular problem?"

"This week?" She consulted her PDA, calling up the calendar. "How does Thursday suit you, Mr. Thibeadaux? Thursday at two o'clock."

"I guess it'll have to do." He didn't sound pleased that she couldn't immediately accommodate him.

"Your address, please. And a number where I can best reach you." Phaedra tapped the stylus against the PDA screen, keeping up with the information that he rattled off.

"CT Inspectorate," she repeated back to him the name of the

company and the address. "What type of inspection company do you work for, Mr. Thibeadaux?"

"Grain, primarily. Wheat. Sorghum. Rice. Why? Does it make a difference?"

"I can't tailor a solution for you if I don't know what you do, can I, now? I'll see you on Thursday."

"One more thing, Ms. Burke-Carter."

"Yes?"

"How much is this going to cost me?"

"I'm not ready to discuss figures with you, Mr. Thibeadaux. Not until I've had a chance to assess your situation."

"Give me a ballpark."

"Not even a ballpark."

"An hourly rate?"

"It varies."

She heard him give a sigh of irritation at her stonewalling tactics, but Phaedra knew better than to toss out a number that would either lock her into a rate she could accept or would scare him off if he figured it was too high. "You know, Ms. Burke-Carter, Solly told me that you can be a bit difficult when you want to be."

"Mr. Thibeadaux," Phaedra said crisply, clamping down on her words. "Is there something that you need to tell me? Something before we meet on Thursday?"

"What do you mean?"

"For someone who claims to need my help, you don't seem very accommodating."

"You mean willing to fall over and let you shove your hand into my wallet? That's what you consultants do, isn't it? Rattle off some crap trying to convince your clients that you're needed. Then inflate the hours on the invoice to charge ridiculous fees. Or skip out before finishing the work?"

"I have no intention of putting my hand anywhere near your wallet," she assured him. "That's what electronic transfers are for."

Here we go again, Phaedra thought to herself. Another one who didn't trust her profession.

"How about making my first consult free for old time's sake? PV alum-to-alum," he eased the question by her smoothly. He was trying to get by with something for nothing. Well, her services didn't come cheap. There was true value to what she did.

"What value do you put on the safety of your employees, Mr. Thibeadaux?" Phaedra responded to his question with one of her own.

"There isn't anything I wouldn't do for them if it'll keep them from getting hurt or killed."

"I'll tell you what, Mr. Thibeadaux. Because Solly suggested that you speak with me, for old time's sake, my first consult will be free. It won't cost you anything for me to listen. So, let's meet. I'll listen to you. You listen to me. And if I can't convince you that I can help, then we'll go our separate ways."

"Then, I'll see you Thursday at two o'clock. Anything I need to do to prepare for the meeting?"

"Yes, I need you to gather all of your employee incident reports for the last two years. Especially those related to accidents and those involving lost work time."

"I've got copies of most of them sitting on my desk."

"An excellent start. And I need access to your documented policies and procedures."

"Most of that information is passed on through on-the-job training, Ms. Burke-Carter. Some of my employees can barely speak English. Others *might* have finished high school. It's extremely physical, repetitive work. Nobody's got time to plow through a bunch of dusty books that are out of date the minute you print them. But I'll gather what I have."

"I can assess how effective your procedures are when I see you on Thursday."

"You're not going to take our company secrets and sell them to your other clients, are you?"

"I'll sign whatever nondisclosure agreements or confidentiality contracts you have."

"Don't you worry your head about signing NDAs," he said smoothly. "We may be a Southern, family-run business. But some of the old ways still work for us, Ms. Burke-Carter. Like that quaint, turn of the century practice of sealing a business deal on the trust of a handshake. Keep your NDA. I've learned from personal experience that they're not worth the paper they're printed on."

"You don't trust consultants, do you?" It wasn't really a question. Phaedra was only letting him know that she recognized his hostility but was still willing to deal with him.

"And it only took you fifteen minutes to figure that out. I'm already impressed with your expertise," he retorted, then hung up on Phaedra before she could beat him to it.

"You should be," Phaedra muttered to the dead phone line hum that echoed in her ear.

Chapter 4

Bastien hung up the phone with mixed feelings. He couldn't count the number of times he'd reached for the phone, started to call Phaedra Burke-Carter and then hung up again before it could ring. It was worse than being in grade school, trying to make that first phone call to his first preteen crush.

It wasn't that he doubted Phaedra's abilities. Solly had recommended her, and Solly wouldn't do it unless he thought she could help. When he'd left the bowling alley Monday night, he'd stayed up until four o'clock in the morning researching her. By the time he made himself call her, he was already fighting a stress headache. Knowing that he had a full day at work before him didn't put him in the best of moods, and he knew that bad attitude came across on the phone. Bastien had contacted her impressive list of clients. They gave her excellent references. Enough to convince him to go ahead and call her.

What Bastien doubted was his ability to convince Remy that the company needed to spend the money to bring her on board. In Remy's eyes, bringing on an outside consultant meant that somebody inside of CT Inspectorate wasn't doing their job. And that somebody had better get their act together quickly, or that somebody would soon be out of a job. Bastien didn't have to read between the lines. Remy made it clear. Bastien was the one who was at risk.

Holding Phaedra's card between his fingertips, Bastien gently, distractedly tapped the card against the page in the yearbook that held her picture. She'd been a junior then. According to Solly, she'd attended the same parties that he went to. Still, he didn't remember her, and it frustrated him that he couldn't. Solly teased him and told him that was one of the effects of getting old, and for his birthday he would buy him a case of ginkgo biloba to help with his memory. In response to Solly's "getting old" cracks, Bastien made Solly's son cover his ears while he told his friend what he could do with that case of herbs.

Bastien compared Phaedra's school photograph with the one posted on the Web site for her consultancy firm. The years had certainly been kind to her. More than kind. Generous. The girl in the college annual was just that, a girl. A girl trying to look more mature than her nineteen years. Her thick, dark, curly hair was teased for volume and ballooned around her head. Large dark eyes were hidden behind wide-rimmed glasses. The blouse she wore was bright pink with an obnoxiously frilly bow that fell in ribbons down the front with bright pink lipstick to match and large plastic hoop earrings.

The woman on the Web site was considerably more polished. Sophisticated. She wore her hair sleeker now. A long bang swept across her forehead from left to right and the rest was smoothed into a french roll. She still wore glasses, but they were modern and accented her eyes, rather than dwarfing them. Her dark eyes stared out cool and assured, giving the impression of confidence and competence.

"Is it safe to come in now?"

Bastien's cousin Chas swung the door open and stepped through before Bastien gave him permission. Chas didn't really need permission. As the company's chief finance officer, he could come and go as he pleased. But Chas didn't operate that way. *Not like Remy,* Bastien thought sourly, who used every opportunity to remind everyone of his position. He wore his title like some kind of cape, smothering the employees with it when he thought they weren't giving him the proper respect.

As Chas came in, Bastien quickly closed the college annual and slid it into a desk drawer. If Chas noticed his hastiness, he didn't say anything about it. Instead, he flopped into the chair facing him.

"Alonzo tells me that you've been holed up in your office all morning."

"Alonzo needs to stop worrying about where I've been and worry about his own business," Bastien said testily.

"Everything all right?" Chas asked. Bastien was edgy and not doing a very good job of covering it.

"Sure…everything's fine."

"Uh-huh." Chas wasn't convinced.

"I'm just under a little pressure right now, Chas."

"When are we not under pressure in this place?" Chas commiserated. "But you can't let it get to you, Bastien. You can't let it mess with your health. It's just a job."

"How can you say that, Chas?" Bastien asked, leaning back in his chair and staring up at the ceiling. It occurred to him last night while he was working on the work rotation schedule for Remy that, even though they were a couple employees short, he was still getting pressure to reduce costs. The most expedient way, according to Remy's plan, was to let someone go. That someone might be him. Bastien couldn't afford to let anyone think that he didn't value working here. He was on a mission to carve out a piece of ownership of this company for himself, just like Chas. Just like Remy.

"Because it's true," Chas said. He planted his palms down on Bastien's desk, leaned forward and said, "The minute G-Paw and Remy make you start thinking that there's nothing else outside of this company, that you've got no life outside the one they make for you, then they've got you, Bastien. You hear what I'm telling you? You have to protect your health. Physical. Mental. Emotional." He ticked off on three fingers as he spoke. "This place can suck the life right out of you if you're not careful."

"Is that why you took a sabbatical and let Remy take over this company?"

Chas was in his early forties, premature gray sprinkled through his dark hair.

As much as Bastien admired Chas, he didn't completely get him. "You had this company, Chas. You had it in the palm of your hand. But now Remy's in line to run it. "

Chas shrugged his shoulders, like it was no big deal to him.

"Remy working your last nerve?" He laughed softly when Bastien muttered an unkind assessment of his cousin's abilities.

"I can't believe you let go of something you've worked over half of your adult years to get. I know you busted your ass to get where you are, Chas. You had to put up with a lot of crap from G-Paw and Remy to do it. And now you're just hanging back and letting Remy take it all?"

"I let go to get something I wanted more," Chas admitted. He opened one fist, imitating releasing the company and closed the other fist, pressing it to his chest over his heart.

"Jacie," Bastien said, knowing exactly what he meant by that pantomime. Jacie was Chas's wife. But that simple word didn't come close to describing all that she was to him. Chas never actually used the words *soul mate,* but he didn't have to. Anyone who ever saw them together could easily recognize the depth of feeling he had for her.

"When I met her, everything changed, including my priorities. I met her, hired her then married her. A year later, we started having kids. Next thing I knew, being up here twenty-four hours a day, seven days a week wasn't all that important to me anymore."

Bastien was almost envious of the spring in Chas's step as he and Jacie, the office manager, walked out hand in hand at the end of each day. Like two teenagers who couldn't get enough of each other, they left the cares of CT Inspectorate behind them while Bastien remained behind to be the good company man that Chas used to be.

"Don't get me wrong," Chas tried to clear up a wrong impression. "I love the work. I can even tolerate making money."

"Tolerate? Who are you trying to fool? The Thibeadaux family wouldn't know what to do with ourselves if we couldn't make money."

"Now you're sounding like G-Paw," Chas accused him.

"He raised you. He must have beaten that into your thick skull, too."

"I'm not saying that he didn't. Just don't lose perspective. Don't let the job make you miserable. When it gets to be like that, it's not a job anymore. It's a prison."

"Yeah? Well, thanks for the advice, *cousain*."

"I know what you're thinking. Only worth two cents. I'm willing to back up my words with action. If you need anything from me, anything at all to make sure you get what you need, you know Jacie and me have got your back."

"I appreciate the offer. But you've got enough on your plate. Let me handle my business. You don't need to babysit me."

Chas got up to pour himself a cup of coffee from the six-cup brewer that Bastien kept in his office.

"Texas. Louisiana. Oklahoma. Those are your territories, Bastien. You run it the way you want and don't take no lip from that old man or from Remy. Don't think I haven't noticed how he's been ridin' you, too."

"It's no secret that my division has had some screwups up in here lately. Everybody thinks that I'm not cutting it."

"Don't get down on yourself, Bastien. Nobody who knows you thinks that. Those accidents weren't your fault."

"Maybe not my fault but my responsibility. Four accidents in four months. Come on now, Chas. How can I justify that? I'm not liking those numbers and neither is G-Paw."

"So what are you going to do about it?" Chas issued a challenge.

"I'm thinking about bringing in a consultant."

Chas made a face at Bastien's response, then tried to play it off as if he were dissatisfied with the coffee. "What kind of consultant?"

"Health, safety and environmental. Solly Greenwood recommended her."

"Her?" There was genuine intrigue in Chas's question.

"Yeah, her," Bastien said, emphasizing her gender. "Her name's Phaedra Burke-Carter."

"Of the Houston Burke-Carters?"

"You know them?"

"I know them. They're a very powerful family."

"Worth the money?" That's what it all boiled down to for Bastien.

"Depends on who you ask. One thing I can say for certain, if you're dealing with a Burke-Carter, you'd better bring your *A* game. When it comes to making their money, just like G-Paw, those people don't play. They're dead serious about making sure that their name stays spotless. If you're going to work with her, be up front about what you expect and get everything in writing. That'll protect you both."

"I already told her that she didn't have to sign a nondisclosure agreement," Bastien confessed.

"Oooh, rookie mistake." Chas laughed at him. He didn't seem too concerned that Bastien had already disregarded his first bit of advice. "There's still time to correct that. When's your first meeting with her?"

"I set up a consult for this Thursday."

"That soon? You don't waste time."

"I don't have time to sit around and wait for Remy to fire me because I can't get the work done."

"Nobody's going to fire you, Bastien," Chas assured him.

"Okay, then. Replace me. Or demote me. I'm not gonna let that happen, either."

"What makes you think she can help you?"

"She's got credentials coming out of her ears. Her client list reads like a roll call for the Fortune 500."

"She sounds expensive. You've got the budget to bring in outside expertise?"

"You mean after Remy blew it on detailing the van? Nope. So, I had to get creative. The first consult is free."

"How'd you manage that? You ain't that smooth of a talker. How did you manage to get on her schedule?"

"Turns out we went to school together. Here, take a look."

Bastien pulled the college annual from the drawer and flipped to the page that he'd marked with Phaedra's business card.

"Hmm…interesting," Chas said, barely managing to keep his expression neutral.

"That's *not* the way she looks today," Bastien said. He swung the computer monitor around and pulled up her Web site.

This time, Chas gave a low whistle of admiration under his breath.

"Hey, cut that out! You're a married man!"

"Blissfully married," Chas affirmed. "But I ain't blind! And I know you aren't either. Don't let that business suit fool you, Bastien," he said, tapping the monitor. "That woman's got it going on. I'll bet she knows it, too, and can use it to her advantage. Don't let her distract you from taking care of your business, Bastien. A woman like that can twist a man's head clean around."

"Do I look like I have time for that, Chas?" Bastien made a sweeping gesture, pointing to the stacks of paperwork on this desk.

Again, Chas laughed at him, pricking Bastien's pride.

"I don't see what's so damn funny."

Chas then rubbed his hands over his eyes and his mouth, pretending to wipe the grin away.

"Let me ask you something, Bastien. And don't get offended. I'm not trying to get in your business."

"What is it? What do you want to know?"

"When's the last time you went out?"

"What do you mean *out?* You mean like on a date? With a woman?"

"No, with a wombat. Of course I mean with a woman. And I don't mean hanging out at Fast Lanz bowling alley with Solly and your crew. I mean when's the last time you got all cleaned up, dressed to impress and took a woman out to a romantic movie? A late night dinner? A concert?"

"What's that got to do with anything?"

"Just humor me, Bastien. You've been puttin' in a lot of hours up here. When's the last time you got yourself a little, you know, sumthin'-sumthin'."

"Is there a point to this conversation?"

"The point is that I've been in your shoes. One hundred percent company man, through and through. Any spare moment not spent up here at the company was spent thinking about the company. Before I met Jacie, that is. Let me tell you. I didn't realize just how alone I was until that woman came crashing into my life."

"And did you get a little sumthin'-sumthin' from her, too?" Bastien asked snidely.

"I had to," Chas said, his expression somber. "G-Paw practically threw me on top of her. Said I needed to handle my business. Made me figure out which one I wanted more, her or the company, so I could get my head back in the game."

"That's not what I'm looking for from Phaedra Burke-Carter, Chas. This is business, pure and simple. I'm fighting for my right to run this company, right along with you and Remy."

"I wasn't looking either. You can't ignore that basic instinct. More than instinct, it's that inescapable sense that nothing's gonna be right until you and she get together. When it hits you, it's gonna hit you hard. I'm here to tell you. I did everything I could to keep from wanting Jacie. Tried to keep it all professional. Even convinced myself for a time that I was doing the honorable thing. Call it what you want—fate, destiny, a taste of good old-fashioned lust. The point is, she showed up in my life when I was at my weakest. One thing led to another…and well, you know the rest. I'm only telling you this because I want you to be ready. Face it, Bastien. You've been off your game for a while."

"So, what do you expect me to do, Chas? Go and grab the first female I see and have a quickie behind the building before meeting with her?"

"Behind the building. In the backseat of that crazy van…yeah, I know about that."

Bastien groaned.

"You do whatever you have to do to keep your head on straight while you're meeting with that woman. I'm looking at that photo of this Burke-Carter woman and I'm telling you, she's got it. If she's anything like the way she looks, you don't stand a chance."

"Well, I didn't ask her to come out here for her looks," Bastien grumbled, swiveling the monitor back around. "I need her for her brains."

"Why not get yours? You'd better believe that Remy's gettin' his," Chas confided. "Nobody needs to spend *that* much time in Beaumont. I think that man's got women waiting for him across three states."

"I'm not like Remy, Chas," Bastien said seriously. "I can't do those hit-and-runs. The next time I fall for a woman, it's going to be for keeps. I'm almost thirty-five years old. I don't have time to play house."

"That's why I respect you, Bastien. That's why I put you here, in this office. I know you'll always do the right thing for this company and the right thing for yourself."

Bastien didn't voice his doubt, but Chas read it in his body language.

"Look, Bastien, I wouldn't have approved you and your employee transfers if I didn't think you all were up to the job."

"I'm going to fix this," Bastien promised. "I won't let you down."

"To hell with me," Chas said, rising from the chair and starting for the door. "You won't let yourself down. Speaking of letting down, you know Jacie's got a surprise birthday party planned for you, don't you? For Sunday afternoon right after church. Make sure you're sufficiently surprised when she springs it on you."

"Don't worry about that, Chas. Solly's planning to ambush me, too. I'll have plenty of time to practice my surprised face." Bastien raised his hands to either side of his face, raised his eyebrows and opened his mouth to imitate the look he planned to give.

"Hmm," Chas grunted. "Needs more work."

"Not the first time I'll hear that today," Bastien retorted, lowering his head back to his reports.

Chapter 5

The railroad crossing arm lowered and warning lights flashed as the cargo train rumbled on, seemingly without end. Phaedra wasn't going anywhere any time soon, so she sat in her SUV, fingertips drumming impatiently against the steering wheel. Several eighteen-wheelers were in front of her. Another half dozen idled behind her. The blackish-gray smoke from their chrome exhaust pipes created clouds of noxious fumes that drifted into the air and seemed to melt into the storm clouds forming on the horizon. Two days ago, when she'd agreed to meet with Bastien, the weather promised to be clear. How quickly things changed.

"Not a good day to be claustrophobic."

She didn't believe in signs and omens. Yet, it couldn't be a co-incidence that the mood of the man she was going to meet was as thick and oppressive as the clouds threatening to pour down rain.

Phaedra was sandwiched in between the trucks, not able to inch forward or scoot back. She wasn't late for the meeting with

Bastien Thibeadaux. Not yet. But that didn't stop the anxious knot in her stomach from churning. Premeeting jitters. She hated being late. In her opinion, it was the ultimate in rudeness. It was certainly no way to impress a new client, especially one as cranky and impatient as Bastien was. She couldn't miss the meeting after all of the research she'd done. Though she'd promised him that the first consult was free, she'd already put enough time into the meeting to pay for a week of her office leasing fees. She'd better come out of this meeting with a signed contract—or at least the promise of one.

As Phaedra waited for the train to pass, she used the time to flip through her notes, committing to memory more details about the company. She didn't want to fumble through papers during the meeting. Nothing turned away potential clients faster than a consultant who didn't perform the most basic research.

Fifteen minutes before she was scheduled to arrive and she was stuck behind the train. This was cutting it too close. She wouldn't have time to collect herself or even stop by the bathroom. She flipped down the visor and checked her appearance in the mirror. Not a hair out of place. Face perfectly made up. Phaedra wasn't conceited, but she knew that she was the model of professionalism and competence. It was an image that she worked hard to cultivate, especially for today. She didn't want to look anything like the girl of her junior year in college. That wild child with the teased hair and the skintight catsuit was a distant memory.

Thirteen minutes until her appointment and the train was still taking its time. Twelve minutes. Eleven.

Phaedra reached over and picked up the cell phone from the passenger seat. *I'm just going to have to call him and apologize for being late.* As she placed the Bluetooth in her ear and scrolled through the contact list, the phone started to ring. It was Bastien.

"Phaedra Burke-Carter speaking."

"Ms. Burke-Carter. It's Bastien Thibeadaux."

"Mr. Thibeadaux! I was just about to call you."

"Really? Let me guess. You're stuck at the entrance?" He didn't sound irritated like he had when he'd ended their conversation on Tuesday. Phaedra found herself thinking how much she liked the sound of his voice when he wasn't snarling at her.

"Yes, I am. There's a train crossing and it seems to be taking forever. Is there another entrance to the facility?"

"Yes, ma'am. About a half mile up the road, off to your right."

She rolled down the window and stuck her head out to see. "I guess it doesn't make a difference. I'm sandwiched between several large trucks."

"Then you'd better sit tight," he advised. "Some of those crazy rig jockeys have been known to whip out into traffic when you least expect it. When the gate lifts, pull forward to the guard station, give them my name and then take the left fork toward the main building. It's a red brick building."

"Got it. Left fork. Red brick building," She repeated. "See you in a minute. Oh, and Mr. Thibeadaux…"

"Yeah?"

"How did you know I was stuck at the train crossing? I could have been just running late."

This time, he did laugh. A deepthroated chuckle that rumbled in her ear and sent an unexpected shiver down her spine. "Ms. Burke-Carter, people like you don't run late."

"People like me?" she said, inviting him to explain.

"Type A personalities," he went on. Phaedra translated control freak in her head.

"Besides, I can see you from the security monitors up here. I've been watching you for the past ten minutes. You *are* driving the charcoal-gray SUV, right?"

"That's me," she confirmed.

"Nice ride," he remarked. He seemed more relaxed than when he had first spoken with her.

"Thank you," Phaedra responded automatically to the compliment. She also sent her thanks to the heavens for small favors. Just because she was prepared for his hostility and resentment didn't mean she wanted to deal with it now. Now, she wasn't sure what to expect from him.

When the last railcar rumbled by, the railroad crossing arm

lifted, she waited her turn as the trucks ahead pulled up to the guard station. By the time it was Phaedra's turn, she already had her driver's license out, presenting it before the security guard requested it.

"I'm here to see Bastien Thibeadaux at CT Inspectorate." The guard recorded her license number on a clipboard and walked around the SUV to list the make and model.

"Have a nice day." He waved her on. She veered left, toward the signs indicating visitor parking. Parking spots were reserved for the CFO and COO. A third sign was planted in front of a parking space that was twice as large as the other two spaces combined. The sign was white, trimmed in red and black with the letters G-PAW.

G-paw? What kind of a company position is that? There were a few other parking signs, a couple of marked spots for disabled employees or visitors. There were also some signs designated for short-term parking—only thirty minutes. The others seemed to be free and open to anyone. Phaedra pulled past the spot she wanted and then shifted the car into reverse to back into the spot.

She collected her briefcase from behind the passenger seat and one more item that she'd remembered to bring along—the college annual of her junior year. If she had any doubts before who Bastien was, they were erased the moment her eyes landed on his pictures in the annual. He was *that* boy. She'd looked up each reference to his name, marking every page. Phaedra also double-checked that there were no pictures of her in that slinky leopard costume. For this meeting, she wanted him to take her seriously. He wasn't going to do it if he was too distracted by thinking of her as she was back then. Since he didn't seem to remember her, she would continue with the meeting as if they'd just met for the first time today. First impression, fresh impression.

She climbed out of the car and slipped the keys into her jacket pocket. One last time check. Perfect timing! She'd made it with one minute to spare. As Phaedra pushed open one side of the double doors, a rush of cool air and music playing softly over the public address system greeted her.

Directly in front of her was a large, curved reception desk.

The desk was black and sleek with a genuine gray-and-brown speckled marble counter. She approached the desk, smiling at the receptionist. A woman with blond hair pulled back into a cascading ponytail sat, elbows planted on the desk, face propped up on her fists. She licked her thumb and turned the page of a fashion magazine.

"Good afternoon." Phaedra greeted and pulled the sign-in book toward her. "I'm here to see Bastien Thibeadaux." In neat, block letters, she printed her name, the time of arrival and the person she'd come to meet. Her eyes scanned down the page, noting the number of other visitors, their arrival and departure times.

"Yes, ma'am. He's expecting you. Can I see your ID please?"

The receptionist took and scanned the ID. Seconds later, Phaedra's information appeared on the computer monitor. A printer whined and spat out a label with Phaedra's image and name on it. *Visitor* and *Escort Required* was stamped across the bottom.

"Here you go, Ms. Burke-Carter. Just attach it to your jacket."

Phaedra affixed the label below her right shoulder.

"If you'll just have a seat, Mr. Thibeadaux will be right with you. Can I offer you something while you wait? Coffee? Soda? Help yourself. It's right over there." The receptionist pointed with her pen at a small glass table across the room holding a coffee bar and baskets of assorted snacks.

"No thank you." Phaedra always refused the initial offer of a beverage. Fumbling around with coffee cups or soda cans could get awkward during first meetings. Bypassing the snack bar, she took a seat.

The seats in the reception room were made of chrome and gray vinyl, matching the gray flecks in the reception desk countertop. They were deeply padded and comfortable, with high round backs and curved arms. After she sat down, she expected Bastien to come through another set of double doors to the right of the reception desk. Two minutes ticked by. Three. She was on time. He was now the one officially late.

Phaedra's eyes drifted to the selection of magazines on the

table beside her. She selected one, not really interested in reading any of the articles, but wanting to find something to do with her hands while she waited.

Ten more minutes passed before she loudly shuffled the magazine, a not-so-subtle hint that she was still waiting.

"I just paged Mr. Thibeadaux," the receptionist assured her. "He's on his way."

Just as Phaedra was glancing at her watch and comparing it to the decorative row of wall clocks indicating the time in various cities, the side doors swung open and Bastien Thibeadaux walked through the door.

No, not walked through, he stormed through like a force of nature. When Bastien Thibeadaux shoved open the double doors, it made Phaedra jump. The resounding echo as the doors flung open reminded her of thunder.

Phaedra looked up from the magazine, meeting Bastien's gaze from across the room. It took her less than a second to collect herself. In that time, she took him in from the top of his closely cropped, but wavy hair all the way down to his steel-toed work boots. Lightning flashed in her mind, and when it faded, left a single, smoking word burned into her brain. Trouble. This man was trouble. He spelled trouble all those years ago for her in school, and he was going to be trouble for her now. She knew that as assuredly as she knew his name. Thibeadaux. Trouble. The two were inextricably linked.

The dark blue coverall he wore was not meant for fashion but function. The long sleeves were rolled up, showing off the fraternity tattoo in the shape of the Greek alphabet symbol omega. The tattoo did its job. It showed off his pride and commitment to his fraternity and had the added bonus of accenting well-muscled arms.

He hadn't exaggerated when he said the work was physical. You couldn't get cut biceps and triceps like that just managing workers. Bastien stood around six foot two or six foot three. Yet, he seemed taller to Phaedra because she hadn't stood up yet to greet him. She was afraid to.

She'd read in novels or seen romantic comedies of people

going weak in the knees, but she'd always thought that was a ridiculous exaggeration. It didn't happen in real life. Certainly not to her. She wasn't the type of woman who was swayed by physical appearances. She wasn't that shallow. Not anymore. Since graduating from college—and her one lapse of judgment at that homecoming party—she'd learned a valuable lesson: forming emotional attachments based purely on physical appearances didn't work out. At least, not for her.

Yet, there she was, sitting in that chair, staring up at the man with skin like sweet golden honey, looking into wide hazel eyes and seriously wondering what it would take to get him to remember her. What would she have to do to get him thinking about her, looking at her the way he did back then—with deliberate attention and single-mindedness of purpose?

Get a grip on yourself, Phaedra! This man is a client.

This man was big trouble. It only took him a moment to cross the room with his long-legged strides before Phaedra came to another snap decision. This was one potential client she was going to drop like a hot rock. Forget all the time she'd already sunk into preparing for this meeting. If she had any real sense, she should end the meeting right here, right now. What made her believe she could face him after all this time and not let it affect her reason?

Phaedra's mind scrambled to find a reasonable excuse for why she'd suddenly have to leave. A mix-up in her schedule. An emergency call from the office. Yes, that sounded plausible. Anything sounded better than telling him that she had serious doubts about her ability to keep business on her mind while he was around. She'd just have to apologize for wasting his time. But she'd only do it from the relative safety of her car, call him from her cell phone as she was burning rubber out of the parking lot.

"Ms. Burke-Carter." Bastien approached her, holding out his hand in greeting. "Sorry to keep you waiting."

His voice had the same sexy Southern quality as she remembered from their phone conversation. Same, yet different, if she could at all explain it. There was no distraction of coffee shop chatter this time or the rumble of railcars passing by her to mute the effects of Bastien's speech. Now she had the full effect of his voice directed at her.

Unprotected, unshielded, Phaedra felt caught in a maelstrom as vivid memories and raw emotions that she thought she'd long buried swirled inside her. Fifteen years was a long time to forget. Not long enough, apparently. It was unsettling, this uncontrollable urge to run for cover. Phaedra wasn't used to feeling this way. She wasn't sure if she liked it. At the same time, she found herself wishing that she could indulge in it more. She had to do something to get her wits about her. What could she do to stall for time?

Chapter 6

Bastien sensed that Phaedra was agitated. He could tell from across the room by the look on her face and in the slow, deliberate way she set her magazine down on the table. She didn't say a word from her chair but stood up to face him first. He'd extended his hand to her, yet she'd left him hanging out there just long enough for him to start to feel foolish. Before he could draw it back, she slipped her hand into his, pressing her warm palm against his palm.

Phaedra's hand was slender with neatly manicured natural nails. No colored polish, her nails were highly buffed until they shone as if lacquered. Her grip was firm and filled with confidence as she pumped his hand several times and looked him squarely in the eyes. When he looked into hers, he experienced a powerful moment of déjà vu. Something about those expressive eyes seemed so familiar. Dark, serious and shining with intelligence and intensity. Chas had been right. This woman meant business.

Maybe staring at her picture in their school annual and clicking through her Web site convinced him that he knew her.

Coupled with the fact that Solly had said they'd gone to some of the same parties, all of that registered with him. That had to be the explanation for his feeling of instantaneous recognition and connection. All of the anxiety that Bastien had felt about asking her to meet with him dispersed into the air of confidence that surrounded her. Everything was going to be all right. Somehow, he knew that before she spoke a single word.

"Mr. Thibeadaux, thank you for taking the time out of your day to meet with me."

She greeted him politely, with an undertone of a gentle rebuke for keeping her waiting. Bastien smiled at her, letting her know that he understood exactly what she was telling him. He admired the fact that she could do it with a smile and not put him on the defensive. This Phaedra Burke-Carter was well put together. Perfect makeup. Not a hair out of place. Tailored suit. She spoke in clipped, clearly enunciated sentences. A woman like that didn't run late. She would always be as punctual, and as tightly wound, as the proverbial Swiss clock.

He had every intention of being there in the reception area to greet her before she got here. First impressions were crucial ones. He'd been gearing up for this meeting since they'd spoken on Tuesday. He'd worked on his attitude, as Solly reminded him. The fact that Chas found some extra money to put back into his budget gave him another lift.

Back in his office, Bastien had all the information she'd asked for neatly boxed and labeled, waiting for her to go through them. A full hour before she was expected to arrive, he kept stepping into the office where all the security camera monitors fed into. As soon as he saw her pull up to the guard shack, he headed straight for the reception area.

Despite his best intentions, when he left his office, three employees came at him at once, each one with a different problem for him to address. Two of them Bastien easily put off; the third required immediate attention. By the time he sorted it out with Alonzo, the receptionist was paging him again.

"Did you have any trouble finding us?" Bastien made polite conversation.

"No, not really. I'm accustomed to navigating around the city."

"This isn't exactly downtown Houston. We're a little out of the way."

"But I made it," she insisted.

"On time, too." Bastien couldn't resist teasing her.

"I don't like keeping my clients waiting. I know how valuable their time is."

"But since this first consult is pro bono, we can splurge a little on the time expenditure, eh, Ms. Burke-Carter."

"Did I happen to mention in our conversation that only the first hour is free, Mr. Thibeadaux?"

"Ready to get started then?" Bastien said briskly. Chas had been right; those Burke-Carters didn't mess around.

"Of course. That's why I'm here."

"Right this way." Bastien gestured toward the doors leading back to the offices. "Through those doors and down the hall. My office is the fourth door on the left."

Phaedra inclined her head in a silent, regal way to say thank you, scooped up her briefcase and started to move ahead of him. As she walked ahead, Bastien hung back, admiring the view. Everything about the deep, cherry red-and-black houndstooth suit she wore boasted success to Bastien. It was a refreshing change from the jeans, khakis and coveralls that were made a necessity around CT Inspectorate by the nature of their work. Phaedra's two-button jacket accentuated her slender waist and flared out slightly over her hips. Hips that had just the barest hint of a roll when she walked. Her skirt was of a sensible length, hugging her curves without straining fabric across her bottom and stopping just at her knees. The silky underlining of her skirt made a soft swish-whoosh as she walked. Barely no-ticeable, yet loud enough for a man whose senses were suddenly made hyperalert by her presence to hear. The heels of her black leather shoes echoed softly on the tile floor. There was just enough lift in those open-toed, three-inch heels to draw attention to her calves.

There was an awkward moment while they were swapping lead positions. He was torn between watching her or moving ahead to push open the door for her. Decisions. Decisions. It was hard to switch between derriere watching to being debonair.

Phaedra stopped abruptly, allowing him room to pass. "Fourth door on the left, did you say, Mr. Thibeadaux?"

Bastien wasn't anticipating the question. He didn't expect her to turn around and catch him watching her, either. He lifted his eyes quickly, clearing his throat in a kind of nonverbal apology. Second time within the past five minutes that he had to apologize to her. He wondered what kind of impression that made.

"Maybe I'd better lead the way," Bastien suggested.

She made a small "go-ahead" gesture with her hand.

Bastien opened the door to his office and allowed her to move ahead of him. When she did so, her scent wafted after her. It was light, sweet and floral with an undertone of spice. The delicate scent contrasted with the dark severity of the power suit and her no-nonsense demeanor. Bastien tried not to draw in a deep breath as she walked by. After being caught admiring her body, she wasn't going to catch him sniffing after her, too. Though, there was an exposed spot on the back of her neck that he imagined he could—

Focus, Bastien. Focus! Don't get distracted.

She walked in, not taking a seat, but pausing to look around his office. Bastien made no apologies for it. It wasn't much to look at. He didn't spend much time personalizing it. No artwork on the walls other than posters of the different types of grain the company inspected. A few interoffice memos and phone lists that he'd tacked up for quick reference. No plants or statuettes to clutter the room. No photos of family or friends. Why bother making it a cozy second home when he spent most of his time out in the field?

There was one large antique leather and mahogany desk that he'd managed to bring from his office in New Orleans. In front of the desk were two matching leather and mahogany guest chairs. One of the chairs had a three-inch gash in the back support and stuffing was starting to poke through. He always promised he would get it repaired. He'd been making that promise for four years.

Jacie, the resident style and decor guru, tried covering the gash with a throw pillow, but the damned thing kept getting in the way when folks sat down in it. To keep from hurting her feelings, Bastien kept it in the office and tossed it on the couch that she'd also purchased.

Jacie had meant for the couch to go in the reception area, but G-Paw didn't want to give anyone the impression that his employees had enough time to indulge in lounging around. Since the couch was a custom job, the manufacturer wouldn't take it back. It was black leather. Leather that was butter soft and felt good to crash on after pulling a double shift. That's where Bastien made best use of those frilly, decorative pillows.

"Here you go." Bastien pulled out a chair for Phaedra. He kept his tone light and conversational as he circled around to his chair behind the desk. "So, tell me, Ms. Burke-Carter, during your initial research what dirty little secrets did you find out about us?"

"I'm not interested in secrets at the moment, Mr. Thibeadaux," she replied. She pulled out a manila folder, neatly labeled with the company name on it, and laid it on his desk. "I'm interested in facts. Only the things that I can observe and help you correct."

Man, she was good. She wasn't going to be baited. Not that he wanted to get under her skin. He did want to crack through that icy exterior, though. She had an excellent poker face. He'd hate to be sitting across the table from her, betting his last dime. But in effect, wasn't that exactly what he was doing? He was betting his reputation and his livelihood on the fact that she could help turn his employees around.

"Then let me rephrase that. What have you discovered so far?"

She slid the folder across the desk closer to him and began to talk about the history of the company—from its founding by G-Paw all the way to how many clients they currently supported.

"You've recently opened another office in Canada, haven't you? And are expanding your Beaumont operations? How have you managed to do that in this sluggish economy?" she asked.

"We cut overhead when we lost the branch office in New

Orleans after Katrina." Bastien didn't have much more to say than that. Not much left of his former life and his work at CT Inspectorate but his furniture.

She lowered her eyes. "I see. I'm sorry." There was genuine empathy in her tone. "I have an artist friend who was born there. He had a studio and is thinking about going back to try to rebuild. Any plans to reopen CT Inspectorate's office there?"

"Eventually, if demand increases. But we've relocated most of the employees here."

"Are those your employee files back there?" She noted the stacks of boxes behind his desk.

"Yes, ma'am. Do you want to go through them now?"

She leaned back comfortably in the antique armchair and crossed her legs. Placing her hands on the armrests, her fingers unconsciously rubbed against the wood that had been worn smooth by over a hundred years of use. Bastien couldn't take his eyes off her slender fingers as they caressed the dark mahogany. His heart rate shot up, knowing that same circular motion if performed against his skin would leave him as stiff and as solid as that armrest.

His eyes strayed to the long lean lines of her smooth, stocking-clad legs. Nothing sexier to him than a woman in sheer stockings and heels. "Or…uh…would you rather hold off until after the tour of the facility. You're not exactly dressed for treading around grain silos."

"You can take me on your tour. I'd love to see the facility. I'm sure I'll be fine, Mr. Thibeadaux."

"Yes…yes you are fine…I mean will be…I mean…"

Aw, hell naw! What's the matter with me?

Bastien mentally slapped his forehead with the palm of his hand. He blamed it all on Chas that he was a wreck dealing with this woman. The woman was a triple threat. Smart. Sexy. Secure. She knew who she was and what she could do. Did she have any idea of what she was doing to him? She wasn't giving anything away by her tone or her expression. As far as he could tell, the only thing on her mind was getting the information she needed from him in order to developing a working contract.

"So tell me, Mr. Thibeadaux, about the specific trouble you've been having with your employees. What kind of trouble? When did it start?"

"Seems like it cropped up recently, all of a sudden," Bastien said, thankful for something else to focus on besides this woman's legs and the fantasy he suddenly had of her wrapping them around him. "Four serious accidents in four months. But when I did some more digging, I've found that there have been several, less serious incidents. Not involving injuries, but loss of product."

"And loss of profit?"

"You bet. And I can tell you right now that it didn't sit well with G-Paw. He's my grandfather and the owner. You just don't mess with that man's money. If I had to put a dollar value on everything combined, we're probably talking about losses upwards of half a mil."

She whistled softly, and his eyes immediately lifted from her legs to her lips. Her red-tinted lip gloss reminded him again of cherries. Sweet, luscious cherries.

Awww…hell, Bastien inwardly complained. Why did she have to look so fine? And why did he let her get inside of his head this way?

"Somehow, I have to recoup that. But I can't do it unless I get my folks working at peak efficiency."

"I'm not an efficiency expert. My primary area of expertise involves helping define policies and procedures that affect health, safety and environmental factors. My suspicion is that your HS&E policies and procedures need a complete overhaul. This means, of course, restructuring your training."

"I'm going to be up front with you, Ms. Burke-Carter. I don't have the budget for all that."

"You certainly can't afford to keep letting your employees hurt themselves because they're not properly equipped to do their jobs," she insisted.

"I've got good folks working for me. They bust their butts to get the job done." Bastien refused to let a squabble over money prevent them from getting whatever they needed to make working there safer, better. He rummaged on his desk for a piece of paper and a pen. After scrawling a dollar amount on the paper he pushed it across the desk at her. "This is what we have to work with, *cher.* You tell me what you can do with that."

Phaedra picked up the paper, stared at it for a moment, then raised her eyes to regard him with a look that he was beginning to understand was her way of buying time while carefully choosing words. Bastien couldn't tell from her expression whether she was going to ball it up or laugh in his face. He suspected that it was nowhere near what she was used to getting for her consulting services. But it's what he had. For him, what she decided to do with it was an indicator of her character. Was money all Phaedra Burke-Carter cared about?

She set the offer paper down again. "I can work with this," she said softly.

"You can? You will? Oh, man, that's good to hear!" Relief flooded his voice as Bastien rocked back in his chair, lacing his fingers on top of his head. He felt as if a two-ton anvil had just been lifted.

"Of course I can…and of course I will, Bastien."

Bastien then leaned forward, grinning at her as if she'd just given him the best news of his life. He covered her hand with his. It was meant to be a cordial expression of gratitude. A totally innocent, incidental touch. A poor substitute for the kind of touching he really wanted.

Holding her hand was a reasonable substitute for his initial, intense impulse. He'd wanted to leap over that desk and kiss her. Not just a peck on the cheek but a full blown, bend her over backward, lip-locking kiss she'd remember for years to come. He could almost imagine her frosty facade melting like chocolate left in a double-boiler too long. Starting with a slow simmer then rapidly scorching as her indignation set in. It didn't hit him that she'd dropped the formality and called him by his first name until seconds after he covered her hands with one of his and gave a gentle squeeze.

"Thank you, Phaedra," he responded simply.

When Phaedra didn't pull away, didn't even flinch at his touch, Bastien was optimistic. Maybe his first impulse to kiss her wasn't such a bad idea to begin with. He pushed the boundaries and added a delicate caress to his hand-holding. Phaedra didn't move, didn't even blink. Neither did he. Didn't dare to. Not even when his office door swung open and G-Paw stood there, glowering wordlessly at him.

Chapter 7

Phaedra didn't hear the door open. Her ears were too filled with the sound of rushing wind. She knew that the sound she heard wasn't the precursor to the pending storm outside. The rush she heard in her head was her heart's pulse pounding when Bastien touched her hand.

At first, she didn't hear the old man come in. But she felt the change in Bastien's demeanor when it happened. Felt it within her soul. She'd seen his eyes light up in delight at her acceptance to help him. That light in his eyes soon shifted, deepened in intensity as the mood of the moment changed. Bastien's eyes glowed luminous and green with an undercurrent of simmering sexual attraction. The warmth of his palm soaked into her skin and drew her into the sphere of his powerful influence. At any moment, despite her best intentions and protestations that she would never sleep with a client, she feared that she was going to have to kiss him. Kiss him and get the curiosity out of her system. Nothing else was going to staunch the instantaneous rush of liquid heat she felt between her crossed legs when Bastien caressed her hand.

The sudden tension in his face communicated itself through his body as his hand tightened over hers again. This time, there wasn't a subtle, sensuous caress but an abrupt clench.

What? She mouthed the word without making a sound. He didn't say anything but indicated with a slight lift of his eyes behind her.

Phaedra leaned back in her chair, withdrawing her hand from his as she turned to investigate the reason for Bastien's mood shift.

The old man shuffled in, leaning heavily on his cane, and breathing hard. His lean, line-carved face was flushed. His mouth twisted down, lower jaw jutting forward.

"Somebody want to tell me why you and Alonzo ain't on your way out to Galveston? Silvie told me that you hadn't left yet and were holed up in your office with some female."

Some female?

Phaedra didn't have to guess who this was who'd crashed their meeting. G-Paw Thibeadaux.

She was irritated at herself for letting her physical craving for Bastien's touch play with common sense. She was even more irritated at G-Paw for interrupting them. She readjusted her attitude before meeting this G-Paw. Even as frail as he looked, there was still enough authority in his voice to make it clear who was running CT Inspectorate.

As he entered the room, the old man ignored Phaedra, directing all of his vitriol toward Bastien. He punctuated his demand with sharp, stabbing taps of his rubber-tipped walking cane against the floor. He held the cane with both hands, one hand resting on top of the other. G-Paw's knuckles were swollen, curved with the onset of advanced arthritis. A couple of fingers on this left hand were missing. That didn't surprise her. Industrial accidents involving the loss of a finger or toe were common.

Bastien reached for his desk calendar and flipped to a page, tapping his finger against a handwritten note on it. "The *Kirov* isn't due to tie off at the Port of Galveston until eleven o'clock tonight, G-Paw. And they won't start loading until tomorrow. I've got plenty of time."

The old man grunted in acknowledgment of Bastien's assessment.

"Just don't be late," he grumbled his warning. "Tommy Dewhurst is a long-time client and a friend. We're not gonna screw him over by not being there to get his grain moving. You're not going to do it, Bastien."

Wheezing with exertion, G-Paw eased himself into the guest chair next to Phaedra. Only then did he swing his gaze around, regarding her in the way a curious child stares at the bug he's about to burn with a magnifying glass. Phaedra got the distinct impression that G-Paw could see right through her. Through her long-practiced mask of professionalism, through her clothing, down to the core of who she was. He was assessing her and dismissing her at the same time.

"What's your name, gal?"

His raspy voice was barely above her whisper. Yet, it grated on her as harshly as her knuckles on a cheese grater. It was his attitude that antagonized her. His blatantly chauvinistic, imperialistic attitude.

"G-Paw, this is—" Bastien began.

"Did I ask you?" He immediately cut Bastien off. G-Paw lifted his cane and slammed it against Bastien's desk with enough force to take a tiny chunk out of the antique wood. Bastien gripped the arms of his chair and started to stand. Inspect the damage? Throw the old man out of his office? Phaedra couldn't tell which he would do by the repressed fury on Bastien's face.

"How do you do, Mr. Thibeadaux?" Phaedra deflected G-Paw's attention back to her to give Bastien a chance to settle down. Turning in the chair to face him, she extended her hand. "My name's Phaedra Burke-Carter."

"Burke-Carter," G-Paw mumbled, "Burke-Carter…seems like I know your people. Out of Killeen, Texas, right? Your great-grandpappy settled in Houston in 1926 or so."

Phaedra blinked, the only indicator that she was surprised he knew so much of her family history.

"Yes, sir. That's my family."

He rubbed his gnarled hands over the grayish whiskers sticking out of his jaw and chin. "So, what are you doing way out here on this side of town, gal? It ain't me you come to see now, is it gal?" His tone mocked her, telling Phaedra by his inflection that he considered her being there to be an inconvenience.

Phaedra glanced over at Bastien again, not sure of how to respond. How long had that old man been standing at the door? Did he see Bastien offer her a price for her consulting services? Had Bastien already told the old man he was considering hiring her? If G-Paw knew, why was he messing with her?

"I came to see Bastien," she said truthfully, "You probably didn't know that Bastien and I went to school together," Phaedra said pleasantly, holding the yearbook out to him. "While I was out this way, I thought I'd look him up. Talk about old times and play catch up."

"Bastien doesn't have time to play with anybody," the old man said pointedly. "Not with you."

"I realize that he's a very busy man, sir. But there's also a professional reason why I'm here. I'm looking for new business contracts and hoping Bastien could give some leads. He was just about to give me a tour of your company. And then I'd be on my way and he could get back to whatever you needed him to—"

"I thought I told you to keep a lid on spending around here, boy." G-Paw cut short Phaedra's attempt to mollify him.

She'd managed to slide the piece of paper with Bastien's handwritten offer into her bag when she reached for the yearbook. She was worried that G-Paw had seen it and was already squashing the idea of helping Bastien's people before she could get started.

When G-Paw reached into his inner jacket pocket, withdrawing a folded stack of papers and tossing them at Bastien, she almost breathed a sigh of relief. His complaint was about something completely different. Bastien snatched the papers in midair to slam them onto his desk.

"I have been, G-Paw," he insisted.

"Is this what you call responsible spending? Look at this. What is this? Vending machine invoices. Office supply invoices. A *hunnert-and-fitty* dollars on toilet paper?"

"Folks have to eat, G-Paw. You tell me there's not enough time to let them go off-site to eat. And they gotta take bathroom breaks. What am I supposed to do?"

"You're supposed to act like you're spendin' your own money. Not mine."

Phaedra stood up abruptly. She stood up because she didn't like the way he was talking to Bastien about his employees. And she didn't like the way he was looking at her for interrupting him. Nothing about his look told Phaedra that he considered her to be a lady, just a hindrance to his grandson's ability to make money.

"I won't take up much more of Bastien's time, sir," she assured G-Paw Thibeadaux. "I know that he's a very busy man."

"Never too busy to show an old friend around, Phaedra," Bastien said, keeping his eyes trained on her rather than on his grandfather. He picked up the phone and pressed a button for the reception desk.

"Silvie, would you check if there's a golf cart charged and ready to go out front? I'm taking Ms. Burke-Carter on a tour of Inspectorate. We'll be out in a minute. Thanks."

Then he reached inside the desk drawer and pulled out a plastic packet containing a hard hat, safety goggles and earplugs.

"Here, Phaedra. You'll need these in certain areas of the facility."

"While you're out, run Remy's new schedules down to the ship lab." G-Paw reached out with gnarled hands, rifling through the papers with his knuckles until he found the ones that he wanted.

Bastien picked them up without reading them, folded them in half again and shoved them into the pocket of his jumper.

"Ready to go?" he addressed Phaedra.

"You ain't dressed for scooting around here in no golf cart," he berated her. "And you'd better not try climbing up any ladders or scaffolds. What are you trying to do, gal?"

"G-Paw!" Bastien cut him off sharply.

Fixing G-Paw Thibeadaux with a forced, polite smile, Phaedra replied. "Don't you worry about that, sir. I'm dressed appropriately for my visit."

"Speaking of which, we'd better get moving. Let's go, Phaedra."

Bastien came around the corner of the desk, grasped her just above the elbow and hustled her toward the door.

"Just make sure you're back in enough time to get your behind out to Galveston to pick up that ship," G-Paw rasped.

Bastien waved his hand to acknowledge that he'd heard his grandfather but he was intent on hurrying Phaedra out of his office.

"A pleasure to meet you, Mr. Thibeadaux," Phaedra called over her shoulder, mimicking the same tone that G-Paw had used on her, designed to bait him to a response.

If the old man had a response, she didn't hear it. Bastien reached behind her and yanked on the doorknob with a mingled look of relief and something else she couldn't quite read.

Chapter 8

Bastien didn't mean to manhandle Phaedra to rush her along. Something about the sound of her high heels clacking on the tile floor, and his boots in stomping lockstep with hers echoing in the hall oddly reminded him of thunder and hail. He wasn't surprised that a storm should come to mind. Outside the building, he figured he had maybe a couple hours before the weather cut up outside.

"Sorry about that, Phaedra. I didn't know he'd be in the office today. He's on dialysis three days a week, and it usually leaves him weak and disoriented. Sometimes he says things."

"But he means the things that he says! That's the frightening part."

She was vexed. She put her hands on her hips and blew out a huffy breath, shaking her head slowly back and forth and narrowing her eyes in the direction of his office. Bastien knew that, at any moment, she was going to forget that she was *supposed* to be a professional and go down there to tell that old man where he could go.

"Who does he think he is? He may know my family, but he doesn't know me!"

Her voice dropped several octaves. The rumble of a storm warning if ever Bastien heard one.

She took a step toward Bastien's office, but he reached up and grasped her by the shoulders and squeezed.

"Hold on a moment, Phaedra."

Phaedra looked up at him with hardened eyes as Bastien witnessed a parade of emotions and considered options march across her face. It took a moment, but Phaedra calmed down. Her hands dropped from her hips then tugged on the hem of her jacket to straighten it.

Bastien felt a pang of regret when she retreated back into her fortress of cool. Even in her outrage, he'd felt an overwhelming attraction to her. She was so incredibly sexy, even when she was steps away from mauling G-Paw. Standing there so close to her, he felt the heave in her shoulders as she struggled to restore her breathing to normal. Her lips slightly parted, Phaedra closed her eyes to center herself. He relaxed his grip on her shoulders and instead massaged away the tension. Bastien wanted to lean in. Wanted to kiss her.

But this wasn't the time or the place. The echo of voices in other parts of the office was a conspicuous reminder.

"Don't let G-Paw get to you. He doesn't say anything that he doesn't mean, none of us Thibeadauxs do. That's what I'm apologizing for. We're not perfect. Hell, we're nowhere near perfect. But if you're going to work with us, Phaedra, you'd better get used to that fact right now, because the rest of us aren't going to be so quick to apologize."

"No worries, Mr. Thibeadaux. I grew up in a straight-talking family, too. Now about that tour?"

She raised her hands and widened them until her outer wrists connected with his inner forearms. She pressed her arms against him, effectively knocking his hands from her shoulders.

"Yes, ma'am." Bastien inwardly cringed. She'd gone back to calling him Mr. Thibeadaux again. Whatever gains he'd made to get her to relax around him were wiped out by G-Paw's appearance.

"Hold my calls, would you, Silvie? I'll be back in about half an hour." He took Phaedra outside to the row of golf carts parked in front of the building.

"In you go." Again, he lightly touched her elbow and helped her into the cart. As soon as she sat down, he watched her adjust her skirt, pulling it down as far as it would go. He remembered G-Paw's crude comments about Phaedra's outfit. Despite her bravado, they had made her self-conscious.

"G-Paw really got to you, didn't he?"

When she only looked at him with a tightened jaw, Bastien went on. "I thought you'd have a thicker skin than that, Phaedra. A beautiful woman like you being in this business. You're not used to roughnecks talking at you like that?"

"Sure they talk, but I don't tolerate it. Not from anybody." She snapped, ignoring the compliment he'd given her.

He moved around to the other side, climbed in next to her. As soon as Bastien sat next to her, the cart shimmied as she shifted over to keep her thigh from brushing against his.

"It's a little tight in here," Bastien said.

"I'm used to it," she assured him. But she braced herself by grabbing onto the hood with her right hand to keep as much distance between them as the two-seater cart would allow.

"Safety glasses on," he instructed.

Phaedra pulled off her glasses, giving him an unobstructed view of her dark eyes, before putting on the plastic, utilitarian safety glasses. She slipped her glasses into her jacket pocket.

"Hat, too," he said, knocking on top of the hard plastic with his knuckles. "Or are you too worried about messing up your 'do?" he teased her.

"This 'do was tailor-made for safety gear," she said, placing the hat on her head.

"Need some help?" Bastien offered.

"No, thank you. I've got it," she answered.

"Earplugs, too?" she asked, holding up the bright green molded pieces of foam for inspection.

"Not yet. Unless you're trying to tune me out. Is that it, *cher?* Heard enough of my talking."

"That's not what I meant, Bastien," she chided him.

"Oh, it's Bastien now? Just a minute ago, it was Mr. Thibeadaux this and Mr. Thibeadaux that."

"I'm just keeping up appearances," she said, brushing a piece of imaginary lint from her skirt. "You know, we're supposed to be such good old college buddies. Prairie View alums."

Bastien backed out of the parking spot, holding off on conversation while the golf cart's reverse warning siren beeped. Once he was in forward gear and the backup siren silenced, he could ask the question that he meant to ask since the moment she walked into his office.

"Tell me something, Phaedra, do you remember me from school? 'Cause I don't really remember you."

"Prairie View A&M has a sprawling campus with thousands of enrolled students. Why would you remember me?"

"Solly said we went to some of the same parties."

"That doesn't mean anything. There were hundreds of people crowded in those frat houses and in those dorm rooms at any given time or at any given party."

Her answer seemed plausible. But it wasn't enough for him. She wasn't telling him all that she knew. He *felt* it. Why was she holding back on him?

"You didn't answer my question, *Phaedra*." He said, deliberately using her first name to separate the business end of this meeting from the more personal turn he wanted to take.

"Ok, if you insist, yes I do. I mean, I did remember you from one of those parties. And it was only one, not dozens like Solly made it seem. I was a straight A student. I didn't have time to hang out with your frat boys."

"And?" He pressed for more explanation.

Phaedra paused, staring straight ahead with an unreadable expression. He glanced over at her, back to the road, then back to her again letting her know that he was waiting, though not very patiently, for her response.

The fact that he was hounding her, didn't seem to faze her. Phaedra clasped her hands in her lap and said, "Nothing about those parties way back then has a bearing on what's going on with your employees now." She'd made it clear to him. She wasn't going to discuss it. "Now can we continue on with the tour, Mr. Thibeadaux?"

Bastien was willing to drop it for now. But there was still quite a bit of ground to cover around CT Inspectorate before completing the tour. He'd have the opportunity to bring it up again.

"Right. The tour. Moving on. Starting with where we just left. My office is at the original site of CT Inspectorate. It's undergone some major renovations over the last few years thanks to Jacie. The original building used to be little more than a warehouse with partitions for our offices, meeting rooms and labs."

After they passed the silos and the rail yard, Bastien circled around to the lab that handled the paperwork for the ships that came to the port.

"Is that your ship lab?" Phaedra asked.

"Uh-huh," Bastien affirmed.

"Where G-Paw Thibeadaux told you to drop off those papers."

"Uh-huh." He repeated and rolled right on past it, giving her a look that told her he had no intention of stopping. At that moment, his focus was on Phaedra. He knew as soon as he stepped into that lab, he would be beset with requests and demands on his time. So he continued with the tour. It was his not-so-subtle way of letting Phaedra know that she was his highest concern at the moment.

He rounded a corner around the backside of the silos. The roads were a little rougher back there, filled with gravel from the rail yard and spilled grain kernels.

"When the ships pull into the port, product is loaded from those silos that we passed back there through those conveyors overhead."

Phaedra leaned out of the cart trying to watch the conveyors just as Bastien took a small dip in the road. Her weight shift coupled with an unexpected push of pre-storm wind, forced the cart to tilt slightly to the right.

She cried out, grasping onto the support frame. Without seat belts, she was going to slide out and land on the rough asphalt.

As the cart teetered on its right wheels, Phaedra clung on desperately. Her safety hat whipped off her head and clattered to the ground, rolling several feet away.

Bastien reacted instantly. His fingers clamped around her arm, and he drew her back to his side to redistribute the weight. The few inches that she'd managed to keep between them as they toured the facility melted away with the heat of electric contact he felt when her thigh pressed against his. Bastien brought his other arm around to embrace her. Through his coveralls, he could feel her trembling.

"You all right, *cher?*" He spoke the question, his lips against her forehead, calming her. He took off her safety glasses and smoothed his hand over her bangs to brush them back.

"Yes, I'm f-fine," she stammered, nodding her head. "I don't know what's the matter with me. I feel so stupid, leaning out like that. I know better."

Phaedra examined the nails of her right hand. Several had broken down to the quick in her attempt to hang on.

Bastien tsked, making a soft sound of sympathy as he raised her hand to his lips to kiss away the pain. He kissed the knuckles of her torn nails, then turned her hand over, palm upward, and kissed it again. A shiver went upward from her palm. But Bastien didn't believe it was the near-accident adrenaline rush that caused it. He guessed it was her reaction to him.

When he lifted his eyes and caught her dreamy-eyed expression, he knew for certain that he was the one affecting her. One other thing Bastien was absolutely certain of, he wasn't moving from this spot until he'd kissed her. He had to taste her, to know for certain whether her mouth was as luscious as the cherry-tinted lip gloss promised.

Without giving himself time to reconsider the consequences, Bastien bent his head swiftly to hers. As he did so, he instantly knew that it was both the best and worst decision he'd made in a long time.

Kissing her satisfied his curiosity about the feel of her lips, but it did nothing to satisfy his deeper, more pressing needs. This one kiss wasn't the cure-all for his loneliness. Touching her made him realize just how lonely he was. All of the energy he was pouring into the company when he could have been giving it to a woman. A good woman. One who was smart and sexy and secure and could complement his life's goals.

"Don't," Phaedra uttered, showing her dismay by glancing quickly around.

They were completely out in the open. Anyone could come up on them at any moment. Another employee. Remy. Even G-Paw. Not the kind of situation Bastien would want them to find him in if he had a chance of convincing them to hire Phaedra.

If they were caught, what would this do to her professional reputation? If anyone even thought that she was open to the idea of sleeping with her clients, she wouldn't be able to find legitimate work.

"Don't what?" he asked, his voice taking on a ragged, raw quality that told Bastien he hadn't talked himself back from the edge yet.

Phaedra braced herself as she stepped out of the golf cart. "I'll be right back."

"Where are you going?" Bastien called out to her.

"Don't worry about me." She altered her earlier admonition to him. "Worry about yourself and the incident report you'll have to complete for this near-miss accident." She swatted at the golf cart, hitting the hood as if blaming it for her lapse, before walking a few feet away from him.

Bastien let her go. A little distance between them was what he needed to put his own reaction to her in perspective. Adrenaline and arousal were a dangerous combination. Bastien leaned back in the seat of cart, adjusting his coveralls across his groin as Phaedra kept her back to him.

"Damn."

Bastien cursed his cousin for pointing out just how badly he had neglected his need for physical contact. Too many long hours up there at CT Inspectorate chasing the green instead of socializing and dating now put him in an awkward position. If he'd been taking care of business, personal business in the bedroom, there was no way Phaedra could come up in here and have him this worked up.

Phaedra kept walking until she found the safety hat. She dusted it off then set it back on her head. As she came back to the cart, she looked as if the prospect of splattering herself all over the asphalt didn't bother her.

"Anything else you need to show me, Mr. Thibeadaux, before we conclude this tour?"

"No. I think we're about done. Unless of course there's something else you'd like to do." Bastien spread his arm out over the back of the seat and acted as if everything was normal.

"What I'd like to do, Mr. Thibeadaux, is review your employee incident reports in more detail. Maybe chat with a couple of employees to get some more information on what they were doing when the accidents occurred."

He shook his head no. "One of the employees is out on medical leave. The other has since left the company. The other two are on duty right now and unless you want to come back around ten o'clock tonight when they're getting off shift, I don't think I'll be able to accommodate you, Ms. Burke-Carter."

If she could get formal, then so could he. Though he didn't like it at all. After the wildly careening emotional roller coaster ride she'd just taken him on, it didn't feel natural.

"You'll be in Galveston tonight around then. I'm not going to talk to them without having their manager present."

"Don't go. Stay here. We can talk more over dinner. From here, Galveston is only about forty-five minutes away. Plenty of time to talk. I'll alert my crew and shift their schedules around so they can talk to you."

"I can't. I have another appointment I have to make tonight."

Another appointment? Bastien wondered what kind of appointment she could possibly have that would go until ten o'clock. Did she mean a date? Not that it was any of his business, but he felt the unmistakable grip of jealousy.

"I've made the copies of the employee files for you anyway. You can pick them up from my office before you head out…after you sign that nondisclosure agreement."

"An NDA," Phaedra said, smiling a little. "So you've changed your mind about that?"

"It's necessary if I'm going to give you what you need to draft your proposal. So, when do you think you can get back out here with it?" Bastien asked, starting up the golf cart again.

"It could take up to four weeks while I research your working conditions."

"That long?"

"I'll do what I can to accelerate the process, but it's unrealistic to expect me to develop a solution overnight, Mr. Thibeadaux."

"Then, I guess the sooner I get you back to my office, the sooner you can begin."

Bastien pulled up to park the golf cart while Phaedra carefully climbed out and walked briskly back to her car. He'd called ahead to make sure Jayden was waiting with the employee files.

"I'll take these, Jayden." He then called out to her, "Wait up, Phaedra,"

Phaedra spun around as Bastien approached her with the files. "Where do you want these?"

Phaedra gestured toward her SUV and opened her door as Bastien tossed them into the backseat. "Thank you."

"So, what time is it you're coming back here *tonight?*"

He continued with the kind of confidence of a man who seldom accepted "no" as a final answer. His voice pitched low, he moved closer and leaned against the SUV with his arm draped across the hood of the car. He was even closer than when they'd ridden in the cart.

Phaedra had nowhere to go. Yet, instead of feeling like she needed to escape, she found herself wishing for the deceptive solitude behind the grain silos where Bastien had kissed her. From where she stood as she faced him he could touch anything he wanted and she didn't think she would stop him. Not this time.

"I'm not going to," Phaedra said emphatically, responding to his verbal question as well as the one reflected in his eyes.

"Think about it some more," Bastien urged.

Phaedra paused, rolling her eyes toward the sky, pretending

to think hard about the suggestion, then shook her head at him. "No. Sorry."

"You're not sorry," he said, lifting his lips into a rueful smile that, if she hadn't been bracing herself, would have made her cave in. "I think you're enjoying seeing me on the begging side of pitiful, *cher.*"

"That's not it at all!" Phaedra protested.

"So, where do you want to eat tonight?" He lifted an eyebrow at her. A sort of smug, triumphant salute that he would eventually wear her down.

"At my dining room table. Serving for one," Phaedra replied.

"You could make a trip out to Galveston," he suggested, "We have a company beach house. We could continue our meeting there."

As he said it, it sounded far-fetched. It was an idea that she shouldn't have even bothered to entertain.

"I couldn't possibly, Bastien." Phaedra said firmly. "Not tonight. I have another commitment."

Bastien dropped his chin in dejection. "Well, you can't blame a man for trying, can you?"

"Listen to me, Bastien," she said. "Get this through up there.

"If I'm going to help you, I'm going to have to set some ground rules. This is the way it's going to be. Part of my success in turning companies around includes having the respect of the people that I work for and with. If they don't respect me, they won't listen to me. And if they won't listen to me, they won't get the benefit of what I know. Do you understand what I'm trying to say?"

"Yes, *cher.* I'm feelin' you."

"Your employees are going to take their cue from you about how they're going to treat me. If we're going to get your employee infractions under control, I have to know that I'll be allowed to do my job without…well, without worrying about what anyone is going to be saying behind my back."

"We can't stop people from talking. People think what they want and say what they want."

"We don't have to give them any fuel for the fire, either. I simply want a chance to show you and your company that I know what I'm doing."

"Go ahead and write that proposal. I'll find a way to get it approved and give you your chance."

"Thank you, Bastien. I'll call you later to touch base with you and let you know how I'm proceeding."

Bastien opened the door for her and helped her into the seat.

"All right. You be careful on the road, now, *cher.* It looks like a nasty one is about to blow through."

Chapter 9

Bastien was on Phaedra's mind from the time she pulled off the lot until the time she headed for the freeway.

Come on, Phaedra! Get your head screwed back on straight, she berated herself. It was just a kiss. How could she let one man consume her thoughts so quickly, so completely? Yet, there she was actively considering meeting up with him in Galveston when she knew it wouldn't be prudent. She was ready to jeopardize her profession, her ethics. And for what? A little physical gratification?

Phaedra pounded her forehead with the heel of her hand, trying to drive away the feeling of Bastien's lips where he'd first kissed her in consolation. Now that she was away from his sphere of influence, her thinking was much clearer. One thing was certain, Phaedra vowed, if she was going to work with him, he would have to keep his distance.

She hadn't gone five miles down the road before the weather that had been so cooperative while Bastien took her on the tour of the facility finally gave in. As she drove along the freeway access road, Phaedra kept a watchful, distrustful eye on the clouds darkening from light gray to black with ominous tinges of green. Flashes of lightning cracked the sky, followed closely by echoing rolls of thunder.

The first splatters of rain hit her windshield with the force of tiny water balloon bombs—intermittently at first, then growing in speed and intensity. The grain dust blown onto her parked car from CT Inspectorate's elevators and conveyers collected with the raindrops and ran like rivers of tan-colored mud down the sides of the windshield, out of reach of the wipers.

A convoy of cement mixing trucks entered on the freeway at the same time as Phaedra. The trucks slowed to a crawl, churning up water and mud and flinging back an occasional rock against her windshield. As the air around her darkened, she turned on her hazard lights and dropped back to give them room. Phaedra's fingers gripped the steering wheel as she concentrated on keeping her eye on the road. She didn't notice her phone ringing at first until the Bluetooth earpiece sitting in a cubby near the dashboard started to flash blue and vibrate.

Phaedra hooked it onto her ear.

"Yes?" she responded tensely.

"Phaedra. It's me, Bastien."

"What is it, Bastien?" She didn't mean to sound rude, but she didn't want to take her attention from the truck that had just cut in front of her, either. No lane change signal. No taillights. Its load of scrap metal tied down by bungee cords slid and shifted precariously to one side and then the other.

"I called to tell you that you left your briefcase in my office."

"I did?" Phaedra took her eyes off the road for a second to check around her. "Just great!" Exactly what she didn't need right now. She'd been so caught up in trying to suppress her reaction to him that she'd left her bag in his office. "I can't believe I did that."

"Where are you? I can bring it to you so you won't have to turn all the way around to come back for it."

"I haven't made it to the freeway yet. It's pouring buckets out here, and the roads are starting to flood."

"Be careful, Phaedra. Those trucks don't always slow down

when the weather gets ugly. Maybe you ought to pull over until the weather passes."

She looked around, getting her bearings. "Not a bad idea. I've just passed a gas station, a convenience store and a barbecue restaurant."

"I know exactly where you are. You should be coming up on a strip center with a tax preparation storefront and a self-service laundry."

"Yes, I think I see it now. I can—oh, good grief! What now?"

Phaedra turned the wheel sharply, trying to avoid debris falling from the bed of a flatbed truck hauling scrap metal.

"Phaedra?" Bastien's voice came back, strident and concerned. "Phaedra, is everything all right?"

She didn't answer him right away but kept her focus on the road. The chunk of metal had fallen so quickly that she couldn't avoid it as it bounced and clattered on the road. She heard it thwack against the SUV's front grill. The sound of metal against asphalt was awful as her car dragged it along, then sucked it under her wheels.

Bastien must have heard it, too. She didn't see how he couldn't. It sounded awful to her. "What was that?"

Phaedra's car fishtailed on the wet asphalt. Concerned, but not panicked, she spun the steering wheel, readjusting as the rear tire punctured, shredded and wound up in partial strips on the road along with the metal debris.

"Hold on, Bastien. I just hit a piece of metal in the road. Pulling over now!" Hazards still flashing, Phaedra coasted off the access road into the parking lot where Bastien said he'd meet her.

He didn't wait long enough for her to park before he demanded, "Where are you now, Phaedra?"

"In that parking lot with the self-service laundry," she confirmed her location as she pulled into a parking spot. Phaedra drew in deep breaths to calm herself. When she held her hands out in front of her, they trembled. She couldn't help noticing that she'd reacted the same way to this potentially fatal accident as she had to Bastien's kiss.

"You stay right there. I'm on my way. I should be there in about fifteen minutes," Bastien promised.

"No hurry, Bastien. I'm not going anywhere anytime soon. I have to call my roadside service to change my flat tire."

"Roadside service? What are you calling them for? Didn't I tell you that I was coming to you?" She heard him moving around his office, opening drawers, slamming them shut again followed by the jangle of keys.

"Bastien, I can't ask you to fix my tire, it's pouring out here! I have a roadside assistance service. That's what I pay good money for."

"I'll do it for you, Phaedra." He sounded offended that she didn't consider him as her first choice. Just as quickly, all seriousness dropped from his voice. "And I'll do it for free…for the first hour, that is. After that, I'll have to charge you."

"You are only talking about changing my tire, aren't you, Mr. Thibeadaux?"

"Why, of course, Ms. Burke-Carter." He mimicked Phaedra's prim tone. "What else could I possibly be talking about?"

"Why, the tire of course."

"Listen to me, Phaedra. All jokes aside. This isn't the best area to break down in. Being so close to the port, we get a lot of traffic, not all of it legal. I want you stay in the car, and lock the doors. Don't open the doors or roll down the windows for anybody. I'll be there as soon as I can."

"Thanks for the warning, Bastien. Don't worry, I can take care of myself."

"I didn't say you couldn't, superwoman," he teased, "But you wait there so I can take care of you, too."

Phaedra didn't know if the smile in her voice and in her heart came over the phone when she said, "All right, Bastien. I'll be careful."

"See you in a minute."

She turned off the engine, checked the locks and waited for him. The rain continued to fall. With the car engine off, the droning of highway traffic and the splash and splatter of the rain against the car surrounded her in strangely hypnotic sounds. Soothing.

She lay back against the white leather headrest and thought about all that had transpired during the day. She thought about her meeting with Bastien, replaying in her head every word, every gesture, every look that said more than what they uttered with their mouths. They'd met to talk about Bastien's safety concerns, but there was a dangerous current running beneath each phrase. For every word they spoke, there were a hundred others that they didn't. And when he'd kissed her. Oh, that kiss!

Phaedra closed her eyes and moaned aloud, her hand inadvertently rising to tentatively trace the curve of her mouth with her fingertips. The memory of the kiss, how she'd felt, how he'd tasted and how he'd tested the boundaries of her resistance made her squirm in her seat. She was glad that she was alone and that her windows were darkly tinted. Anyone watching her might assume she'd lost her mind.

The sputter of another vehicle approaching her caused her eyes to fly open.

Bastien?

No. Not him.

Phaedra's heart sank as a battered red wrecker truck pulled up. It came from around the corner of a building on the far side of the parking lot and rattled toward her. Its headlights cut through the rain and blinded Phaedra for just a moment. The tow truck idled for several moments, gears grinding as the hauling hooks and pulleys readjusted. Then, the driver side window rolled down and the driver leaned out.

"You called for a tow, ma'am?"

Through the window, Phaedra shook her head no. Even if she had called her roadside assistance service, they couldn't have gotten here that fast.

"Ma'am, you wanna roll down your window?" The driver tapped at his ear as if he couldn't hear her. She reached for the button to roll down the window to repeat her denial, but then paused as Bastien's warning came back to her. This wasn't the safest of places to be. Instead of rolling down the window, Phaedra pressed the door locks again, the driver heard her lock the doors.

"No thanks," Phaedra called out loudly through the raised window. "I've got someone on the way."

Either the driver didn't hear her or wasn't going to take no for an answer. She saw him turn away and speak to someone on the passenger side. The wrecker driver's partner leaned forward to get a good look at her and the SUV. For an instant, their gazes connected across the span of their vehicles. He waved at her from the other side, smiling. That smile did nothing to put her at ease.

Maybe her nerves were getting the best of her or maybe she was alarmed by Bastien's warning. Still, Phaedra didn't like the vibe she was getting from this tow truck team. Something inside of her clenched in irrational fear when one of them got out of the truck and walked toward her car, even though she'd told them that she didn't need their help.

The man was huge. He had to weigh over three hundred pounds. His rain slicker was too small, exposing coarse, hairy arms covered in tattoos. His grease-stained gray jumper was too long and caught on the heels of his cowboy boots as he shuffled on the pavement, sloshing through pools of water collecting in potholes in the ground. He lowered his head, covered by a sopping wet, faded yellow bandanna. It was hard to tell where the bandanna ended and the straggles of his dishwater blond hair began.

Phaedra waved him back. "I don't need your help."

He ignored her, circled around the car once, shaking his head, and toying with the toothpick he had stuck in the corner of his mouth. He sloshed around to the rear of her SUV, and Phaedra could feel the entire SUV shake as he hefted a couple of times on the rear hatch, trying to lift it open.

"What are you doing?" Phaedra twisted in her seat and shouted at him. "Stop that!"

"Ma'am, your rear tire is all chewed up. Open up yer hatch, and we'll fix it for you. Swap it out for ya real quick and git ya on yer way."

"No."

She couldn't have made it any plainer than that. Yet, he came around and leaned his hip against the driver's side door. With his weight against the door, she couldn't open it. If she wanted to get out of the car, she'd have to scramble to the backseat or scoot over to the passenger side. The wrecker driver took that as an option, too. He'd climbed out of the tow truck and was now resting his arm against the hood of her car, leaning forward, peering into it. It seemed to her that he was checking to see if she was alone.

Feeling trapped in her own vehicle, Phaedra pressed the redial button on the cell phone, hoping to catch Bastien before he left the office. It rang for several seconds. There was a moment of silence on the line while the phone rolled over and began a fresh round of ringing. Finally, he picked up.

"Yeah?"

"Where are you?" Her question came out sounding like the demand of a silly, frightened child calling out for help against imaginary things that go bump in the night. She felt foolish for feeling afraid but was not going to discount her fear. Phaedra understood all too well that a healthy fear could sometimes save your neck.

"About two minutes away. What's wrong?"

"N-nothing." She didn't want to alarm him. These two hadn't done anything. Not really. But their tactics seemed too aggressive to be helpful. "Nothing," she repeated. "Just get here. Okay?"

"I'm on my way. Are you all locked in? All the doors? Windows up?"

"Yes," Phaedra assured him then added. "Would you do me a favor and stay on the phone with me until you get here? I've got company."

"What kind of company?" The question came back fast and filled with wariness.

"I'm not sure. They drove up in a tow truck."

"Did you call them?" There was more accusation in his tone this time.

"No, I didn't. You asked me not to. They just showed up on their own."

"Don't you worry now, Phaedra. Tow trucks cruise the freeways all the time looking to pick up business."

"I know," Phaedra said. She knew this to be true. She also knew that he was saying that to allay her fears. The only thing that would really make her feel better was him getting there.

"I told them that I didn't need them to change my tire, but they're not budging. Where are you now?"

"I'm coming up on you right now."

Phaedra lifted her eyes and watched as Bastien drove up in one of the white company vehicles that she'd seen parked in front of CT Inspectorate. Tension drained from between her shoulder blades and from her voice.

"I see you," she said softly, gratefully. "Thank you for getting here so fast."

"Not a problem," he said, snapping the cell phone shut.

Phaedra watched as Bastien got out of the truck, seemingly unbothered by the rain or the two men who circled her car. His steps were unhurried, his head was unbowed. As he walked toward her, he was loosely swinging a tire iron in his right hand—a completely appropriate and reasonable tool for her situation. Yet, the sight of which made the wrecker driver and his partner back away from her toward their own vehicle.

Bastien raised his free hand in greeting. "Nasty time to be out, huh, boys?"

The driver of the tow truck folded his arms across his chest and shifted his weight from foot to foot. As he glanced at his partner, Phaedra could feel the uneasiness communicated between them.

"Yes, sir. It sure is."

Even the big man got out of Bastien's way as Bastien positioned himself between her SUV and the wrecker crew. He glanced over his shoulder and winked at her before turning his attention back to them. He put his hands in front of him slapping the curved business end of the tire iron into the palm of his hand. The smack of the thick iron rod against his wet palm sounded unpleasant. It probably looked even worse from that wrecker crew's perspective.

"You…uh…need any help, bruh?" the driver offered.

"Naw, man. I've got this," Bastien said, taking a step closer to them, still hefting the tire iron. "How much do we owe?"

"Nuthin', man. Nuthin'. Just trying to help a lady out."

"Yeah, we were just trying to get her back on the road. Make sure nuthin' happened. You know," the big man chimed in.

"I know. Real angels of mercy." Bastien lifted the tire iron and rested it on his shoulder.

The big man forced laughter. "Angels of mercy. I like that. We just might paint that on the truck. New advertising."

"Uh-huh. You go on and do that," Bastien advised. "Go on now." He gestured toward the road with the tire iron. He only had to do it once before the wrecker crew mumbled their goodbyes, piled back into their truck and spun out of the parking lot.

Phaedra rolled down the window. "Is it safe to come out?"

"They're gone. And they won't be coming back."

"I meant you, John Henry."

"John Henry, the steel driving man. I like that. I just might have to paint that on my truck."

"You do that," Phaedra advised, mimicking his words and his inflection when he'd warned them off.

"Are you all right, *cher?*"

"I'm fine. I don't know why I panicked like that. I don't scare so easily."

"Don't worry about it. Those were some skanky-looking characters." His quick eyes took in the open glove box, the papers that had fallen out while she'd searched through it, finally resting on the item sitting, dark and sleek, on the leather seat beside her.

"And what were you planning to do with that?" There was curiosity in his tone as he indicated the nonlethal Taser sitting within her hand's reach.

"What do you think? Same thing you were going to do with that if it came down to it," Phaedra retorted, pointing to his tire iron.

Just because she'd never been assaulted on any of her assignments didn't mean that she went blithely through her career without preparing for the eventuality. Thank heaven she never had to use that Taser. Having it made her feel better. Just as having Bastien come to her aid had.

He nodded and said, "I'm glad that it didn't resort to that. For either of us. Been a while since I've had to throw down."

"Me, too," Phaedra said gruffly, pretending to crack her knuckles and pound her fist into her palm.

Bastien laughed. "You're something else, lady. Where's your spare tire and jack?"

Phaedra pointed her thumb over her shoulder, toward the rear of the SUV.

"I've got an extra umbrella in the truck. Let me get it for you," he offered.

"I'll hold it over you while you work."

"No, ma'am. I want you to use it to walk into the restaurant over there while I change your flat."

"And leave you out here in the rain all by yourself? I can't do that."

"In that case, set the parking brake and give me your lock lug key. Be back in a minute."

The rain had not let up. Bastien's coveralls were soaked by the time he went back to his truck to retrieve the umbrella and her briefcase. He didn't open the umbrella as he returned but waited until Phaedra opened the door and climbed out of the SUV, holding it over her head so she wouldn't get wet.

"I'll take over now," she said, taking the umbrella from him.

Phaedra shielded Bastien from more rain as he retrieved her spare tire and jack. Just like in the golf cart, there wasn't much room for them to maneuver under the umbrella. Phaedra stood close to Bastien as he knelt down by the tire and started to loosen the lugs.

"Whatever you hit tore this tire up good," he remarked, his words staccato as he worked the jack handle up and down.

"A truck hauling scrap metal cut me off and lost part of its load. Metal bounced all over the place. I'm fortunate it didn't bounce up and hit my windshield and that I could reach you. You came out all this way just to bring me a briefcase. In case I haven't said it enough, thank you, Bastien."

"Do you really think my being here is about that briefcase?" He glanced over his shoulder as he worked.

"Then what is this all about, Bastien?"

"You know what they say, don't you?"

"Say about what?"

"About people who leave things behind."

"Umm…they say that they're absentminded?" Phaedra suggested, lifting her eyebrows at him.

"Noooo," he countered, heaving the shredded tire off and putting the spare on. "They say that people leave things behind because, subconsciously, they want to come back."

"I didn't go back to you. You came to me," she argued with him.

"Which brings me back to my original question. Do you think *my* being here is only about your briefcase?"

Nervously she toyed with the umbrella, spinning the handle in her hand and making it twirl. "What else could it be?"

"Come with me to Galveston tonight…and I'll tell you. Better still, I'll show you, *cher*."

Bastien's back was to her as he worked on the tire so she couldn't see his expression.

"The house is right on the beach. Twenty steps and you're right there. It's got three separate bedrooms. Separate full baths. Fully stocked kitchen and, if you didn't like what I served up, there are several restaurants nearby."

"You're not making it easy for me to say no," Phaedra complained.

"Then don't."

"No," Phaedra said with conviction. She was his consultant. He was her client. Nothing was going to happen between them. Period. "I can't. I've already told you."

"I'm surprised you'd let other people dictate to you what you should and shouldn't do. You're an independent woman. You don't have to do anything you don't want to."

"Easy for you to say, Mr. I-don't-have-a-budget-to-do-what-I-want-for-my-employees," Phaedra was stung into saying. "You don't know how it is with me. My career…my family. I have other obligations. People depend on me to make certain I stay at the top of my profession. I can't just do whatever I want to do, whenever I want to."

"No, *cher*. It isn't easy for me to say," he corrected. "It's not easy for me at all. Aside from my work issues, I'm not used to having to work so hard for a 'yes' from a woman. I want to get to know you better. Getting you to visit me in Galveston is the best answer I can think of."

He tightened the last lug and then pushed the shredded tire and rim to the rear of the SUV. Phaedra followed closely behind him, holding up the umbrella and stubbornly shoring up her will-power. If only he knew how close she was to caving.

"There," he said, putting all the tools back and slamming the hatch shut. "You're good to go."

Good to go? She didn't want to. She didn't want to go and neither did he. So, they stood for a few minutes barely inches away from each other, face-to-face. Not talking. Not touching. Simply huddling under the umbrella with sheets of rain falling all around them and the sounds of the freeway filling the silence.

Bastien broke through the invisible wall first, leaning forward to brush a kiss on her cheek. "Drive carefully."

Phaedra closed her eyes at his touch and leaned forward into his chest. As she moved to be closer to him, she felt her feet step deeper into a puddle. Water sloshed over her shoes, soaking her feet. She had the crazy image of sinking deeper and deeper into that puddle. She had that unmistakable feeling that she was getting in over her head.

"How long will you be in Galveston?" she murmured.

"Only a few of days. I'll be back Saturday night. Solly's throwing me a surprise birthday party."

"I didn't know it was your birthday, Bastien."

"See? If you came to visit me, there's so much more you could find out about me. Come to Galveston and celebrate with me."

Phaedra took a deep breath and spoke quickly before she could talk herself out of it. "I might not be able to come out there to Galveston, but maybe I could call you and continue my research. You know, get to know you better…I mean, more about the company and…and…"

"Phaedra," he began, stopping her nervous ramble.

"Yes, Bastien?"

"Get back into your car. Back to your obligations." He held the door open for her, waited while she buckled up. That wasn't what he was originally going to say, but at that moment, it was the safest thing.

"That's not a full-sized spare," he reminded her, "As soon as you can, get to your mechanic to have it replaced."

"I will," Phaedra promised, nodding.

"I'll talk to you later, Phaedra."

"Just talk," she stressed. "I'll call you when I'm ready to arrange for employee interviews. I hope you understand, Bastien. In order for us to work together, we have to respect these boundaries."

Chapter 10

Bastien hit the Galveston County limits sometime around eleven o'clock that night. He rolled along the causeway between the Texas mainland and Galveston Island with all of the windows of his truck rolled down. The evening turned out to be better than he'd expected. After the cloudburst that kept him drenched while he changed Phaedra's tire, the rain clouds eventually cleared out, leaving a clear summer night sky filled with stars and a bright yellow moon. The breeze blowing off the Gulf was steady and strong, stirring the tropical palm plants that grew in this part of Texas.

There would have been less traffic congestion on the back roads of Galveston. But he'd taken that road a million times and felt in need of a change of scenery. Bastien still had some time left before he had to check in with the port authority. The crew of the *Kirov* hadn't been cleared to tie off the ship. The captain and first mate had his cell phone number and would call when they were available. Besides, they weren't going to load all two million bushels of wheat before he got there. He wasn't worried. Not about work, anyway.

Tonight, he was going to take Chas's advice. When was the last time he relaxed? Enjoyed the sites? Bastien figured that he'd earned a little "me" time.

Actually, he took this detour to give him time to plan. He was scouting out locations along the Seawall Boulevard. Locations where Phaedra and he might possibly wind up. Cafés. Coffee bars. Piano bars. Little known, out of the way night clubs that played twelve bar blues. Didn't matter where they went as long as she was there with him.

By the time he could smell the Gulf breezes, he'd made up his mind that he wasn't going to be satisfied with just another phone call from her. Bastien wanted to see her again. Not next week or the week after when she'd made vague promises to return.

Getting her to come to him wasn't going to be easy. Even in the few hours that they'd spent together at Inspectorate, he'd observed some things about her personality. Spontaneity wasn't a word that fit easily or naturally into her vocabulary. Getting her out here was going to take a lot of convincing. He needed a plan that didn't sound like he was running a game on her. She was a smart woman and could smell a game coming a mile away. If he was going to win her over, he had to be smart about it, too.

Every time he thought about how he was going to change her mind, intelligence collided with instinct and intuition. It didn't make sense for him to ask her to jeopardize her reputation, by crossing that thin, but clearly defined line between personal and professional. Bastien could list a thousand reasons why what he wanted from her was inappropriate, from certain points of view.

Yet, at the moment, Bastien didn't really care about those other points of view. As he cruised along the Seawall Boulevard, watching all of the happy, contented couples walking hand in hand, he wanted what they had. Where was his own slice of contentedness? Up until he'd left New Orleans, he didn't think he could have the life of a deeply committed relationship. He hadn't found a woman who made him entertain the possibility.

"Just my luck," Bastien grumbled aloud. He had to find one woman he shouldn't want and couldn't have. Intelligence was telling him to let it go. Yet, instinct was telling him to hold on. There was something there for them. He felt it deep down in his gut where instinct lived. When he'd asked her out, she'd declined because she was obligated to. She didn't *want* to refuse him. Her head and heart were waging a debate. Which one would win would depend entirely on him.

Bastien had all the evidence he needed to press forward. He'd seen the conflict in her eyes. He'd heard it in her moan when he'd touched her. He'd tasted her struggle when he kissed her. As long as there was the possibility that her heart would win, Bastien was going to do whatever he had to do to tip the balance in his favor. Forget about doing the smart thing. Instinct and intuition promised him that his heart would later thank his head for keeping out of the way.

Get this through up there, Phaedra had said before she left him earlier that afternoon, tapping him on his forehead. She'd done it because she understood what a stubborn hardhead he could be. Bastien laughed to himself. We'll, that wasn't the first time he'd been accused of being hardheaded. And he fully anticipated that his heart would drive his head against several brick walls before he was willing to give up. No, not brick—ice. The solid icy walls of Phaedra's resistance. He was willing to take a couple knocks to get what he wanted. He'd proven that every day for the last four years since walking through Inspectorate's doors in Texas.

Bring it!

Bastien sent his challenge to Phaedra to the open air. He pulled out his phone, thinking that he'd check in with the office. That was what his head was telling him what to do. He wound up dialing Phaedra's number instead.

It was late. Almost midnight. Before the second ring, he was already forming the perfect message he would leave when her voice mail picked up, a message crafted for winning hearts.

"Hello?"

"Phaedra? Hey. It's me. Bastien," he stumbled over his words. So much for witty repartee.

"Yes, I know."

"Did I wake you?"

Bastien listened closely in the background for telltale sounds that she was not alone. This obligation that she had to keep, that kept her from being with him, had *it* followed her home? Did *it* live with her? Was that *it* actually a *he?* Was *it* her man?

"No, you didn't wake me. I was working late anyway." There was rustling in the background and the soothing strains of piano music.

"Yeah. Me, too."

"Could you hold on just a minute? Let me turn down the music."

"Sure. I'll hold on."

The noise in the background faded. No more music. She'd either turned it down or moved to another room. Moments later, she returned to the phone.

"Okay, I'm back. So…did you make it to Galveston okay?"

"I got into town about half an hour ago."

"I'm glad the weather cleared up. I felt terrible for you out in the rain changing my tire."

"Don't you worry about that now, *cher.* You've apologized enough for something that wasn't your fault. Besides, the weather's turned out fine. Just fine."

"I'm so glad to hear it."

"Hear it? Naw. You oughta be here to see it. Not a cloud in the sky. A big ol' yellow moon is hitting the water just so. Enough stars to dazzle your eyes. So close, I can reach out and pluck one out of the sky for you."

"I had no idea you had a poetic streak in you!"

"Matched only by my mean streak, huh?"

"I wasn't going to say that."

"You didn't have to. I saw that look on your face when I sent those wrecker drivers off. I didn't make you nervous, did I?"

"Noooo," she said, drawing the word out.

"I sense a *but* tacked on the end of that," Bastien said.

"I was just wondering what you would have done if they'd tried something."

What she was really asking him was if he was capable of

violence. Did he have a temper? Could he, would he, ever turn that temper on her?

Bastien chose his words very, very carefully.

"I don't know what I would have done, Phaedra, if those guys had pushed it. I just know that I wouldn't have let them hurt you. I wouldn't let anyone, and I mean anyone, hurt you."

Did that give her the assurances she needed?

"Those guys made me nervous. That's why I called you in the first place. I knew you'd handle it."

"So, Phaedra, did you get that information I sent you?" He'd sent a text message with the address of his beach house to her cell phone, an e-mail and for good measure left a message on her office voice mail.

"You mean the address in Galveston? Oh, yes, I received it," she acknowledged.

"What about the rest of my invitation?"

Phaedra cleared her throat and coughed delicately away from the phone. "No, Bastien, I'm sorry I won't be able to make that appointment."

"Appointment? Phaedra, that wasn't a meeting request that I sent you. I asked you if you wanted to come out here and celebrate my birthday with me."

"I know," she said, laughing. "The singing e-card gave me the clue."

"And?" he prompted.

"And nothing. I've already sent you a response. I can't go. I can't be there with you."

"Why not?"

"Because I have too much work to do."

Maybe she did. Maybe she didn't. Maybe she was using work as an excuse to keep that thin, clearly defined line between them. Bastien barreled over that imaginary line like he just blew through that streetlight changing from green to yellow.

"I want to see you again, Phaedra."

"And you will. Next week when I come out to interview your employees about their accidents and review your working conditions," she promised.

"It doesn't have to be that long until we see each other. You can bring your work here tonight."

"That's not possible."

"Why not, Phaedra. What's stopping you?" he pressed.

"It's late," she said, sounding to Bastien like that was the first excuse she could come up with. "I'm not going to be driving around at this time of night."

Bastien mentally kicked himself. Of course he shouldn't have asked her to come out this late. But he wasn't quite ready to give up.

"What about in the morning?"

"I have appointments first thing in the morning."

Bastien pulled up to the next stoplight, tapping the palm of his hand against the steering wheel in silent frustration. That light was the perfect metaphor for what was going on in his conversation with her.

"Then what about after your appointments?"

Phaedra sighed dramatically into the phone. "You don't give up, do you?"

"Is that a yes?" Bastien said hopefully. "Sounded like a yes to me."

"Then you need to check your cell phone's reception," she contradicted. "That wasn't a yes."

"What if I tell you that I can keep it strictly business? You don't want to come to my beach house? Fine. I just thought you'd be able to work comfortably there. You pick the location. You pick the topics. Could you make time for me then?"

"Believe me, I really wish I could. But it wouldn't work. It would feel…well, like a date. And, the truth is, Bastien, I don't date my clients. It's unethical and I could get into serious trouble for it. We both could."

Bastien's cell phone beeped. Another call coming in. He checked the caller ID display then swore softly. It was the manager of the grain elevator at the Port of Galveston calling him to the *Kirov*. Not the best timing, so he ignored it.

"That's the last thing I want is to get you into trouble, Phaedra," he said.

The phone beeped again.

"Maybe you'd better answer that," Phaedra said, recognizing the sound.

"It's the *Kirov*. It can wait," Bastien said, fighting to keep the irritation at the interruption out of his voice. He wasn't ready to hang up on her just yet. If he could just keep her talking, keep her thinking about him, maybe she would—

"Bastien, if it's your job, then you have to answer it. I can't be the reason for you getting into trouble," she said resolutely.

"I know…I know…okay, then, if that's the way it has to be. Is it okay if I call you tomorrow?"

"Of course it is, Bastien. As long as it's business related."

"Absolutely," he said in a dry manner meant to make her laugh.

"Somehow, I don't believe you."

"You just be sure to answer the phone anyway."

"I will, Bastien."

"And Phaedra."

"Yes?"

"Thanks for…you know…watching out for me, *cher*."

"You see, Bastien," she said. "You're not the only one making sure that neither of us is hurt."

Chapter 11

Well after midnight, Phaedra hung up the phone with Bastien. As she held the phone in her palm, it felt warm almost to the point of discomfort. They'd been on the phone for almost an hour. Logically, she would have blamed the warmth on the battery overheating for being on the phone for so long. But Phaedra wasn't feeling very logical at that moment. Just the opposite. She wasn't feeling logical, or motivated to work, for that matter. The phone was hot because *she* was hot. Hot to the point of discomfort.

And it was all Bastien's fault!

She sat in the middle of her bed, papers scattered around her and a half-filled bottle of chardonnay sitting on her nightstand. Phaedra's computer rested on her lap as she pecked at her keyboard, a half-hearted attempt to type up her notes. She'd only gotten as far as the cover page when Bastien called her and practically begged her to come out to see him.

"I had to say no," Phaedra spoke out loud to the empty room, hoping the sound of her voice would convince herself that it was true. "It's better this way. No sense in starting anything we can't finish."

What was it they said in all of those tough gangsta movies? Don't start nuthin', won't be nuthin'.

"A truer and more eloquent sentiment has never been spoken. So, that being said, here's to profit before passion." She toasted herself, taking another sip of wine to empty the glass.

Phaedra fell back on the bank of pale pink and green satin-covered throw pillows that decorated her bed. She was a little buzzed; she could tell by the way the room was spinning.

"Take my keys, bartender. Call me a cab," she whispered then giggled at the silliness of her emotional state. She blamed her giddiness on the two glasses of wine that she'd had on a practically empty stomach. She hadn't eaten much dinner. She blamed it on being tired. The truth was she wasn't tired; she was tempted. Distracted by thoughts of Bastien Thibeadaux.

With only cheese, crackers and fruit to counter the effects of the wine, she wondered what she'd have to do to counter the effects that Bastien seemed to have on her.

She grabbed one of the pillows, hugged it close to her chest, and like a love struck teenager, pretended as if she were holding Bastien. A poor substitute for the man in the flesh.

Phaedra closed her eyes, trailing her fingers along the pillow as she traced from memory the tattoo on his upper arm that proudly proclaimed his fraternity.

"Your own fault you're lying here all alone, Phaedra. You could have him if you want him."

And she did want him. There was no denying that. If she could only let go of her fear of being judged, she could have had him close to her just like that.

Closing her eyes, Phaedra pictured every detail that could have been if she'd only said "yes" to him tonight. It would have been so romantic, sitting out on the open patio of his beach house. An exquisite seafood dinner. Flowers. Candles. Soft music and the feeling of strong Gulf breezes blowing against her superheated skin, ignited by his touch each time he reached out to her. The image of her and Bastien curled up, sated and sleepy after a night of making love settled in her mind. The image was so sharp, so clear, that she could hardly believe that she hadn't gone through with it. With the way her body reacted, as if reliving a recent memory rather than indulging in a secret fantasy, no one could convince her otherwise that she hadn't been with him.

Phaedra couldn't help herself. As she thought about how he would feel against her, face-to-face, chest to chest, his body fused with hers inevitably as he moved over her and gradually into her, prolonging his own pleasure while he saw to hers, she squeezed the pillow even tighter. Reality was quick to tell her that it was only cold foam cushions and lace and satin that she held on to; but in her fantasy, it was the vibrant warmth of Bastien's skin. Her fingers splayed against the pillow, willing herself instead to feel the broad planes of his well-muscled back. She caught her lower lip between her teeth, wishing that it was he who was nipping at her and wishing that she could feel his tongue plunging into her mouth.

Without consciously realizing what she was doing, Phaedra's hands slid from the pillow, following the trail she imagined he would take if she'd relented and given him the opportunity. Over the peaks of her breasts, down over her stomach, glistening with a sheen of perspiration as her breath came faster and faster. Then dipping between her clenched thighs. A sharp inrush of breath when she felt how completely the fantasy had affected her.

"Bastien!"

Phaedra called out his name, wondering if she could send her desire through time and space and instantly transport him there. Curling up into a ball and drawing her knees up, she rocked back and forth as she fantasized how he would rock her to soothe her after tremors of long-denied physical release wracked her from head to toe.

"See what you've done to me, Bastien?" Phaedra complained. God, what was she going to do? How was she going to face him knowing that if he even looked at her the wrong way, she was likely to relent. What would all of her colleagues think of her if they knew that she turned one of her clients into her own personal love toy?

She shut down her computer and pushed her papers off the end of the bed.

"All your fault!" she grumbled, shoving the pillows away for good measure.

By the time she arrived at the office Friday morning, she was in no better mood. Her sleep was fitful, filled with dreams that she didn't remember but saw the effects of when she looked in the mirror during her morning routine. Phaedra applied a touch more makeup than usual, dabbing concealer to the dark circles beneath her bleary eyes.

Phaedra avoided her usual coffee shop. She'd arrived at her office at 6:30 in the morning to pull the files she needed for her daily appointments. Her first appointment wasn't until 9:30 a.m., but by 7:00 a.m., she was already feeling her craving for the sweet indulgence affecting her ability to focus. Reading through her notes from a legal pad in her left hand, Phaedra reached for the small pot of freshly brewed dark roast with her right.

"Ouch! Sh—!"

Phaedra clamped down on the curse when her finger collided with the warm side of the coffeepot.

"Are you all right, Ms. Burke-Carter?"

Phaedra's administrative assistant, Summer Davis, looked up from the mail she was sorting at her desk.

"I'm fine," Phaedra said sharply. She resisted the impulse to stick her finger in her mouth and instead blew softly on it to take away the sting. Holding her hand out in front of her, Phaedra frowned at the two bandages that were wrapped around her fingertips.

"What happened to you? Did you burn yourself?" Summer asked. "I mean…just now…on the coffeepot."

"Something like that," Phaedra muttered. It wasn't the coffeepot that had given her this pain but getting too relaxed around that Bastien Thibeadaux. And if she didn't stop thinking about him, letting him distract her, Phaedra had no doubt that she was likely to suffer more than a few broken nails.

"Oh, Ms. Burke-Carter," Summer hailed her before Phaedra

returned to her office. "I didn't get a chance to update your calendar. Your two o'clock today from that oilfield services company asked if we could move the meeting to Tuesday. I already checked. Tuesday is open."

Phaedra blew on her coffee to cool it. "Thanks, Summer."

No afternoon meeting. Just one appointment today and she was free. Free to…to do what?

Don't even think about it, girl.

Phaedra pushed aside the thought that eased its way past her resolve not to see Bastien again until she was ready to discuss his company's safety issues.

Profit before passion. Profit before passion. Profit before passion. The mantra resounded in her head, crashing her thoughts like she imagined the waves of the Gulf crashed against Galveston Beach.

Chapter 12

The main conveyor system at Pier 30 was broken. The report finally came down to Bastien around noon. He didn't need a report to tell him that. The acrid smell of burning, grinding gears mingled with the scurry of technicians scrambling to troubleshoot the problem was evidence enough. There would be no grain loading today until the problem was resolved. So Bastien stood on the pier where the *Kirov* was docked and shot the breeze with Grigoriy, the first mate. Grigoriy knew very little English, and Bastien knew even less Russian. Most of their conversation was in pantomime, with universally understood expressions of frustration at the delays.

Grigoriy grumbled, kicking at the crushed shell gravel covering the ground. Several chunks kerplunked into the water, dropping into the channel beyond the slick oily layer covering the surface to over forty feet below.

"*Da,*" Bastien responded in the affirmative, sharing the sentiment. He'd expected to be underway by now. There were nearly 12,000 megatons of wheat waiting to be loaded. Even at top capacity, it would have taken them ten hours. And now they were a full day behind. Bastien drained the last of his bottled water, crushed the plastic, and tossed it into a recycling container on his way out.

Twelve hours wasted since he'd gotten off the phone with Phaedra and reported for work. By 1:30 that afternoon, Bastien called back to the office and gave them the status.

"What do you mean you're not on your way back yet?" Remy had questioned. He had been waiting for Bastien's call. While Bastien was in Galveston, Remy was responsible for holding down things at Inspectorate. He wasn't all that happy about having his weekend plans put on hold.

"Just what I said. The whole operation's shut down."

"What are you doing about it?" Remy demanded.

"Not much I can do, Remy. I can't hand carry the grain and dump it on the ship, can I? I'm going back to the house until they call me out again," Bastien told him.

He climbed into his truck and sat inside for a moment to write up a brief report to go along with his time log. Twelve hours. Man, what couldn't he have done with those twelve hours if Phaedra had been there.

Bastien shook off the shoulda-woulda-couldas then snapped the cover of his binder closed. He checked his phone to see if he'd missed any calls. That is, any that he really wanted to return. He was disappointed that Phaedra hadn't tried to call him; but he didn't really expect her to. She'd told him that she would be busy with appointments today. That didn't stop him from hoping she'd find time to sneak away. A text message. A phone call. Something to let him know that she was thinking about him.

"Happy birthday to me," he sang to himself, cranking up the engine and backing out of the parking spot. As he drove toward the beach house, he went over the contents of the fridge. He hadn't eaten much while he played the waiting game. Snack foods mostly. The last time he was out here, he'd stocked the freezer with meat that would keep well—burger patties, chicken. Maybe he'd fire up the grill and...

"I don't believe it..."

He shook his head back and forth, trying to squash the ear-to-ear smile that spontaneously lifted his lips. As Bastien turned off the main road onto the soft sandy approach to the beach house, he caught a glimpse of over two dozen helium metallic balloons tied to the railings leading to the first floor. The beach house was elevated on stilts to allow for high tides. The balloons, in alternating colors of purple and gold, his fraternity colors, whipped back and forth in the high winds.

"Jacie," he said aloud.

This looked like the kind of stunt she would pull. Chas had warned him that she was planning a surprise party for him. Wasn't that supposed to be on Sunday? He wondered how she managed to pull this off. He slowed down as he drew closer and noticed in the shadows underneath the house a car parked in his spot. Was Jacie still here? There was only one car. Had he arrived too soon? Maybe he should drive around another twenty minutes or so and practice on his appropriately, pleasantly surprised face.

No, that wasn't Jacie's car. The tender smile for his cousin's wife faded. Nervousness and anticipation took its place. Bastien maneuvered his truck onto the parking slab next to the charcoal-gray SUV that was parked there. As he pulled parallel to it, he leaned forward and peered through the tinted window.

Slowly, the SUV's window rolled down and Phaedra looked back at him from behind large frame sunglasses. She lowered her head, pulling the glasses down on the tip of her nose.

"You're late," she chastised him.

Bastien nodded, accepting her rebuke. "What can I do to make it up to you?"

"You can make sure I don't regret my decision," she replied and got out of the car.

Bastien lifted an eyebrow in response to her request. He didn't want to assume anything, but he didn't want to rule out any possibilities, either.

Phaedra came around to meet him at the foot of the stairs carrying a gift bag tied together with another purple balloon. She lifted her sunglasses until they rested on top of her head. Her hairstyle was much more casual today. It was still twisted up, but held off her shoulders with a mother-of-pearl barrette.

"What's that?" he asked, indicating the bag.

"What do you think it is?" she said. She held the bag up in front of him then swung it playfully out of his grasp as he reached for it. "No, you have to guess."

"Hmm…let me think." He leaned back against the truck, folding his arms across his chest. "That bag's too small for a Harley-Davidson V-Rod."

She laughed at him. "Don't get your hopes up."

"And it's *definitely* too large for a string bikini and tanning oil." He placed his hands on either side of her hips, close, but not touching, pretending to measure her.

"You know, that was my first choice, but I didn't think any of the styles I selected would fit you," Phaedra said, moving toward the stairs. She wore a long, black-and-pink floral halter dress that fell to her feet, brushing the tops of backless leather sandals. As she started up the stairs, she held the gift bag in one hand and lifted her dress in the other to keep from tripping.

"Then, what is it?" Bastien asked. Like yesterday, when she came to the office, he watched the alluring sway of her hips as she climbed the stairs. He waited at the bottom, staring up at her, knowing that she would soon realize he wasn't immediately behind her. At the moment, Bastien was in no hurry to move.

Seeing her stand there reminded him of why he'd chosen this particular house for Inspectorate. This house, like Phaedra, was a perfect complement for him. Both were classically elegant. Both were natural in their beauty. Both gave him a sense of un-failing strength and ability to withstand the fiercest of storms. And both, Bastien secretly admitted to himself, gave him a sense of serenity. A sense that this is where he could retreat from the world and know that he was safe.

Phaedra turned around, trying to keep her expression bland. It was the same look she'd given him when she'd caught him watching her at Inspectorate. Only this time when he met her gaze, she shared with him a shy smile of encouragement.

"I'm not going to give you your present out there, Bastien. You have to invite me inside and then I'll show you."

Oh, the possibilities!

She stepped aside and let him open the door.

"I haven't had a chance to air the place out since I got here," he said, by way of apology. He moved around the front room, opening the white, plantation-style shutters and throwing up the windows. Phaedra set the gift bag down on a wicker table with a "no peeking" warning and opened the windows on the other side of the room. As the cross breeze blew through, she paused at the window and admired the landscape.

"It's so peaceful out here," she murmured.

Bastien came to stand beside her. He leaned his hands on the window ledge. "It certainly makes coming to work more bearable," he said.

"Bastien, can I ask you something?"

"Sure…"

"This is the one and only time I'll talk about work today, I promise."

He grimaced and indicated for her to continue.

"Do you like your job? I mean, does it give you personal satisfaction?"

"You want me to be honest, or do you want me to give you the answer that'll make the company look good?"

"I'd appreciate honesty."

Bastien took a deep breath. "Honestly, Phaedra. I hate it. I get a sick feeling in my stomach whenever I wake up and know I have go back to that place. The hours are long. The work is hard…but that's not what turns me off about it. It's Remy and G-Paw. They make it a living hell."

"Then why do you do it?"

"When I ran my own division in Louisiana, it wasn't so bad. I had good people working for me. Everybody worked hard, pulled together. They respected each other. And even when we had disagreements, we worked it out. Then we closed the New Orleans office and consolidated here. That's when everything started to go wrong. I've wracked my brain trying to figure out why."

"That's why you called me," Phaedra interjected.

"Uh-huh. To help me see what I wasn't seeing. To answer your question, I stick with it because I'm the only thing standing between my crew and Remy and a march to the unemployment line for them. He wants to fire them and I won't let him. As long as I've got Chas backing me with numbers that show we can still turn a profit without letting them go, I'm going to hang in there."

"It must be awful for you," she said sympathetically.

Bastien shrugged. "I'm a big boy. I can handle my business."

Phaedra turned around, resting on the ledge next to him. "I guess that's why I decided to come to see you, Bastien."

"And why is that?"

She shrugged her shoulders then laughed self-consciously. "Because you're trying to go it alone. And no one should be alone on their birthday. So…happy birthday, Bastien. But, if you're expecting me to sing, you can forget it. I can't carry a tune if my life depended on it."

Phaedra lifted a wagging finger at him, one of them she'd injured on Bastien's site tour.

Bastien clucked in sympathy and took her hand. He kissed the bandage, massaging her hand. When Phaedra swayed toward him, resting her forehead against his chest, Bastien curved his arm around her and drew her closer to him.

"You don't have to sing, *cher,* if you don't want to," he said, brushing the top of her with another kiss. "Just you being here is present enough."

He placed his hand on the small of her back, caressing her there. The material of her dress was silky to the touch. It made the softest rustle as the breeze caught and drew it tighter against her body. With her pressed against him so closely, Bastien perceived in an instant that Phaedra wasn't wearing much underneath it.

Bastien gently moved her away from him.

"Give me a minute to wash up and change?"

"Sure, take your time."

Bastien ducked into the bedroom and turned on the shower. "Have you had anything to eat yet?" He shouted over the running water.

"No, I haven't," Phaedra answered back. She took a seat on the stool beneath the wet bar that connected the kitchen and the front room and helped herself to one of the nectarines in a fruit basket.

Bastien came out of his room, his hair still wet and glistening from his quick shower, tugging a crisp, white linen shirt over jeans.

"Grilled chicken okay?"

"It's fine." Phaedra gulped down the last of her fruit and discarded the peel and napkin into the kitchen trash. "That was fast."

"I'm not one to waste time. So, how was the drive?" he asked, moving to the kitchen and pulling out spices and utensils. "Did you run into much weekend traffic?"

It was small talk but it kept Bastien's mind focused in directions other than the softness of Phaedra's lips glistening from the fruit.

As he made preparations for the meal, he congratulated himself on how well he managed to keep up his end of the conversation. Phaedra made it easy; he had to give her credit. She was intelligent, able to converse on a wide range of topics—from global politics, to local sports, to which movies would likely win awards that year. She laughed appropriately at his attempts at humor and came back with funny rejoinders that caught him off guard and made him appreciate her dry sense of humor.

Bastien set up to have their meal out on the balcony, where they could enjoy the warmth of day. His intention was to keep her there, sharing this day with her, until they could watch the sunset together. His father had always told him that a woman who was content to sit patiently with him and talk with him, who could easily enjoy his company, would be the one he should pay serious attention to. Passion was easy to find and quick to fizzle. But true companionship could be the bond that would hold him and his woman together long after the heated moments had passed.

With the meal eaten and the dishes cleared, Bastien turned his attention back to the gift bag still waiting on the table.

"So, do I get to unwrap my present now?" he asked, rubbing his hands together with the impatient exuberance of a little boy.

"Yes," she said, smiling at him. She went inside to retrieve the present. While she was gone, Bastien pulled the chair she'd been sitting in and moved it closer to him.

"Happy birthday, Bastien!" she said grandly, holding out the bag to him.

"For me? Oh, you shouldn't have!" he teased.

"Okay then, I won't!"

"You'd better give me that, *cher.*" He gave a mock warning. He set the bag on the table and peeled aside the sticky tape that held it together. Inside he found a large, coffee table book. It had a glossy jacket cover with a picture of a porcelain harlequin mask lying in the grass with Mardi Gras beads tossed haphazardly around it.

Wordlessly, Bastien flipped through the book and gazed at several more photos, seventy pages worth, of various scenes of New Orleans and the surrounding parishes. People, structures, countryside and other eclectic compositions from the artist filled the pages, all reminiscent of his home.

Bastien flipped to the first page and noticed a personalized message and signature of the book's author. "Phaedra, where…where did you get this?" he asked.

"Do you like it?" She didn't sound very sure of herself. Her expression was guarded as she waited for his answer.

"It's incredible," he said, putting a pleased smile on his face.

"All original," she said. "I told you that I have an artist friend. This is his work. I know with you working so many long hours that you probably don't get a chance to get back much and that you might be feeling a little homesick. So I thought I'd bring a little Louisiana here to Texas."

"I don't know what to say." He reached out and squeezed her hand, communicating all his emotion with that simple gesture.

Phaedra suddenly stood up, dragging him out of the chair. "Come on."

"Where are we going?" Bastien asked, knowing where he *wanted* to take her but letting her set the pace and direction of this private party.

Chapter 13

Phaedra kicked off her shoes. "Take off your shoes, too. I want to walk on the beach," she said.

"The beach?"

"I don't get many chances to kick back and relax. I can't imagine a more perfect way to end the evening." She paused when she noticed his reluctance. "What's the matter, Bastien? Don't you want to go? Oh…sorry. I forgot. A walk on the beach probably isn't new or fun for you, is it? You can come out here any time you want."

"That's not it," he said. "I'd love to take that walk with you, Phaedra. It's all this talk of you ending the evening that's getting to me."

"It's getting late. I have to get back."

Twilight would quickly fade to night, and she hadn't planned on spending the night. She deliberately didn't pack an overnight bag. No change of clothing or toiletries. And no condoms.

"I know," he said, pulling himself out of his funk before it ruined the time they had left. Spontaneity didn't come easily for

Phaedra. If he squashed her enthusiasm now, he didn't know what that would do for future attempts of her stepping out of her comfort zone.

"We should head that way." He pointed in a direction. "There are fewer tourists and beachcombers."

Bastien knelt down and rolled up his pant legs a few inches above his ankles. As they started down the path toward the beach, away from the shelter of the house and the sandbanks, the wind became even stronger. And, Phaedra noted, dramatically cooler. She edged closer to Bastien, encouraging him to put his arm around her bare shoulders.

They walked along in silence, the water's edge slapping at their feet. Bastien didn't speak until the tide started to rise, splashing higher against his legs, soaking his pants and the hem of Phaedra's dress.

"We should turn back. The tide rises high here and will be up past your knees before you know it."

Phaedra nodded. She stopped, tilting her head up to watch the stars wink on in the sky, one by one.

"You were right," she whispered. "The stars….they're so close. You can't really see this in the city. Too many buildings and artificial lights, I guess."

"How did you know?" Bastien asked.

"How did I know what?" Phaedra returned, sensing that he wasn't asking her about city lights at that moment.

"That I'd still be here at the beach house today," Bastien clarified.

She shrugged her shoulders. "I didn't, really. I'd hoped. And even if I hadn't waited for you, I'd hoped that you'd see the balloons and know that I was thinking of you."

"Have you been thinking of me?" He sounded pleased, with a hint of smugness that Phaedra was willing to let slide. This trip was designed to make him feel better. She shouldn't be surprised if he was a little puffed up at the attention.

"Why don't you ask me, instead, if I've been able to stop thinking about you since yesterday?" Phaedra said. "It's the craziest thing. I can't understand it…and I can't stop it. Even though I know it's wrong that I shouldn't even consider the possibility that…you and I could…"

"Could what?" he wouldn't let her leave her thought hanging.

She stopped and turned to face him. "Bastien, I'm not going to deny that I don't feel a powerful attraction for you. You're a very….um…compelling man."

"Compelling?" he said, sounding wounded. "Is that all? How about irresistible," he said, lifting his eyebrows at her. "What about sexy? Strong? Smart?"

She put her hands on her hips. "Well, you've certainly said it all for yourself, haven't you?"

"I haven't even gotten started, *cher*."

"That's what I'm afraid of."

He approached her again, wrapping his arms around her waist and drawing her close to him again. "You don't have to be afraid of me. I told you before. I wouldn't let anyone hurt you."

He held on to her until the next wave crashed upon them, almost at knee level.

Phaedra laughed and shivered as the chilly water splashed against her.

Bastien took her hand while she took a handful of her drenched dress, and they made a dash back for the beach house. By the time they made it back, Phaedra's feet and legs were covered with clumps of damp sand and stray pieces of seaweed.

She bent down, trying to dust some of it off before climbing the stairs to retrieve her shoes and car keys. Then she noticed the fine layer of sand on her arms, face and neck.

"That's the only thing about living on the beach that I would change," Bastien said, "With the winds around here, you wind up taking half of the beach with you when you go. It ends up tracked all over the place."

Phaedra looked up in alarm at that statement. "I just had the car detailed when I had that flat tire replaced. I am not tracking all this sand inside with me."

"Come with me. This will help," he said, guiding her around the corner of the far side of the house.

The beach house was equipped with an outside shower and

faucet enclosed behind a five-foot lattice stall. Bastien turned on the water at the lower faucet. It sputtered, pushing out air bubbles, then ran free and clear. Bastien stuck his feet under the water, rinsing the sand away. Then he held his hand out to Phaedra.

"Careful," he murmured. "Don't slip." As she moved closer to the spray, Phaedra lifted the hem of her dress and stuck her feet under the water faucet. Bastien knelt down and began to smooth his hands over her legs, just below her knees, to wipe away the sand.

Phaedra clung tightly to her dress, looking down at him as he brushed up and down with confident strokes. He kept his face turned from her, just like yesterday when he'd worked on her tire. But unlike yesterday, when she'd sat next to him and tugged her skirt down, Phaedra struggled with the desire to lift her hem higher.

She held her dress in bunches at her knees with both hands. But as Bastien continued to massage her skin, she gathered her courage and inched the material higher. Barely perceptible at first, then with increased boldness, she exposed more of her skin to him. Inch by inch, the hem crept upward and so did Bastien's attention to her. When her dress was well above her knees, clinging damply to her thighs, Phaedra gathered the material and tied it into a loose knot to hold it in place. Bastien glanced up with questions in his eyes. Did she want him to proceed? Would she let him? If he continued, would it give her reason to regret her decision?

Looking down at Bastien, Phaedra cupped her hands behind Bastien's head and caressed him. Her fingertips lightly touched a long-healed scar that she hadn't noticed before.

"Bastien," she said, her voice filled with tender concern. "How did you get this?"

He leaned his head away, taking it out of her searching fingers. "Ask me again some other time." He planted a kiss on each of her thighs, then turned off the water before standing up.

Cradling her face, Bastien soothed away the gritty sand, leaving streaks that, when mingled with the water from his hands, caught the moonlight through the lattice walls and glittered against her skin like finely crushed diamonds. He brushed her hair back then, on second thought, released the barrette clasp that bound up Phaedra's dark hair, letting it fall in soft waves to her shoulders.

"If you're going to leave, Phaedra, now's the time." His breathing was harsh as he leaned close and whispered in her ear. "If you don't leave now, you're staying…all night…with me. You understand what I'm telling you, *cher?*"

"I should go," she whispered back, clinging to him. Every touch made a liar out of her, proclaiming her intention to do just the opposite.

Bastien rubbed his hands against her arms to brush away more sand and erase the goose bumps that appeared on her flesh.

"No. Stay with me tonight," he urged. Bastien reached for the halter tie around her neck. He paused, resting on her shoulders, waiting to see what she would do. When she didn't flinch, he began to tug on the ties.

"Phaedra, you don't have to go any farther than you want to. You don't want me to touch you, just tell me. I want to see you. Just let me look at you." He released the dress straps, letting them dangle down her back. Yet the dress remained in place, hugging tightly to her curves. Bastien didn't lower the dress but waited for Phaedra to show him the boundaries of where he could go.

Phaedra reached for Bastien's linen shirt and tugged upward. He shrugged out of it, draping it over the shower wall. She splayed her hands against his chest, feeling heat emanate from his skin. Bastien's unique scent wafted to her—smelling to her like all the best things of summer. She couldn't resist. She had to know if he tasted as good as he smelled, as delicious as he looked—like a honey-dripped, sweet treat. Phaedra stood up on tiptoe, wrapped her arms around Bastien's neck for leverage and touched the tip of her tongue to his bottom lip. As Phaedra rose on her toes, the dress fell away, pooling at her feet.

Her bare skin to his, Bastien's response was immediate and unmistakable. He caught her underneath her bottom and lifted her closer. Two steps forward and she was pinned securely between him and the wall. Phaedra gasped out loud, as much for the swiftness of the move as she was for the craving desperation that told her he couldn't move fast enough for her. A sense of urgency rose inside her, a secret fear that she was running out of time.

"Phaedra," he muttered against her mouth. "Please tell me that you brought protection."

"No…no, I didn't." Her tone was mournful. "I never thought it would get this far."

"Neither did I," Bastien groaned as he lowered his head to rest on the wall behind her.

"Bastien?" she ventured.

"Wait…" he replied. "Just give me a minute."

While he stood there, Bastien concentrated on the chilling night sounds of the beach to cool his superheated skin. When Bastien's cell phone started to ring, he ignored it, letting the voice mail pick up.

"You're not going to answer that?" Phaedra questioned. She was still holding on to him as his shoulders slumped with disappointment.

"It's work."

"Then you'd better—"

"I know…I know…" He tried not to sound ungracious as he let her go. Bastien stepped back, giving her a dejected look when Phaedra stooped down to pick up her dress. She frowned at the sopping wet material, not looking forward to putting it back on. Phaedra started to wring the water from it as Bastien's phone rang again.

"Yeah," he answered tersely, looking back at Phaedra apologetically. "What's up, Remy? They did? When…All right, then. I should be back within the hour…All right…Sure…No problem. I've got it covered."

Bastien snapped the phone shut, looking at the ground for the moment.

"Don't tell me," Phaedra said, sympathetically. "You have to go."

"The repair crew got the conveyors working again. They should start loading soon. I'm sorry, Phaedra."

"Don't apologize," she said, with forced brightness. "You have a job to do."

"Any chance you'll be here when I get back."

"No. I won't be."

"I didn't think so. But I had to ask."

Phaedra closed the distance between them, wrapping her arms around his waist. "If it's any consolation, I really enjoyed myself today, Bastien."

He planted a kiss on her nose. "Thanks for my birthday present. I really appreciated it."

"You really like the photo book?"

"That, too." He grinned at her. "Before you head out, Phaedra, if you want to slip into some dry clothes, I've got a spare shirt upstairs," he offered.

"What about pants? Your pants won't fit me," she objected.

"What? You walking around in only my shirt wasn't part of my birthday present?"

Phaedra pursed her lips at him, giving him a *don't be greedy* glare.

"Stay a few minutes while I get dressed for work. You can toss your dress in the dryer and let it spin dry for a while." He paused for a moment, then looked into her eyes.

"When will I be able to see you again?" he asked.

"I'll be working the rest of the weekend and through the week playing catch-up on the interview questions for your employees."

"I'll see you on Monday, then?"

Phaedra paused before responding. Bastien knew that look. It was the look that said she was searching for the perfect answer. One that would suit her and soothe him.

"Not this Monday," she corrected. "Next Monday. In a week, maybe. If I get caught up. We'll see how it goes," she said, enough to appease him without making promises. "I'll call you to let you know when."

Bastien heard it in her tone. She didn't have to say it. Don't call her.

Chapter 14

A week later, Bastien sat at his desk, turning through the pages of his calendar. Like a bizarre countdown, each day that passed without speaking with Phaedra was marked with a large red X.

He leaned back and stared up at the ceiling. As he stared, he counted the pencils that he'd launched up there. They were stuck in the ceiling tiles, sling-shotted by rubber bands and the force of his frustration.

He'd gotten into work around five that morning and started shooting sharpened pencil darts at the ceiling at eight o'clock, the time he'd expected Phaedra to show up. She'd said a week, hadn't she? That was the soonest he could expect to hear from her. She didn't show, and she didn't call him to say that she was running late. Phaedra never ran late. If she wasn't there, Bastien figured, it was because she didn't want to be.

He was starting to second guess himself. Sure things took a crazy turn back at the beach house. He never expected her to meet him there, even though he wanted her to. And when she did and stayed with him until he had to return to the *Kirov*,

Bastien thought that everything was cool between them. Maybe she'd worked through her issue of never dating her clients. Then, just like that, she cut off all communication.

Bastien glanced over at his computer. Okay, maybe not all communication. She'd sent him a couple e-mails asking him to clarify some information she found in his employee files, but that was it. No emotion. No hint that she was feeling anything at all for him. Not even a smiley face emoticon.

By five o'clock that evening, Bastien stopped checking his messages and stopped bugging the receptionist to see if any packages had arrived for him. He'd stuck his cell phone way back in the drawer. Having it on him was a constant reminder of how she hadn't called and how he'd deliberately refrained from calling her. He spent the next half hour busily sharpening more pencils.

"It's going to be a long night," Bastien muttered.

Bastien gave up. He put his feet down and lowered his head onto the desk with a thud. He banged it several times until it started to sting. That's how Jacie finally found him when she came in to say good-night.

"Knock, knock," she announced before opening the door.

"What do you want?" he growled at her, his voice muffled because his face was pressed against the desk calendar.

"Rough day?" she observed. When he glanced up, she pointed at the ceiling.

"You might say that."

Jacie came in and slid the guest chair across the floor, moving it closer to the desk.

"You know I'm taking those out of your office supply budget, don't you?" she said as she rustled around on his desk, moving aside at least five empty pencil boxes and the remainder of the rubber bands that he'd started to mold together into a grapefruit-sized ball. "And speaking of budgets, I need you to sign these before I can process them."

"What are they?"

"Requisitions for more safety equipment. Safety goggles, earplugs, gloves. Stuff like that."

"Where did these come from?" Bastien sounded irritated,

taking the requisition forms from her. "I'm not supposed to be spending any money."

"I know that, Bastien." She fluttered her eyelashes. "If you need this stuff, I'll make sure you get it. And the requests came from you. Remember? Right after Eduardo's accident."

"Man, I must be getting old. I don't remember filling these out at all."

"You've been working too hard," she commiserated as he flipped through the pages and scanned through the line items. "Remy said you gave these requests to him a couple weeks ago, but he's been sitting on them, not wanting to spend the money."

"Somehow, that doesn't surprise me," Bastien complained, scrawling his approval signature across them. "Remy would sit on an exploding land mine if he thought he could squeeze a few extra pennies out of it."

He flipped to the last pages of the requisitions, made a few corrections to some of the order numbers that he'd committed to memory from the supply catalog. "Wrong item number. These won't do us any good. We need dash 354, not 854."

"Just make the change and initial it. I'll make sure it gets changed in the system when I send the order off."

"Is Remy sitting on any more of these?"

Jacie shrugged. "I dunno. He might be."

"Let me know if he is. I want to check them out before you put the orders through."

"Sure. I'll keep an eye out for them…And speaking of eyes…"

"I wasn't speaking of eyes," Bastien said, suspicious of Jacie's too-casual tone.

"I was," Jacie said, "I was making conversation. Chas said you were supposed to meet with that consultant again today."

"Uh-huh."

"Well?"

"I guess something came up. I haven't heard from her today. I've been hanging around waiting, but—"

"You haven't eaten anything, have you, Bastien? I saw you around lunchtime, but you weren't eating anything."

The thought of food hadn't even occurred to him today. "I haven't left the office. Too busy."

"Uh-huh. Too busy vandalizing it," she retorted. "You should eat something before your blood sugar drops and makes you crankier than you already are. I don't know why you keep that little fridge over there, Bastien. I keep it stocked for you and you just keep ignoring it."

"Stop filling it full of healthy crap like wheatgrass and tofu and I might take you up on it," he teased her. Both of them knew there was very little chance of him giving up his kind of snack food for Jacie's.

"So," she continued, leaning her elbows on the desk. "Why do you think your consultant friend ditched you?"

"How should I know?"

"What do you mean you don't know? Didn't you try to contact her?"

"Nope." Bastien hadn't told anyone about Phaedra's visit to the beach house. Not even Chas. As far as he was concerned, they were the only ones who knew. If Jacie did have an inkling, she wasn't letting on.

"Why not? Something might have happened to her. Like when you went tearing out of here to help her change a flat tire."

"Who told you about that?" Bastien demanded, sitting up from his slouch in the chair.

Jacie grinned. "Bastien, just because you're in your own little world when you get on that phone doesn't mean that no one else isn't that world with you. Our offices are connected. I heard you talking to her through the air vents." She pointed up and over his shoulder.

"You can hear me?" It was a little unsettling to know that private conversations weren't always private. Bastien couldn't help wondering if he'd been heard all of the times he'd vented in his office about Remy.

"Yep."

"Since when?"

"Since Remy changed out those air filters for a cheaper brand. When you're standing in a certain spot and if the air is blowing in the right direction, I can sometimes hear every word. You know, you shouldn't cuss so much when Remy pisses you off."

That answered his question.

"Change 'em back," Bastien ordered. "You don't need to hear half the things I want to say about him."

"Speaking of saying, why didn't you call Phaedra when she didn't call you?" she insisted. "It's pretty obvious to me that she's got your nose wide open."

"What do you mean obvious?"

Jacie leaned forward and whispered, "The next time you two want to get your freak on, do it back behind Silo 6. There's a blind spot there that the security cameras can't hit."

"Aw, hell," Bastien groaned. He was afraid of that. He'd better not tell Phaedra.

"Okay, I admit it. Is that what you want to hear? I'm physically attracted to her. What my eyes see my body responds to. Can't help the way I'm wired."

"But God also gave you a brain, Bastien. Hopefully some common sense as well. You can't jump every female you see."

"That's not fair, Jacie! You know I've been a good boy."

"Only because Remy won't let you off work long enough to get into trouble."

"Jacie, if it was just about climbing into bed with any woman I saw, I could have found someone anytime I wanted to. This thing with Phaedra, whatever it is, is different. This is something I feel deep down…something that isn't going to be satisfied with a quick tumble. You get what I'm saying?"

"You hardly know her," Jacie reminded him.

"I know…I know…common sense should tell me that I shouldn't be tripping this hard over her. But the reality is, I am. No matter how many times I tell myself that I'm being a fool, I can't stop myself from feeling the way that I do. I really like Phaedra. Sure, I like the way she looks. I also like what she's about and how she handles herself, too. She's smart and competent and completely dedicated to her work."

"Sounds boring." Jacie passed judgment.

"Oh, trust me. The lady's not boring!"

Bastien wouldn't give Jacie some of the details of conversations that he'd had with Phaedra at the beach house. He wished that he could so she could see Phaedra as he saw her. She could be as passionate about the ills of the world as she was about people who poured ketchup over a perfectly good porterhouse steak. She made a convert out of him with her inflexible stand on international injustices while compelling him to participate in her discussions on various makers of high-heeled shoes. She was a fashion plate who knew which styles of clothes accented her best features. Yet when Bastien complimented her on them—her clothes and her incredible body—she grew genuinely self-conscious. She'd made many business contacts over the years as she built her career but had few close friends. Most of her best friends were family members, not unlike his own family situation. The only topic that she carefully avoided during their private time together was their shared history in undergraduate school. That was all right with him, too. Bastien didn't like dwelling too far in the past anyway. He didn't know that Phaedra of "way back when." Maybe one day he would. For now, he wanted to get to know more about Phaedra the way she was now.

Maybe he didn't know her in an expanded length of time; but the glimpses she gave him of what she was about were insights into her soul. He knew what was important to her, what she was devoted to and what she despised. He could make her cry with laughter and sigh with irritation. Intuitively, he knew where all the buttons were. She'd shown them to him. Practically given that secret knowledge to him. Bastien had known couples who'd been together for years and still not gotten the depth of understanding he and Phaedra developed. His reaction to her when she'd first come to meet him at Inspectorate was immediate and irrefutable. No other woman had raised the same response in him.

"Bastien," Jacie said, reaching out and covering his hand with hers. "If you really do have feelings for this woman and she's not ready for it, I suggest you back off, too. Give her a chance to process her own feelings in her own way and in her own time."

"You haven't told me anything I haven't told myself."

"Great minds think alike," she announced. "That's how Chas and I were able to make it. I couldn't force him to admit he wanted me. I had to allow it to happen naturally."

"No chance of that. I think I pushed her too hard. She was supposed to be here today. I've been waiting for her and, well, you can see what happened to that plan. I think I scared her off."

"You're wrong, Bastien. Phaedra doesn't scare easily."

"What makes you so sure?"

"Because I happen to know that Phaedra's sitting out there in the waiting room."

"Is that supposed to be some kind of a joke?"

"No joke, Bastien. She had the guard at the guard shack call the main desk to announce her, but by that time, Silvie was already gone."

"Why didn't she just call my cell phone?"

"Good question. Why aren't you picking up? She said that she left you a message."

Immediately, Bastien's hand went to his hip pocket, slapping it to check for the phone. Then he realized he'd shut it off and hidden it away.

"Why don't you go out there and get her? She's been waiting for you, Bastien. Don't keep her waiting any longer."

"Why'd you make me wait?" Bastien demanded, as he stood. "Why didn't you tell me sooner?"

"Because you needed to talk…to work out your feelings. I wanted you to have a clear head when you talked to her. She came out all this way to see you. Don't mess it up!"

"I won't. Thanks for looking out for me. Next time your performance review comes across my desk, I'm recommending you for a raise."

"Don't waste your time. I've already signed your name to a three percent raise. And an end-of-year bonus, too!" Bastien heard her call after him as he took off down the hall, heading for the reception area.

Bastien slapped his hands on the double doors, forcing them open. That's where he found Phaedra in the reception area, standing with her back toward the door. She stood, staring up at the wall clocks, with her hands behind her. In them, she held on to a black leather portfolio. She didn't speak when he came in but waited for him to address her.

He stood at the entrance and tapped the crystal face of his watch. "You're late."

"It's still Monday," she came right back at him, pointing at the clocks on the wall.

"I was expecting you first thing this morning. I did what you asked. Kept out of your hair. You were supposed to be here early. A reward for my good behavior."

She lifted one eyebrow at him and said, "I didn't set that expectation, Mr. Thibeadaux. I told you that I'd *call* you on Monday. I did call you, like I promised, and you didn't pick up. You can't blame me for that."

There was no playfulness in her conversation. She was so coolly in control that he imagined silver hoops weren't dangling from her ears but tiny icicles.

"Then I guess, if we're going to do this deal, we need to get a better line of communication going, Ms. Burke-Carter."

"I completely agree, Mr. Thibeadaux."

"Are those your interview questions?" Bastien asked.

"Do you have time to review them now, or would you rather I leave the packet and come back some other time?"

"Right this way, Ms. Burke-Carter," he said holding the door open for her. As she passed him, he whispered, "I didn't think you'd show, Phaedra."

With a perfectly composed face, she looked at him and asked, "Did you miss me, Bastien?"

"Miss you? Naw, I was too busy working to be thinking about you."

Phaedra's face relaxed into a smile. A smile that told him she didn't believe him.

Good. Because I didn't believe me either, Bastien rationalized.

He ushered Phaedra into his office. She stopped short, taking in the pencil-covered ceiling, and covered her mouth to suppress a giggle.

"What's so funny?" he challenged. "I'm trying out a new decor."

She settled herself into a mahogany and leather chair and placed the folder deliberately on the desk. Bastien didn't open it right away but sat on the corner of the desk.

"Well," she prompted, meeting his gaze while pointing to the portfolio on the desk. "Do you want to review those interview questions? I think you'll find them very carefully structured. They're meant to collect information without assigning blame or culpability."

"In a minute." Bastien dismissed the offer, moving the portfolio farther away from her so that she couldn't reach it. "Before we get down to that business, we have some more pressing business to get out of the way."

She placed her hands on the chair, gripping the smooth mahogany arms. "Fine, Bastien. If that's the way it must be. Where do you want to start?"

"Let's start with what happened today. What happened to you? And don't give me any bull about working. Why didn't you call me sooner?"

"Because…because it took me this long to decide whether or not I wanted to continue with our…"

"Partnership?"

"For lack of a better word."

"Then what would you call it?"

"Oh, I don't know, Bastien!" She threw up her hands in exasperation then forced herself to clasp them tightly on the arms of the chair again. "I thought I had it all figured out. But after Friday…after I left you at the beach house, I've become more confused and angry at myself for not keeping my head clear and angry at you for putting me in that state of confusion."

"Phaedra, if I did anything to make you feel that way, if I did anything to disrespect you, I swear I didn't mean to." Bastien reached down and pried her hands from the chair. Smoothing her hands between his palms, he couldn't help but notice how cold they were. She was so nervous. He felt the erratic fluttering of her pulse.

"It wasn't you!" she protested, squeezing back. "You were only being honest about your feelings. You're not responsible for my feelings. I am. So, if I got mad, it wasn't on you."

"So tell me, *cher,* why are you so mad?"

"Because…well…that's the first emotion I could call up after being pulled out of my comfort zone. You make me come outside myself, Bastien. You make me do things, say things and…and feel things that I'm not used to feeling. Certainly not from people I work with."

"Hey, I'm not just any ol' body. I'm me."

"Don't take it personally. I don't like feeling out of my element. It's a control thing."

"I understand. For now, that comfort zone of yours has only got room for one. It's gonna take time getting used to me being around, time I'm willing to put in. But I'm not going there by myself, *cher.* I won't push you if that's not what you want. You tell me once more and I'll respect your decision. You say no, make me believe it, and I'll leave you alone. But if you're feeling anything for me, anything at all, I'll be willing to wait until you can make room for me. Tell me right here, right now, have we got a chance or no?"

Phaedra's face remained impressively composed. The only indication that she'd heard him at all was to pull her hands out of his and grip the arms of the chair even tighter.

Bastien moved closer into her personal space, invading it, but ready to pull back at the first sign of panic. "Are you feelin' me, Phaedra?" He leaned forward, whispering emphatically to her. "Do you have feelings for me?"

"Yes," she whispered back.

"Yes, what?" He needed clarification.

"Yes, I have feelings for you, too, Bastien. I didn't want to. God knows that I don't. But I do…I have…and I…I don't know what else to do!" She threw up her hands helplessly.

"Relax, *cher.* It's gonna be okay. For now, don't do anything. You don't have to do anything. We'll just let it be and see what happens next."

Bastien knew what was going to happen next. He knew because he was going to *make* it happen. He was going to kiss her and hope to heaven that she kissed him back with as much fire and commitment as she had when she wasn't worried about her professional image.

Leaning down to kiss Phaedra probably saved his life and hers. One minute, Bastien was leaning over her. The next he was tumbling over the desk, his heels flipping over his head in an unexpected somersault.

The walls of his office shook, and plaster from the ceiling and all of those pencils rained down on them as concussive explosions rocked the air outside of the building. Seconds after the first explosion, the air screamed with warning sirens. A series of long and short bursts from a horn warned all of Jacinto Port and the surrounding community.

Instinct, rather than deliberate intention, made him reach out to Phaedra, grabbing her by the arm and pulling her to the floor as he slid. Another explosion. This time his windows shattered, spraying shards of glass in all directions. Phaedra cried out, covered her head with her hands, even as Bastien covered her with his body.

"Stay down!" he whispered harshly to her. When she didn't answer, but looked up at him with frightened eyes, Bastien grasped her by the shoulders and pulled her up so that her back was resting against the desk, shielded from any more flying glass. He wasn't even sure if she could hear him. His own ears were painfully ringing and felt as if someone had shoved cotton and glass in them.

Bastien pounded the heel of his hand against his temple and ear to clear his head.

"Phaedra, are you all right? Are you hurt?" He scanned her face and hands for cuts.

She shook her head, swallowing back her initial shock in huge gulps. "I don't think so. My ears are ringing!" She pressed her palms to her ears, opened her mouth wide. "Those warning sirens…that's the signal for fire at the port!"

Bastien hauled himself up, peering over the desk and through the gaping hole where his windows once were. He watched in stunned silence as an orange glow lit the night sky.

"I can't tell if it's one of the tankers in the channel or somewhere in the shipyard. Not sure how close it is to us."

Phaedra sat up to see for herself. They stood for a moment, motionless, speechless, both fascinated and horrified at the fierce flames arcing toward the night sky. The entire shipyard was bathed in the glow so that every building, every rail car, every typically darkened nook and cranny was revealed. The trance was broken as shouts from somewhere inside of the building brought them back to themselves.

"That's Chas." Bastien recognized his cousin's voice. "Come on." He took her hand. On the way out the door, Bastien grabbed a clipboard hanging on its hook. It was the duty roster for the night shift. He'd need that for roll call. Every employee would have to be accounted for.

"I've got this side," Phaedra indicated that she would take the right side of the hall. Bastien took the left. On the way out of the building, they tested each door, making sure no employees were injured inside of the offices.

"All clear," she called out to him and listed the name or number on the door.

Within minutes, they'd gone through each room on that side of the building. Bastien then took Phaedra to the lobby where they met up with Chas.

"You all right, Bastien?" Chas noted the scrapes on Bastien's cheek and the tiny chunks of glass still falling out of the crevices of his coverall. Chas was covered with dusty white chalk from the ceiling. It was caked in his hair and streaked his face. He swung his gaze to Phaedra and noted how tightly Bastien held her hand. "You must be Ms. Burke-Carter."

She nodded. "Phaedra."

"Are you all right, ma'am?"

"I'm fine. Just a little shaken."

"Where's G-Paw?" Bastien asked Chas. "Is he all right?"

"He was in my office. I sent him to the conference room while I figured out what's going on."

"And Remy?" Bastien had almost forgotten about his cousin.

"He went to the Beaumont site earlier this morning I talked to him not more than an hour ago."

"Then it's just the three of us to get our folks through this. We'd better get at it."

"Four," Phaedra included herself, squeezing Bastien's hand in calming assurance. "That makes the four of us."

Chapter 15

Several employees stopped Bastien as he weaved his way through the conference room and bombarded him with questions. Questions to which there were still no answers.

"You know as much as I do," he assured them, looking toward the wall-mounted flat screen television. Someone had the remote control and was rapidly scrolling through each of the news stations, trying to get more information. But each station that came in showed the same news coverage of the explosion. Local news helicopters swung over the area, spotlighting several fire trucks pumping water onto a barge that was rampantly burning in one of the channels.

Bastien stood with his arms folded and watched for a few minutes along with his employees. This feeling was all too familiar. It was only a few years ago while he stood, just like this, and watched the news coverage in helpless frustration as his home, and all that he knew, was destroyed. Only it wasn't fire that swept it all away. It was water. Waves and waves of water that poured in when the levees around the Big Easy collapsed.

"You think terrorists had something to do with this, Bastien?" Dennis Keagon, Bastien's second shift supervisor, stood next to him watching the newscast. Dennis was one of the ones Bastien had brought with him from the New Orleans office.

"That's not what the reporters are saying."

"You think they'd tell us the truth if it was? They might be holding something back to keep us from going into a panic."

Bastien forced a smile. "I'm not panicking. Are you, Dennis?"

"Who me?" Dennis huffed. "No way, man. I'm cool. But my wife isn't. She's been blowing up my cell phone, calling me every five minutes to make sure I'm all right. She's been watching the news and thinking that there's something toxic in that barge."

"Tell her not to worry. Did you see the name on the barge the last time that helicopter did a flyby? It's the *Dulce Magdy*."

"The one that was supposed to be loaded with wheat and sorghum." He recalled the name on the schedule.

"That's right. We've been waiting until the last train pulled in so we could start loading. Remember? No dangerous chemicals. No toxic gases. You call your wife and tell her that nothing but regular ol' tanker fuel is the cause of the fire. Will ya do that so she can stop worrying? She's five months pregnant, isn't she? She doesn't need to be worrying at a time like this."

"Sure thing, Bastien. I'll let her know and tell her you said so. That ought to get her to ease up on me."

"Go call your wife, Dennis."

Dennis relaxed his shoulders and moved to another side of the room to make his phone call. With that small bit of comfort Bastien had given Dennis, he'd also given the grapevine at Inspectorate a fighting chance to kill the rumor of a terrorist attack. When Dennis left him, Bastien took that opportunity to approach Phaedra.

"Hey," he said in greeting, "Are you all right?"

"I'm fine."

"Good. That's good to hear, Phaedra," Bastien started toward her with the look that said he needed to hold her.

Phaedra held up her hand, stopping him with the slightest tilt of her head. "The only thing I want to hear from you right now, *Mr. Thibeadaux,* is that the roads are clear and I can be on my way. If that's not what you came over here to tell me, then you'd better keep moving. Go see to your people."

"You've heard the horns, Ms. Burke-Carter." He got the hint. "You know they haven't sounded the all-clear. No one is going anywhere."

Phaedra rubbed her eyes. She was trembling with fatigue and something else that he recognized from his eighteen or twenty-hour days of running on sheer willpower alone.

"Have you had anything to eat tonight, Phaedra?"

She shook her head no, admitting. "Just coffee. Coffee and corn chips."

Bastien turned his body so that only she could read his lips. "Now, what kind of meal is that for a growing girl, *cher?*"

"Corn. Corn's a vegetable. That's healthy, isn't it?"

"I wouldn't be a proper host if I didn't do better than coffee and corn chips."

He linked his arm through hers. It was an intimate gesture that, under normal circumstances, he'd never exhibit and she'd never permit. Not in front of the employees. Bastien knew that if she was anything like him when he'd been working all day and neglecting to eat, he expected her to drop from exhaustion.

For a moment, he thought she might pull away. By her hardened, disapproving expression, she was considering it. Phaedra straightened her back and flinched, as if to jerk away from him. Bastien edged even closer to her, keeping his hand firmly cupped around her arm to prevent her from disengaging. When she saw that he wasn't going anywhere, that he was literally at her side, she relented.

"You need to eat," Bastien advised.

"A bag of snickerdoodles to go along with my corn chips? That's all that's available in the vending machine."

"I've got a fridge stocked with something a little more nutritious than snickerdoodles in my office," he promised, then gave a mock shudder. "Jacie keeps it stocked, so I know it's healthy. How about it? It's not grilled chicken. But is wheatgrass and tofu okay?"

Phaedra bit her lip to keep from laughing. Still, Bastien could see the inner debate going on behind her eyes. Phaedra was worried about what his employees and relatives would think or say about her. All he was worried about was making sure this woman—*his woman*—didn't collapse.

Chapter 16

"Careful where you step," Bastien warned Phaedra when he took her back to his office.

"Oh my God," she gasped, noting the shards of broken glass scattered around the room. The glass crunched beneath her feet as she walked. "We got out of here so fast that I didn't realize it was this bad."

She looked around, taking in the collateral damage the blast at the port had created. Shattered glass. Fallen chunks of plaster. She wandered over to the gaping hole where the window used to be.

"Bastien, I'm so sorry."

"You don't need to apologize," he said, standing behind her and rubbing her shoulders. "I'll get someone in here to board up that window as soon as I fix you something to eat. Go on, Phaedra, and take a seat."

He led her to one of the guest chairs. Yet, Phaedra's eyes strayed to the couch and the comfortable-looking pillows that were propped up there. Without meaning to, she yawned behind her hand.

"Oh, excuse me. That was rude."

"Hope that's no reflection on the present company," he joked as he walked over to the far side of the room. Nestled in the corner next to a lateral file cabinet was a space-saver fridge, custom-built to match the wood grain of the file cabinet.

Resting her elbow on the chair's armrest and her cheek on her fist, Phaedra watched Bastien through bleary eyes as he plucked a hastily scrawled note that was stuck to the front of the fridge with a swatch of gray duct tape.

"B," he read aloud. "Took food to the conf room, but left some 4 U and PBC. Thanks. J."

He waved the note at her. "This is Jacie's doing. Let's see what she left us. Hopefully she took the wheatgrass and sprouts with her."

"The what?"

"It's what I call all the health food she keeps purchasing for me. Jacie says I eat too much red meat and need to get more natural foods into my diet."

"Nothing natural about eating grass," Phaedra commented, "unless you're a cow."

"You know, I keep telling her that and she keeps on fillin' up the fridge with that stuff. I thought when I left it in there long enough for the sprouts to start sprouting, she would take the hint and bring back my processed meat and cheese and my sugary sodas." Bastien turned back to the fridge, opening it up.

"Seems to me you eat healthy enough," Phaedra said under her breath, running her eyes up and down his backside.

As far as she could tell, beneath that utilitarian coverall there was absolutely nothing wrong with that man's physique. She caught her lower lip, remembering how she'd felt when Bastien pulled her out of the way of flying glass. Bastien had covered Phaedra with his body, pressing her close to the floor. Heavy. Solid. But not crushing. He knew how to manage his weight lying on top of a woman.

"How do you feel about deli-sliced turkey and ham on wheat bread?" he called out, his voice slightly muted.

"Hmm? What?" Phaedra didn't hear him. She was distracted by images of him holding her after their walk on the beach. Phaedra pressed the heels of her hands to her eyes.

Stop it, she chastised herself. This wasn't the beach or Bastien's hideaway bungalow. This was CT Inspectorate—a place of business. If ever she needed to maintain decorum, it was now.

"I said how about a sandwich."

She cleared her throat, sitting up straighter in the chair. "A sandwich sounds fine."

He reached into the fridge and started piling items into his arms. "Let's check the expiration date. Still good. Still within the calendar year. Close enough to good."

Bastien turned around and spread the sandwich fixings out on the desk before him. When he sat down in his chair on the other side of the desk, he started to prepare the sandwiches. Bastien opened the bread while Phaedra opened the condiments and sandwich meat.

"Not quite the ambience of our first dinner date, is it, *cher?*" he remarked, reminding her about his birthday dinner.

Bastien didn't need to remind her. Despite her will, every detail about that evening was replaying itself in Phaedra's mind. Her feelings started to churn again with the same intensity as that night. She didn't need chardonnay and soft music and starshine. Being here with him was intoxicating enough. Phaedra lowered her eyes, forcing herself to focus on the makeshift meal.

"No worries," she said, taking a bite into he sandwich.

"You've got a spot," Bastien said, his voice taking on a deeper level of huskiness as he reached and out wiped the corner of her mouth with his thumb.

"I'll take care of it," Phaedra said, leaning her head away. She couldn't forget where she was. As much as she wanted to recapture the safety and solitude of her time with Bastien, wishing wouldn't make it so.

She covered her attempt to put some space between them by removing the top from a bottle of water, preparing to take a sip. She couldn't raise the bottle to her lips. Bastien was still tracing the outline of her mouth. His thumb touched her lower lip, traveling lightly over the edge.

"Please, don't," Phaedra pleaded.

It would have been oh-so-easy for her to part her lips. All she had to do was touch her tongue to his fingertip and send the same electric current he was shooting through her back to him to complete the circuit. It wouldn't take much. A hint of his touch was all that was needed ignite those feelings she had to douse when he was called back to the *Kirov*.

"What? I'm not doing anything," Bastien said, laughing at her. There was nothing but the suggestion of his caress that kept her captive in that chair. She gripped the armrests, squeezing convulsively, gouging her fingertips into the padded leather and wood.

"This is *not* a date, Mr. Thibeadaux. This is neither the time nor the place."

Bastien took his hand away.

"Not a date, huh? If you say so." Bastien didn't sound as if he believed Phaedra or accepted her claim. He rocked back in his seat, ripping off pieces of his sandwich and stuffing them into his mouth.

"I do say so," Phaedra insisted.

"Ah, but you don't think so," he said, pointing his index finger at her.

"How do you know what I think?" Phaedra didn't have to try too hard to make herself sound irritated.

Bastien refused to be baited into the argument.

"Phaedra, it took me a while, but now I can see right through you. Right now, you're probably asking yourself what in the world you are doing here. Why aren't you at home, safely tucked in bed instead of trapped out here with me? You're exhausted. Hungry. Frightened. Vulnerable. Angry. And *curious*." He placed a heavier emphasis on that last word as he counted them off on his fingers, lifting each one from a balled fist as he spoke.

"What do you mean I'm curious?"

"That's right," Bastien said, folding his arms on his desk and leaning forward. "Curious about me. Curious about us. Curious about just how far we bend all those rules that tell us what we should and shouldn't do. Come on, Phaedra, admit it. There's a part of you right now that wants to spit in the face of convention and do your own thing."

"At the moment, the only thing I'm curious about is your

employee infractions," Phaedra said, redirecting the flow of the conversation. She avoided his gaze by leaning down to pick up the portfolio that she'd brought to him. "Maybe that's the cause of all your employee troubles. All of that spitting and everyone doing their own thing."

"That's not fair, Phaedra," Bastien said.

"Are you interested in seeing what I've developed for you or not? If you're not going to take my offer to help seriously, Bastien, then—"

"You really are trying to work, aren't you?" He sounded incredulous. "How can you focus at a time like this?"

"Keeping my head in a crisis. Isn't that what you're paying me to do?"

"Nobody's paid you yet."

"A technicality." Phaedra dismissed the statement. "You know what I meant." She got up from the desk to sit on the couch. Propping the throw pillows against her back, Phaedra lowered her head to the information she'd brought to Bastien.

"Well, if you're not going to admit it, I am. I'm curious," Bastien confessed. "I'm just trying to figure out what makes you tick."

"Work," she retorted. "Paying my bills, my employees and my tithes makes me tick." When Phaedra licked her thumb and turned another page, he stood up abruptly.

"I'm going back to the conference room," Bastien announced. "I need to be there with my folks until all of this has blown over."

"That would be wise." She nodded in agreement.

"I'll see about getting that window boarded up for you."

"Okay. Thanks." Her head still lowered, she kept her eyes trained on the paper.

"Be back in a while," he said, starting for the door.

"Then, I'll be here when you get back."

Phaedra wasn't sure how long a while was. After Bastien left her to join his employees, she kept staring at the pages, not really focusing, for at least another hour. Maybe two. When the words started to blur on the page, swimming before her eyes, she rubbed them, then laid her head back for a moment. It was only going to be a moment. She hadn't intended to sit there for so long. She had every intention of getting up and joining Bastien, maybe even apologizing to him for picking a fight to keep from giving in to her desire.

Yet, the next thing she knew, she was sitting up, crying out and grabbing her calf with the feeling of tiny needles jabbing up and down her leg. When Phaedra's stocking-clad feet connected with the rough cloth of Bastien's coverall, she shifted, causing all of her papers to slide onto the floor. She sat up, moving quickly to collect them and to reclaim the distance between them; but a voice filled with the irritation of a sleep disturbed muttered, "Aw, *cher!* Leave 'em down there and go back to sleep."

Phaedra had taken up most of the room on the couch. He'd left her enough space to recline in comfort while he sat cramped on the opposite end. He leaned back, his long legs stretched out in front of him. He'd taken off his work boots and propped his feet up on a chair. He'd given her most of the blanket for warmth, too, while he kept just a corner to toss over across his lap and partially to his knees.

As Phaedra tried to slide back, she pulled the covers off of him. Bastien's hand shot out, grabbing the edge of the blanket and yanked it back.

"You didn't list blanket hog as one of your many accomplishments, *cher.*" He tsked in mocked sympathy. "I feel for your future husband."

He was teasing her again. That told Phaedra that if he'd left upset with her, he'd gotten over it somehow.

Phaedra smiled back at him. "What time is it?" she whispered.

The blanket rustled as he drew out his arm and checked the luminescent glow of his watch. "Almost three in the morning."

It didn't seem odd to Phaedra that they would be whispering to one another. His office was dark and silent. Her ears strained for the sounds of any noise throughout the entire building.

"It's so quiet."

Lifting up on her elbows, she tried to peer out the window. It hadn't been boarded up, as Bastien had promised, but a huge blanket was tacked over the opening. The blanket didn't stretch all the way across, though. Between the gaps, it was still dark outside. No orange glow from the fire. No red and blue swirling lights from the emergency vehicles.

"Most everybody's gone home now."

"The fire's out?"

"Uh-huh," he said through a yawn. "Some time around one-thirty this morning."

"And the road block?"

"Lifted. Word came down from the port authority emergency management command center. So, we let everyone go home."

"That means I can go home, too!"

"That's right. You're free to go anytime you want."

"Oh, thank God!" Phaedra's soft cry was exuberant as she twisted her torso, fumbling around on the floor for her shoes. Though her eyes had not yet adjusted to the darkness, she could sense the waves of unspoken disappointment coming from Bastien over her eagerness to leave. He'd given off the same waves when she'd prematurely ended their dinner date.

Phaedra felt remorse. As much as Bastien had done to take care of her, she could have at least shown him a little more gratitude. All night long he'd watched over her and kept her comfortable. And what did she do? At her first opportunity, let him know that she wanted to get up out of there as soon as humanly possible.

"You've been a lovely and most gracious host," Phaedra said. "But I really must be leaving."

As soon as she leaned over, the same charley horse that woke her up stung her again.

"Ouch! That hurts!" Phaedra gave a muffled cry. She reached for her calf with her right hand while trying to keep herself from falling off the couch with her left.

Bastien grabbed her elbow and kept her from sliding.

"I'm not the kind of man who needs his woman at his feet," he replied, hauling her up again. "But at my side."

Chapter 17

It was the second time that Bastien had kept her from falling. The first time was during the site tour as they rode in the golf cart. Now, he'd saved her falling off the couch and landing unceremoniously on her backside.

But who is going to save me from falling hard for Phaedra Burke-Carter? Bastien wondered as he held on to her arm. That's exactly what he was doing. Falling fast and hard. He knew the moment the all-clear report came down from the port authority and he didn't wake her up that he'd lost his sense of perspective. Why didn't he wake her up to let her know that she could go home, too? He told himself that he was only trying to let her get her rest. To him, it sounded plausible that it was safer for her to stay there with him than to get on the road at this time of night. Hadn't that been one of her objections about coming out to Galveston to visit him?

Truth was, Bastien admitted to himself, he was being selfish. How long did he sit there waiting and watching while she slept? How long did he sit there, letting the minutes tick by, while he debated whether or not to wake her? Not to encourage her to go home, but to encourage her to stay. He wanted her to stay with him tonight. And not to sleep through it, either. When she woke up and almost pulled the covers off of him, Bastien had to yank them back in order not to make a fool out of himself.

"What's the matter?" Bastien asked when Phaedra grimaced in pain and reached for her leg.

"Charley horse," she said through clenched teeth. She balled up her fist and pounded her calf through the covers.

"Cut that out," he said, deflecting the next blow. "Let me see."

"I know what to—" Phaedra started to argue with him.

"And I know what to do, too. Not enough potassium in your diet." At least, that's what Jacie told Bastien whenever he complained about leg cramps after pulling double shifts for weeks at a time. She had him eating bananas until he was sick of the taste of them.

Bastien flipped the blanket back, exposing Phaedra's long, incredible legs. "This one?" Pointing to the spot on her calf she was massaging, Bastien touched her leg. She confirmed by wincing.

He wondered if she saw the concern on his face. More than Bastien wanted to touch her, he wanted her to trust his touch.

"Do you want me to massage it for you?"

Silence followed while Phaedra considered his question. Then she relented. "Would you, please?"

"Sure. No problem." Bastien didn't want to sound overly eager. Phaedra had to know that it didn't have to be all about sex with her. He could be her friend, too.

He rubbed his hands together to warm them before placing them on her skin.

"Lie back and relax."

"I am relaxed."

"No, you're not. You're so tense, you could snap in two."

"Sorry. It's just that I'm not entirely comfortable with the thought of you touching me like this, Bastien. Not here on your job."

"Trust me, Phaedra. I'm not going to hurt you."

And he meant that in every sense of the word. He had every intention of keeping the massage therapeutic. He used only enough pressure to let her know that he only wanted to make her feel better.

"Flex your foot," Bastien instructed. "Point your toe toward the ceiling. Now point over at that door. Back and forth. Back and forth. That's it. Easy does it. Stretch out your calf muscle. Any better?"

"Umm…hmm." Phaedra leaned back, closing her eyes. "Feels much better. Thank you, Bastien."

"You're welcome. But I gotta admit, Phaedra, you have the most incredible calves I've ever seen."

"Do a lot of women watching, do you, Bastien?" She opened one eye and peeked at him.

"I'm pleading the fifth and not answering that question."

"You can answer," she gave permission. "I'm not a lawyer, and you're not on trial."

"Like hell I'm not," he replied, laughing. "When a woman tries to get you to admit that you have eyes for other women, any man had better keep his mouth shut. I don't care how enlightened or sophisticated women think they are, no woman wants to feel second to any other woman in the eyes of her man."

Phaedra also laughed. Bastien felt the tension draining from her as he continued his massage.

"Is that what you are, Bastien? My man?"

"I was speaking hypothetically. But now that you've brought up the possibility…"

Bastien let the sentence hang there as he massaged down Phaedra's calf and across the bottom of her foot. When he pressed his thumb against her arch, she let out deep, mewling sigh. "Oh, yes! That's the spot right there. Now the other foot."

She pulled her right foot from his grasp and slid her left foot between his hands.

"I think you've got a run in your stocking," Bastien noted, his index finger following the line from her manicured toe, tracing her instep and then continuing up the line just below her knee.

Phaedra arched her back, clamping her hand over her mouth to suppress a giggle.

"What? Are you ticklish?" The rip in her hose went beyond the hem of her skirt. But he stopped his massage at the hem, his fingertips lazily tracing a line from her calf to just behind her knee.

"It's good to know you can laugh. You were so serious with me tonight."

"Employee safety is serious business," she answered. "And it's been a tough day. Hasn't it been for you?"

"Of course it has."

"You're not showing it," she said in a mixture of awe and irritation.

"You want me to show you the run in my stocking, too? Would that make you feel better?"

"Bastien!" she chastised, nudging him with her foot. "Get serious. What's your secret? Why aren't you exhausted? I want to know."

He shrugged. "You don't want to know half of what I go through around here, *cher.*" Bastien kept his voice low, mindful of Jacie's warning that voices carried. "Every day is a new crisis. If it's not an explosion like the one last night, it's some other kind of calamity that needs addressing. That's what I do all day long, solve other people's problems. You learn to hang in there."

"If you don't like your job, why don't you quit?"

"I told you. I have to take care of my crew. If I leave, I know that the door will barely close behind me before Remy replaces them with cheaper labor."

"Your crew are all grown men and women who can make decisions for themselves. Your responsibility only goes so far."

"If I could make myself believe that, I would have been gone a long time ago. But I can't. I made a promise to them when we shut the New Orleans office that I'd take care of them."

"That's been four years," Phaedra said. "How much longer are you going to carry their weight?"

"I've got big shoulders. I can handle it. Besides, I knew what I was getting into when I stepped into the family business."

"Okay then," Phaedra said, trying a different approach.

"What if you quit, went to another company and took your folks with you?"

"You mean poach Inspectorate's employees?"

"You can't steal something that isn't valued. Or, you could start your own company. Run it the way you want to."

"Don't think I haven't thought of that, too. Maybe someday… In the meantime, *cher,* I'm gonna stick it out here and endure whatever craziness this business can throw at me. Gotta have stories to someday tell the grandkids."

"Grandkids," she echoed, sitting up. "I didn't know you even had kids, Bastien. How many children do you have? Boys? Girls?

"I'm not married."

"That doesn't mean you don't have any little baby Bastiens running around somewhere."

"Not *this* Thibeadaux," Bastien said firmly, wanting to be very clear on that. "Don't get me wrong, I love kids. But when I talked about kids, I was talking about my five-year plan."

"How far along are you in this five-year plan?"

"Not as far as I want to be," Bastien admitted. "Anything else you want to ask me?"

"Ye-es," she said drawing out the word. Phaedra clutched the blanket in her hands, nervously scrunching and twisting it. "How are we going to make this work?"

"What *this* do you mean exactly?"

"You know what I mean. By now, all of your employees have already assumed that we're sleeping together. I can't do my job under those conditions. I'm a professional and my reputation is very important to me. My family's spent generations building it."

"You trying to tell me that one little night spent in my office and it's all gonna come tumbling down? You don't give your family reputation enough credit?"

"Okay then. Forget the family and the image. I'm not a one-nighter type of woman. Did you know I almost didn't go to meet you in Galveston?"

"I know that, Phaedra. I'm glad you did, though."

"So am I, Bastien. That's what's torturing me. I say that I'm not this and I'm not that and then I turn around and do exactly the opposite. How does that make me credible if you can't believe the words that come out of my mouth?"

Phaedra paused then said, "I need to tell you something, Bastien, and it won't be easy for me."

"Phaedra," Bastien said gently. "You don't have to share anything with me that you—"

"No, let me finish! I need you to know who I was so you can appreciate what it took for me to become who I am now."

"You're talking about us in college, aren't you? When we were undergrads."

"Yes," Phaedra said. "Meeting you changed me back then, Bastien."

Bastien groaned. He leaned back and laced his fingers on top of his head. "I almost wished you hadn't told me that."

"Why not?"

"Because I feel like a jerk. You drop this deep revelation on me and I can't remember how and when we first met."

"I don't think we can move forward with any of your plans until you do remember."

Bastien kept massaging her feet and calves, warming her skin under his touch.

"Did something happen to make you want to forget me? Was it something I said or did that made you push me out of your mind?"

There was a vulnerable quality about Phaedra's voice that made Bastien carefully consider what he would say to her next. He considered how much he should tell her about his past. It was all ancient history. Dredging it up again never seemed like a useful exercise so he seldom did. But now, he had to if he wanted to earn Phaedra's understanding and trust.

"I'd never deliberately want to forget you, *cher*."

"Then, what is it?" she demanded. "Did you deliberately blot me from your memory?"

"Come over here, Phaedra." Bastien opened his arms to her and let her settle against his chest. Bastien folded his arms around her, holding her close to him.

"Phaedra, do you remember at the beach house when you asked how I got this scar?" He pointed to a spot behind his head. "I told you that was a story for another time."

She nodded, not saying a word.

"I guess the time is now. I'm going to share something with you. No one but my family and Solly know the whole truth of it."

"Are you sure you're ready to talk about it?"

"If I don't talk about it, you and I will never get beyond where we are now. I'm willing to take the chance."

"I'm listening."

"I…uh…used to indulge in some pretty self-destructive behavior way back then. I was the typical college boy away from home, out from under my parents."

"Like any other senior impatient to get out and set the world on fire," Phaedra observed.

"I wasn't worried about the world. My world was already laid out for me by my folks. If a pro team didn't pick me up, they'd get me on with Inspectorate. I didn't have to worry about anything, so, I didn't. I partied. Never did any drugs, though. I was wild, not stupid. But I did some heavy binge drinking. Especially at the start of my senior year. I was gonna make up for all the parties I'd skipped out on. By the fall semester of my senior year, I stopped my grade-grubbing. I figured I'd earned some 'me' time. I had a lot of time on my hands because I only had a couple of blow off classes that I needed to graduate. Too much time and money and plenty of other folks looking for any excuse to party. There are gaps in my memory that I can't fill in, no matter how hard I try."

"Maybe I can help you remember me?" she suggested, looking up at Bastien. "You were a senior. I was a junior. It was homecoming on The Hill. A costume party. I was wearing this—"

"Skintight leopard catsuit," Bastien interrupted.

"You remember?" Phaedra was both appalled and encouraged.

"No. Solly told me when he was trying to get me to remember you."

"Oh…uh…yes…That's what I was wearing. Me and my girlfriends went to one of the unofficial homecoming parties some-where off campus." She lifted her hands and hung invisible air quotes around the word *unofficial*. "And you'd had too much to drink. Even if you hadn't told me now, Bastien, I'd remember that."

"Sounds like any party I'd ever gone to," he admitted.

"You tossed back at least ten whiskey shots," Phaedra recounted for him. "You were playing some stupid drinking game, and it was down between you and one of your football teammates."

"That night was especially rough for me. I'd taken a bad hit during the game. Had to sit out a full quarter. Didn't find out until later that I'd had a concussion. Phaedra, half that night's a blur. All I really remember is I eventually woke up, half naked, stum-bling around. Some of my other teammates thought I was still drunk and laughed their tails off when my vision went double on me and I couldn't stand up. If it wasn't for Solly getting me to the hospital, I think I might have died."

"Oh, Bastien, I didn't know." Phaedra wrapped her arms around his waist, hugging him to give him comfort. "I just thought that…"

"Thought what?"

"Nevermind. It doesn't matter."

"Go on. Say what you were going to say. You don't have to hold your tongue with me. You can always say what's on your mind."

"When we met that night, the way you acted with me, I just thought you were being a jerk. At first you started off so nice, so sweet, then I thought the alcohol was affecting you, showing me an uglier side that…well, the self-destructive side."

"Can you fill in some more pieces for me, Phaedra? Please. I want to know. What else did I do?"

"It's not so much what you did," she clarified. "But what I did to take advantage of your…um…condition. I was indulging in my own self-destructive behavior, Bastien. That weekend, me and my girlfriends went to that party with the sole intention of…of…oh, I'm too embarrassed to even admit it. It sounds so stupid when you say it out loud."

She lowered her head, burying her face in his chest.

"Sole intention of what, Phaedra? What were you going to do?" Cupping the back of her head, he stroked her hair, burying his fingers in the silky thick mass.

"There were three of us. Me, Duchess and Kiyanna…you probably don't remember them, either. Those were the girls I ran with. We were like sisters. We made a stupid, schoolgirl pact. We were all still virgins and…at least, that's what we all claimed…and…um…we were going to see which one of us could…oh, this gets more humiliating to say every time I even think about it. I still can't believe that we went through with it."

"Wait a minute," Bastien said, understanding suddenly coming to him. "Phaedra, are you telling me that you and your friends planned to lose your virginity at that party?"

"That was the plan," Phaedra said, her voice squeaking a little. "When we started out, it didn't matter who we picked. We weren't looking for love and commitment. It was all about being first to be 'made a woman.'

"Duchess and Kiyanna disappeared from the party early. I'd lost the bet, but I hadn't lost my virginity yet. I was determined to stay at that party until I found someone. The problem was none of the guys I talked to that night seemed right to me."

"Did Solly help you with your bet, Phaedra?" Bastien didn't hide the fact that he was bothered by the possibility, even though it was long ago.

"No, Bastien. It wasn't Solly. When I wouldn't go up to the room with him, he left me alone. He tried though. Everyone started pairing off, either leaving with their own dates or hooking up with the ones they'd wanted to. That's when I think Solly steered you over to me. When they started playing the last song. You know the one…" She cleared her throat nervously and started to hum a few bars. Bastien grinned, remembering how she'd claimed that she'd never sing for him.

His smile faded as he recalled the words. He hated that song. Always had. With the surge of memories and emotions tied to that song, past and present collided together and shattered the wall that had blocked him from remembering Phaedra.

He saw himself dancing with Phaedra in the darkened room

of somebody's house turned campus house party. A few couples remained, but they were lost in their own moment. His arms folded around her. When the last notes of the song faded, his hand took hers, leading her up a stairwell littered with beer cans, stubbed out cigarettes and moaning, gyrating college bodies behaving as if no one could see that acts best kept private were played out in public view.

He remembered the feel of congratulatory slaps on his back from his frat brothers. He'd won the prize. The one they'd tried and failed to impress. Someone pressed something into his free hand. Another beer bottle. A foil packet.

One door locked. Another door locked. Third door open but the room was occupied. More bodies. Squeaking bed springs. Sighs and moans. One more door. One more try. A few whispered words of encouragement when he'd felt Phaedra's hand grow cold. At the sight of the bed, she'd drawn back. Protests formed and died on her lips. Shades of second thoughts. They'd gotten that far. All she needed was a little coaxing.

Bastien recalled when his hand slid up her inner thigh, resting between her legs. He massaged until warmth and moisture collected, camouflaged by the spots of her leopard costume. She trembled, clutched his arm. More gaps in his memory pushing to the front of his mind. Vague impressions of flesh upon flesh. Eyes, wide and dark, filled with wonder as his fingers first prepared the way. Eyes squeezed shut, as tightly as the legs that closed around him. As her breathing and anticipation increased, his fingers were quickly replaced. Not quick enough. Not before he recognized the flash of her pain reflected in her eyes as he moved over her and into her. The last of her resistance gave way to insistent, indifferent thrusts. He didn't stop to think. To check to see if she was on that journey with him. He couldn't stop the throes of release. Not until his back became slick with sweat and his own moans of release were added to the orgies going on in the rooms all around them.

Bastien's heart squeezed in panic as his arm tightened around Phaedra lying with him now. *Could it have happened that way?*

"Phaedra." His throat closed up. "You and I…"

"Yes, Bastien, we did." Her admission broke the stillness of the room. "You were my first time."

"Did I…did I…" This time, Bastien was the one who couldn't bring himself to say the words. "Did I force you?"

"No, you didn't force me. Bastien, I could have left that party anytime I wanted to. Nobody forced me to do anything I didn't want to do. I wasn't drunk. I wasn't high. I wasn't drugged. I just…I just wanted you. I stayed in that room all night. I stayed even when you got up and left me there to find my way home the next morning."

"Son of a bitch." It was an indictment of his own behavior. "Phaedra, I swear to you I didn't know. All I remember was getting sick and Solly taking me to the hospital."

"I didn't know," she repeated. "No one told me. You simply dropped out of sight, and I was too humiliated to ask about you. I didn't want anyone to know what I'd done."

"Not even Solly?"

"I didn't know him well enough to confide in him. In his eyes, I was just some girl he couldn't get next to at that party. If anyone saw us together that night, they were all too drunk to remember."

Bastien tapped his forehead. "They opened up my skull to relieve the pressure. And while I was recovering in the hospital, Solly told my folks when they came to visit me that I had a drinking problem. I tried to convince them that I didn't have one. But you can't convince your parents of that sitting in a hospital bed, can you now?"

"No, I guess not," she agreed. "What did they do to you?"

"They pulled the plug on my independence here in Texas. Just like that, I was out of there. They made me come back to Louisiana to finish up."

"You were so close. Couldn't they have just let you stay?"

Bastien shook his head.

"G-Paw pulled some strings, and I finished my undergraduate degree at LSU. I settled in there and started my graduate work."

"So, how'd you wind up back in Houston?"

"G-Paw. I had a debt to pay to him. So I moved back here and started work in the office on the bottom rung as a sampler. That gave me time to study online and get my MBA."

"But then you went back to New Orleans?"

"Like a yo-yo on a string, G-Paw kept jerking me around. Shaping my career. He opened a branch in New Orleans and put me there to help run it…up until about four years ago when… well, you know the rest."

"All that time and you never once thought about me?" She couldn't have sounded any more hurt if he'd ripped her heart out with his bare hands.

"Believe me, Phaedra, if I'd remembered being with you, if I'd remembered anything about that night, I would have looked for you."

"I thought it was something I did that made you avoid me," Phaedra confessed. "I never told anyone about what happened about that night because I was too embarrassed. I told my girls that they'd won the bet, and I left it at that."

"Didn't you try to find me?" Bastien wondered. "With the Internet, you can find just about anybody."

"Why would I put myself through the shame and embarrassment of locating you? Why would I want to know that you had moved on…and was probably living with some other woman? When I graduated, I purged you from my memory and made sure that all my other relationships were on my terms. It made me stronger and for that I have you to thank for."

Chapter 18

Bastien was truly disturbed by what Phaedra had confessed to him. He got up from the couch and stood at the window with his back turned to her. He stared, blank-faced, at the makeshift curtain, his mood as dark as it was outside. He didn't say anything, not for a very, very long time. Phaedra didn't speak either.

The sounds of the day were breaking in. Out in the rail yard, rolling railcars announced that the day was on the move. No time for sitting still. No time for worrying about what had been. It was a new day.

"Bastien?" She called out to him. "Say something. Tell me what you're thinking."

"I'm thinking about the way that I treated you. How can you even stand to look at me?"

"It wasn't your fault. You were hurt," she rationalized.

He spun around, clasped his hands together in a praying position and pressed his fingers to his lips. "Don't you see? I used you."

"I went to that party looking for somebody to use as well."

"It's not supposed to be that way, Phaedra. Your first time

shouldn't have been taken so lightly. It should've been with someone who loved you."

"Don't you think I know that? I didn't have such a level head on my shoulders back then."

Bastien spread his arms, apologizing. "Phaedra, if I could take it back…undo what I did to you—"

"But you can't," she interrupted him. "It was what it was, and there's no changing it."

He rubbed his hand over his head then down the side of his face.

"Even if we could turn back time, Bastien, I'm not sure I'd want to."

"How could you say that? It couldn't have been a pleasurable experience for you."

"How could you say that with certainty? You don't even remember. And like I said, I could have left anytime I wanted to. It's not our making love that hurt me. Not having you afterward was the deepest wound. It hurt my pride."

"Sorry to break it to you, *cher.* But we didn't make love, and I was someone you randomly chose."

Furious that he could be so callous, Phaedra shoved the blanket aside and stomped in her stocking feet across the cold floor to face him.

"Is that what you think happened?" she snapped.

"It's what I know. How could it have been anything more than that? Isn't that what you said you wanted from one of us at that party? You let me take you on a bet. Tell me something, Phaedra. Why me? Why not Solly or a dozen other frat guys who would have gladly stepped in?"

So that was it!

Phaedra took a step back, shocked by his response. He wasn't upset because of how he'd made her feel. It was *his* pride that was wounded. Bastien didn't want to admit the fact that it could have been any man. Her selection was random and without forethought.

"What I did was wrong," she confessed. "It was an impulse aided by the perfect opportunity. The moment I saw you, I knew…I just knew. I'd been watching you all night. The way you talked, the way you laughed, the way you moved. You were perfect. The person was right, Bastien. The timing was wrong."

The look of jealousy and suspicion left Bastien's face. It wasn't just any man for her. It was him. Only him.

"Something happened that night, Bastien. Something mystical," Phaedra said.

"Oh, please!" He was derisive. "Don't make it out to be more than it was. We were just two college kids messing around. Playing with fire. We're lucky we didn't get burned."

Phaedra wrapped her arms around his waist, leaning into him just as she'd done so many years ago when they'd danced. There was a connection between them, Phaedra insisted. She was determined to make him acknowledge it.

"I believe we connected on a level that goes beyond physical attraction. If sex was all that we shared that night, why are you and I like we are today? Why are we still alone if we weren't supposed to find each other again? Why have we both let our work take the place of the love? Have you thought about why we haven't wound up in committed relationships before now?"

"Because we're both workaholics," he replied, caustically countering her nostalgic view of their lives. "It's as simple as that. We're not in college anymore with all of our problems taken care of us by our mommies and daddies. We're adults, having to live adult lives."

"You're right," she conceded, nodding her head. "You're absolutely right." Phaedra wondered when he had become the practical one.

"We aren't kids anymore. And this isn't college frat party. So tell me this, Bastien," she said. "Do you want to be with me or not? I have to know that I have good reason before I risk my hard-won reputation. "

Bastien clenched Phaedra by her shoulders, squeezing so tightly that she had to stand on her tiptoes to relieve the pressure. She tilted her head to look up at him.

"Well?" she demanded. "Tell me, Mr. Thibeadaux. Is this merger likely to happen or not?"

Bastien moved swiftly, taking Phaedra with him. They moved

back onto the couch. Eager, roaming hands slid from her shoulders, pulling her suit jacket from her arms. She lifted her hips, her pelvis connecting with his, and felt the power of his arousal straining through his coveralls. Phaedra curled her leg around his for leverage and lifted higher. She moved rhythmically against him. Each time she did so, Phaedra's skirt lifted higher, aided by Bastien's tugging and pulling.

Bastien clutched at the zipper of his coveralls, yanking so frantically that she thought he'd tear into the T-shirt and his skin beneath it. She grabbed on to the two halves and helped him shrug his shoulders out of his clothes, pushing down as far as she could.

"Bastien! Shh!" Phaedra warned him as he moaned aloud. Her free hand covered his mouth as she looked nervously toward the door.

"Don't you worry. Nobody's comin' through that door. Everybody's gone."

"Did you lock it?"

"Yeah, I think so," he muttered.

"Are you sure?"

"Sure enough," he growled, burying his face at her neck as he began a line of kisses that trekked toward the opening of Phaedra's blouse. Clumsy fingers fumbled with the tiny buttons so that he cursed under his breath each time one of the buttons caught in the silk, disobeying his will to be undone. Pushing his hands away, Phaedra clutched at the buttons that he had managed to undo, denying him access.

"Would you double-check for me please?"

"You kidding me?"

"No, I'm not kidding. Please, Bastien. I don't want anyone walking in on us. Like G-Paw," she reminded him. "Remember how well that turned out?"

Bastien groaned again and heaved a dramatic sigh. Clutching his coveralls around his hips to keep them from falling to the floor, he stood up and walked to the door. As he turned the lock, he made sure the click was audible.

"There. Satisfied?" he taunted as he shuffled back across the room.

"Not yet," Phaedra said, encouraging him. "You still have some more work to do."

"Then I'd better get on my job," Bastien said as he joined Phaedra on the couch again. She quickly undid the remaining buttons and allowed the blouse to fall from her shoulders.

Bastien dropped to his knees before her, staring at her with intense eyes. He scooted forward until his torso just touched the edge of the couch. Resting his hands on her outer thighs, he massaged up and down.

"Take that off, too, Phaedra." He indicated with a slight dip of his head.

Phaedra went for the front closure of her bra, unclasping the two hooks.

"And those too." His eyes dipped lower to her waist. The only touch he would allow himself was to keep his hands at her thighs.

Phaedra hooked her thumbs within the waistband of her stockings and panties, leaned back and drew them down with agonizing slowness. Bastien stopped rubbing her legs long enough to take up where she'd left off. Her hands brushed his as he finished removing her underwear. She was completely bare now. Completely exposed.

Phaedra put her hands on either side of Bastien's face, forcing him to look up at her as she searched his face.

Phaedra wanted Bastien. All of him. She wanted to feel him against her.

Bastien started with a kiss. A kiss that seemed to go on and on and on. The more his lips took from hers, the more Phaedra needed from him in return. Where his lips went, Phaedra followed. Where his tongue plunged, she plundered with equal enthusiasm. She kissed him back until she was breathless and panting.

Her arms wrapped around his head and back, keeping him captive against her. Her breasts demanded their own share of Bastien's attention. He was still kneeling before her; and when he lowered his head, planting kisses across her cheek, chin and down her neck to her breasts Phaedra rasped in a mixture of pleasure and dismay. Her lips were swollen with sweet aching, but she wanted more.

His tongue darted forward, teasing one nipple to full erectness, and then the other. Back and forth, he devoted his attention. Each time, he spent a little bit longer, swirling his tongue until Phaedra writhed on the couch, sliding forward so that her core connected with the muscled planes of his chest. Bastien gave an involuntary grunt, a break in his concentration when he felt her slip closer to his shaft. His hand dipped between them, pulling aside his briefs and completely freeing himself from his clothes.

"Bastien." Phaedra's voice was hoarse when she called his name. "I can't wait anymore."

He pulled back, looking at her. "You satisfied yet, *cher?*" There was laughter in his voice.

"Yes!" she hissed, not ashamed of her impatience.

"No…No, I don't think so." He shook his head, smirking at her. "Not yet. You can handle a little more."

"Oh…oh….oh!" She threw her head back against the couch, gouging her hands into the cushions. He went lower still, lathing her with an experienced tongue. Phaedra was so conflicted. Her hand caught the back of his head and encouraged him, showing him exactly how she wanted him.

Bastien didn't need further explanation. He didn't stop, wouldn't stop, even when she clamped her hand over her mouth to smother the shriek that he was seconds away from wrenching out of her.

"Don't you hold back on me, *cher.*"

Phaedra couldn't reign herself in now if her soul depended on it. Her thighs quivered as the shock waves of her orgasm rocked her. Pure electricity coursed through her, making her want to rise from the couch. Bastien clung firmly to Phaedra's legs, keeping her rooted, even as she felt she could soar.

As the tremors subsided and Phaedra's breathing restored to normal, Bastien sat back on his heels, placing the flat of his palms against his upper thighs, waiting patiently. She blinked several times, trying to bring her eyes back into focus. Phaedra ran her fingers through her tangled hair.

"Bastien." She beckoned for him, asking him to join her. Phaedra then scooted to the back of the couch while Bastien lay on his side. He folded one arm under his head for a pillow. The other lazily caressed her hip. His arousal hadn't lessened by waiting for her. As they lay face-to-face, chest-to-chest, thigh-to-thigh, he pulsed against her, heated and hard.

Phaedra reached for him and he closed his hand around hers.

Chapter 19

"Phaedra, wait. Wait! Stop…" She had barely begun when Bastien grasped her wrist, halting her.

"What's the matter? Am I doing something wrong?"

"Naw, *cher*. You didn't do anything wrong. You're perfect. Too perfect. We gotta slow down and let me catch my breath. Catch myself before I erupt."

"Oooh. I see."

"I've only got one condom," Bastien confessed. "I've had it for a long time. A very, very long time. Kept it more out of habit than anything. It might not be any good anymore. The thing's probably disintegrated by now."

"Shh…Bastien, you don't have to explain anything to me." She placed a finger against his lips to silence his confession.

"I do," he insisted. "You gotta know that I'm not a one-nighter kind of man, either, Phaedra. I don't mess around."

"Did I say that you did?"

"People look at me and they assume I'm a certain way."

"People. You mean women?" she said, using the same jealous tone that Bastien had used when he questioned her about Solly.

"Do you have women throwing themselves at you, Bastien?" She teased.

"I'm not a dog. No matter what my fraternity mascot says."

"I know what kind of man you are, Bastien. I can feel it here." Phaedra placed her hand over his heart and closed her eyes.

"What's it telling you?"

"It's telling me to tell you that since you've only got one condom, you'd better do your damnedest to make it last." Her response sent a flash of fire through him.

"You're killing me, *cher*."

The way she caressed him stoked Bastien until he had no intelligible, verbal response. All he could do was lay there, biting his lip and praying that he would maintain control.

"Phaedra." Her name came out on a groan. A clear indicator that he'd reached the limit of his endurance. "My wallet is in my jumper on the floor," Bastien rasped. "The condom's in there."

"Umm…sounds like a problem." She purred. "We're all the way up here on the couch, and it's all the way down there on the floor. One of us has to move to go and get it. Do you want me to stop what I'm doing while you go groping around in the dark for it?"

Time to get creative, he decided.

Bastien slid his left arm under her waist and hooked it around her.

"Hold on," he muttered.

"Hmm? What?" she said, focused more on what she was doing than what he was about to do.

"I said, hold on."

Without another warning, Bastien rolled to the right, with just enough momentum to send them both sliding off the edge of the couch onto the floor. He landed with a soft thud on his back, Phaedra now resting on top of him. He felt her laughing as his free arm flailed out to pound the floor, groping for his discarded jumper. One handed, he dug it out.

Though she lay on top of him, she never released her claiming hold. Phaedra rested one elbow on the floor to support herself and planted her knees on either side of him. She only allowed Bastien room to maneuver long enough to sheath himself in the condom.

"Problem solved," Bastien murmured as he placed his hands on either side of her hips and applied gentle, insistent pressure downward.

Phaedra slowly rocked back, allowing him to enter her in controlled, gradual increments.

"Relax, *cher*," Bastien coaxed her. "I won't hurt you."

"I trust you, Bastien."

Bastien resolved to do his best not to disappoint her. It had been a long time for him. Too long. And he could tell by Phaedra's tightness as she closed around him that she hadn't been with anyone either. She was his, all his, for the taking, just like before. Only this time, he thought solemnly, this time it was going to be different.

He eased into her, waited for her to catch her breath and get accustomed to him before guiding her hips away from him. As Phaedra's face drew closer to his, Bastien kissed her, holding the kiss as long as he could before he felt the need to move again. Each ripple growing stronger.

They kept that rhythm. Careful. Controlled. Keeping a tight reign on their instincts that would otherwise tell them to hurry. Bastien let Phaedra set the tempo. She was the one who determined the length of the kiss, the pauses between pulses. He lay on his back with his hands resting lightly at her hips rather than insisting that she take in all of him. He wasn't going to rush her. He needed her to know that they had time. He'd wait for her.

When she finally completely surrounded him, Bastien felt her tremors building again. As Phaedra cried out, she fell forward. Bastien rolled over once more, curling his leg around her, cushioning her head from the floor with his arm. As they switched positions, Bastien entered her—a deep, deliberate thrust that pinned her down even as Phaedra tried to lift her hips to meet him.

With more leverage and momentum, his motions intensified. He was still resolved not to hurt her. But he was also determined to push the boundaries of pleasure. Her whispers of encouragement told him to delve deeper and deeper still. Phaedra wasn't shy about showing him what she wanted. She wasn't a college girl anymore, nervously seeking affirmation of her womanhood by random selection. She knew what she needed. He knew what she wanted. And it was him.

Nothing could have pleased Bastien more to oblige her. His own satisfaction was directly connected to hers. The more she demanded of him, the more he was willing to give. And give. And give. Limited only by the frailties and the breaking point of the human body. When she widened her knees, allowing him unrestrained access, Bastien gripped the edge of the couch for leverage, fearful that the power of his emotions would crush her if he held on to her. His free hand cradled her bottom as he connected with her.

Breathing was timing. The faster Bastien took air into his lungs, the faster Phaedra took him into her. She reached up with both hands, clawing at the leather couch as if she was also afraid of hurting him with her enthusiasm. Her hands grazed the blanket. Phaedra snatched it down, stuffing the corner into her mouth to keep from crying out. Bastien pulled it aside and instead covered her mouth with his own—taking her breath as his own and claiming her cry of release as his own. As she tightened around him, Bastien felt the last of her resistance and the last of his restraint slip away. He let himself go, even as he clung to her. Bastien held on to her for what seemed like a very long time, breathing heavily and willing his heart to cease its breakneck pace.

"Are you all right, Bastien?" The sound of Phaedra's voice, calm and concerned, brought back a semblance of sanity to his whirling head.

"Don't let go, Phaedra." He pleaded with her as he rested his forehead against hers. "Just don't let go of me."

"I won't," she promised and soothed him by smoothing her hands up and down his back.

Bastien supposed that he should have gotten up, moved them back to the couch. He was in no mood to move and neither was she. What else could he do but pull down a few more throw pillows and toss the blanket over them.

He intended to get up, go to the washroom and bring them both back warm towels. One minute stretched to five. Then fifteen. Then almost a full hour before Bastien had the presence of mind to stir again. He hadn't felt that relaxed, satisfied in...well...ever! He'd never had this feeling of utter completeness before. This sense of all being right in the world. He didn't want it to end.

Bastien stretched, trying not to disturb Phaedra as she slept next to him. When she stirred, murmuring, Bastien whispered to her, "I'll be right back."

As soon as he moved, Phaedra whispered in complaint. She didn't want to move either. Or want him to leave her. She inched closer to him, yawning as she said, "Don't go, Bastien. Stay here with me."

"I won't be gone long," he promised. He stood up and strode across the room to his private restroom. When Bastien came back, he knelt down beside her. Phaedra was already sitting up, with her arms folded, her expression perplexed.

"What's wrong, *cher?*" Bastien asked, sensing the shift in her mood.

"I thought you said you'd sent everyone home?"

"As far as I know, all of my employees are gone? Why? What happened?"

"While you were in the restroom, I thought I heard talking in the hallway."

"Don't worry about anybody else," Bastien consoled her. "I told you. Nobody's coming through that door that I don't let in. Okay?"

"Okay," she sounded dubious as she glanced back at the door and gathered the blanket around her.

"I brought you something," Bastien said, making a peace offering of a warmed towel. She took his hand, guided him to the juncture of her thighs. When Bastien was finished, she took the towel that he'd brought for himself and treated him to the same cleansing ritual. It was as intimate, as giving a gesture as anything they'd done. She awed him and aroused him at the same time. Under her gentle hands, Bastien was frustrated and firm all over again. There wasn't anything he could do about it.

"You're quiet," Bastien observed while she rubbed the towel over his skin.

"I was only thinking after this, you know this means I can't work here for you or with you, don't you, Bastien? It's a serious conflict of interest, if not breach of ethics."

"So, what are you going to do?"

"I won't go back on my word. I'll help you. I suppose I'll ask one of my associates to work with you. Or give your information for another consultant I know and respect. He's good. Very good. His name's Logan Davis. We've worked together in the same industry for seven years and I trust him. If he doesn't suit you then we can talk about my other associates tomorrow."

"Tomorrow," Bastien promised. "We can talk about work tomorrow. In the meantime, we have some other catching up to do." He reached for her again, then immediately pulled back.

"I forgot. My last condom went with an undignified flush down the commode."

Phaedra laughed and said, "Look what I found." She reached behind her, hidden from underneath a blanket, and pulled out three condoms taped together. Stuck to it was one of Jacie's signature notes; yet, it had both Chas's and Jacie's handwriting.

A little sumthin'-sumthin'. Bastien recognized Chas's handwriting. Followed by a heart-shaped smiley face. That could only be Jacie's contribution.

"I should have known I couldn't keep anything private in this office," Bastien grumbled, then turned his thoughts to the woman who inspired his cousin's gifts.

Chapter 20

G-Paw and Remy walked back and forth through the office, searching for signs of life. Each time he found an empty room, G-Paw cursed at Remy because he was the closest one to him.

Remy wasn't in the mood to listen to the old man complain about how nobody wanted to work anymore. As hard as he tried, he couldn't do anything to assuage G-Paw. Chas and Bastien had both agreed to send their employees home. What was the point of keeping them there? After the all-clear siren went off, no one was going to be a lick of good anyway. How could they expect them to work when they were so worried about getting home to their families?

"Look at this place. It's like a damned tomb around here," G-Paw complained.

"That's not true, G-Paw. I'm here. And Chas and Jacie are in his office."

G-Paw rumbled phlegm in his throat. "He won't be no more good after Jacie's finished with him. What about Bastien?"

It was Remy's turn to be derisive. "I heard he was holed up, too, with that woman that he brought in to consult. He took off as soon as he let the employees go home."

G-Paw laughed. "You haven't met her yet, have you, Remy?"

"Don't need to. I know what kinda woman she is. She's laid up in there with him now, isn't she?"

"You'd better get a clue, Remy. That gal's pretty smart. When everybody else was running around here, like chickens with their heads cut off, she jumped right in and took over tendin' to the wounded. She didn't have to. Could have sat back and cowered in a corner."

"You sound impressed." G-Paw didn't use that tone often, certainly never in reference to he or Bastien. Chas was the only one G-Paw ever respected.

"She's a Burke-Carter, if that means anything at all to you, boy."

"You're going to let her do it, aren't you, G-Paw? You're gonna let her come up in here and run things. I'll bet she's gonna cost us. Weren't you the one who always told us not to let women get between us and making money?"

"And I still stand by it."

"So, how can you—"

"Listen to me, Remy. That woman knows her business. And she knows what it takes to run a business. I know her family's reputation. I may not have agreed with all of Bastien's decisions, but hooking up with that Burke-Carter will be one of the better ones. He'll turn his division around. I know he will."

"G-Paw, you and I both know that this is just a job to Bastien. His heart isn't in it. Not like Chas and me. We were born to do this work."

"You mean to say born into it, don't you, boy? I built this company with my own two hands. You're nothing but a bunch of lazy, good-for-nothing leeches."

"You didn't build this all by yourself. Me and Chas helped you. For almost twenty years, we worked right by you. Side by side. We've earned the right to be here. Not Bastien. He hasn't earned a damned thing."

"Bastien might not have been here as long as you or Chas, but he's pulled his own weight. He's good at his job, and he's got the loyalty of his employees to help him along. If you ain't careful, he's gonna bump you out of that number two spot and take over as chief operations officer. He has it in him, I can see it. And if that gal manages to squeeze any more efficiency out of his division, I am of a mind to replace you."

"Like hell you will. I'll burn this place to the ground before I see him pull ahead of me," Remy threatened.

"Don't let your mouth write a check your butt can't cash, boy."

G-Paw didn't appreciate Remy's point of view. He didn't understand that it wasn't an idle threat. Remy meant every single word. Before he'd let Bastien take his position away from him, he'd torch this place, and scorch it so that nobody would have anything. No more company. No more legacy. Nothing!

"G-Paw, I'm not gonna let him take what I've worked so hard these years to get."

"Worked? What do you mean? All you did was ride Chas's coattails. You don't think I saw how he carried you?"

Remy simmered. His nostrils flared as he faced his grandfather. He always knew that Chas was G-Paw's favorite. The only reason he was promoted to chief operations officer was because Chas didn't want the job.

"Well, you gonna stand there with your mouth hung open, looking like an idiot, or are you gonna get me to my office? I'm tired."

"Sure, G-Paw," Remy said grudgingly holding out his arm for him to lean on. "Do you want me to take you home?"

"What are you talking about? Trying to waste my gas and my time? I have to turn around and come back in a couple of hours."

Once they'd made it back to G-Paw's office, Remy helped to ease his grandfather into his chair.

"Oh, mercy! Time for my medicine," G-Paw said, pointing to his desk drawer.

Remy reached for his cache of pills. Instead, G-Paw slapped his hand away and cupped his hand around the neck of his whiskey bottle.

"What're you waiting for, boy? The second coming?" G-Paw rasped at him.

"Maybe you need to be cutting back on this G-Paw. What about your dialysis?"

"What about it?" he said belligerently, glaring at him with red-rimmed eyes.

Remy shrugged, knowing that he could either sit and drink with the old man, monitoring how much he took in, or he could get himself thrown out of his office—in which case, he'd drink as much as he wanted anyway.

Remy filled his glass halfway but G-Paw complained. "Don't be stingy with that, boy."

"Just trying to save some for myself."

G-Paw found another glass and poured one shot for Remy. Tossing it down his throat, Remy ignored the familiar burn that soon followed. He'd barely gulped down the first one when he poured himself another. Then another. Then another. And still another.

"Easy on that, Remy." G-Paw was now the one setting limits. He reached for his bottle and tried to pull it away from Remy, who was too quick for him. At least, he thought he was too quick for G-Paw. His vision suddenly blurred and his hand wobbled. Remy wound up knocking the bottle over on G-Paw's desk, soaking papers with the amber liquid.

"What's the matter with you? You've lost your feeble mind!" G-Paw lifted his cane and tried to thwack him with it.

"You!" Remy said raggedly. "You're what's the matter with me. Ready to pass me over again just to make a stinking dollar! You tried to do it with Chas, and now you're trying again with Bastien. You'd put a blind monkey in that spot before you chose me, G-Paw. Why?"

"What I do, I do for the good of this company, so ya'll will have something when I'm gone."

"Gone? What are you talking about, old man? You're not going anywhere, G-Paw."

G-Paw thrust forward his lower jaw. "Don't patronize me, Remy. I know I ain't got much longer. Dialysis has only bought me a little more time. I'm dying."

"No." Remy wasn't ready to accept that. "You can't be dying."

"Listen to me, Remington." G-Paw leaned forward, his gaze boring into his grandson. "I don't expect to see Chas's boys grow to teenagers. I'd hoped that when they turned fifteen that I'd have them here with me. Like I did with Chas. Like I did with you. But that ain't gonna happen. I know that. I can accept that."

G-Paw drew several deep breaths through his nostrils, calming the quivering in his voice so that he could go on. It was the tremor of age, mingled with fear and barely suppressed rage. He felt cheated and misused by time.

"That's exactly why I gotta do whatever I have to in order to make sure this company stays strong. I have to know that I've got good, solid leadership at the helm. If that means I'll hurt some feelings along the way, then so be it. If I make a mistake now, I'm hurting the future Thibeadaux generations to come. I'm not going to my grave knowing that I could have done something to ensure my family's future and I didn't."

"Haven't I shown you that I can lead, G-Paw? Haven't I proven my worth to you?"

G-Paw stared up at Remy. For a moment, Remy thought he saw pride reflected in the old man's eyes.

"About as useful as a one-legged man in an ass kickin' contest," G-Paw spat.

Just like that, the tender sentiment was dead, strangled in its infancy by G-Paw's inability to show any kind of decent, human emotion. G-Paw poured himself another drink, warming the shot glass between his palms before lifting the glass and pouring the liquid down his throat. The glass barely touched his lips, but he wiped his mouth with the back of his hand and kept talking.

"You let Bastien creep up on you, boy. Pull ahead, even. You let your guard down, and he came up in here and blew you away. What do you expect me to do about that?"

"And after hearing this, what do you expect me to do about it?"

"You raising your voice to me, boy?"

"No. No I'm not." Remy backed down, though he felt like shouting some sense into that old man.

"Remy, do you remember what Chas told you the day he came

back from his honeymoon? You remember how he walked in on you talking to your crew? I saw that look on your face. You were scared spitless. You thought he was coming back to take your job."

Pressing his fists to his eyes, Remy tried to remember. It seemed like so many years ago. The whiskey was doing a number on him.

"He said…he said….he told me to handle my business. That I was to keep on doing what I knew how to do."

"That's right. That's all I ever taught you. No matter what you do, no matter who you do it with, you have to always handle your business. Don't let anyone get in the way. You get what I'm telling you, boy? Is anything getting through that thick skull of yours?"

"Yeah, G-Paw. I get you."

Remy got him all right. He hadn't hung in there all this time to let Bastien take it all away from him now. He was in his way. And G-Paw had just given him tacit permission to do whatever he needed to in order to take care of it.

As Remy sat there, nursing the last few sips of his drink, his muddled head raced along with his hot blood. He didn't stop to think that infighting between them could be destructive. All he could think was that G-Paw only wanted the best for CT Inspectorate. Wasn't he better than Bastien? If he could throw Bastien off his game, get him messing up worse than he already was, G-Paw would see his new golden boy fall. Since Chas didn't want to play company man, that number two spot was his. His for as long as he wanted it. Remy figured that he could even be number one if G-Paw truly was making final preparations.

First things first, he had to take Bastien out of the running. Not as easy as he thought. Remy's first tactics to put him in his place didn't work. When he'd kept his foot on Bastien's neck, watching his every move, trying to point out where he was going wrong, he always turned it back on him and showed him up.

Remy once made the mistake of cursing Bastien out in front of his people. It shamed Bastien the first time because he'd been ill-prepared. Discomposure quickly turned to determination. During their morning planning meetings, when he tried to bust him again, Bastien got increasingly better and better at anticipating what Remy was going to do and say. Instead of standing there looking dumb, Bastien pointed out where Remy's information was faulty and how the decisions he'd made were sound.

Remy switched tactics. He tried backing off, not giving Bastien any direction at all. That's when Bastien took the opportunity to make a bunch of sweeping changes. Changes that Chas agreed with because they made sense and made the company more money. So, while Remy was off, thinking that he was giving Bastien enough rope to hang himself, he was busy tying knots around Remy's job, pulling it closer and closer to him. To hear G-Paw talk, Bastien was just a few dollars away from becoming the new COO.

Remy knew that it was getting harder to trip Bastien up. Bastien was getting too damned smart for him. His crew, though, was another avenue that Remy could use to shake Bastien's confidence. No opening there, either. Remy couldn't get to his loyal employees. He'd never seen such a tight-knit crew.

After facing the uncertainty of Hurricane Katrina together, there wasn't much Remy could do to tear them down. Bastien's weakness, his concern for his employees, was his greatest strength. Yet, Remy was convinced there had to be one other soft spot he could press, one that he knew would shake Bastien if messed with. The opportunity would present itself. Maybe it already had.

He looked back over his shoulder, toward Bastien's office where he knew that Bastien and that Burke-Carter woman were still together.

Maybe the opportunity was right before him. All he had to do was be patient. Keep his eyes open and his mouth shut and wait for his opportunity to show G-Paw that he had what it took to run this business.

Chapter 21

For the past few weeks since the explosion at the port, Phaedra hadn't put in much face time at her own office. She'd spent much of her time auditing the training course that Logan Guillory was conducting at Inspectorate. Her extended absences showed by the high stack of mail sitting in her inbox when she finally got in around five o'clock in the morning. It was too early in the morning for anyone else. But that was generally when Phaedra was most productive. As long as she was in the office that early, there were no impromptu meetings, no casual stop-bys. Just her, her office and a stack of to-do's as high as her head. She accessed her voice mail and picked up her messages.

Only one message that she hadn't gotten around to addressing. As she put the phone on speaker, she picked up a letter opener and slit through several envelopes.

"Hello, sister Burke-Carter. This is Pastor Ellis. Sorry to call you at work. I've also left messages on your cell. Just calling to remind you about the planning meeting for tonight. We'll be finalizing the plans for the Helping Hands picnic this Saturday.

You said you wanted to participate. I know you've been really busy with work, but we could still use your help. If you're still able, we'll see you tonight. Have a blessed day, sister."

Phaedra made a note in the PDA to call the pastor back. As she was sorting through her stack of letters, her office phone rang. Only two people called her that early in the morning. Bastien and her mother. And since she'd just spoken to Bastien last night she knew who it was.

"Hello, Mother," she greeted, pressing the speakerphone button to keep her hands free.

"You're in the office early, Phaedra."

"So are you," she said, noting the number displayed on the caller ID. "What are you doing in so early?"

"I'm preparing for an emergency board meeting. Did I tell you that one of the members is stepping down?"

Maybe she had. Phaedra didn't remember. She'd been so preoccupied with Bastien and CT Inspectorate lately. The company had successfully completed the first phase of Logan Guillory's revised training program. Phaedra had gone back to her office to review Logan's proposal for the second phase—a comprehensive plan to roll out to all of CT Inspectorate's divisions. They were going nationwide!

"Who's stepping down?" All of the members of the board of her mother's foundation were carefully selected. Many were longtime friends. Phaedra couldn't imagine one of them leaving her with so much work still left undone.

"Savannah Cox."

"Mrs. Cox is leaving? Why? Is everything all right?" Mrs. Cox was her mother's first appointee. She was so full of commitment and bright ideas. Phaedra had a hard time imagining the foundation running without her.

"Savannah has some health challenges, dear. She wants to concentrate on treatment."

"Oh, I'm so sorry to hear that, Mother. Is there anything she needs? Anything I can do to help?"

"She needs our prayers."

"Of course," Phaedra murmured. "I'll add her to the prayer list at church. So, what are you going to do about filling her position? I know it will be difficult. No one can truly take her place."

"Interesting that you should mention that, Phaedra."

"Oh?" Her mother's casual tone didn't fool Phaedra. She didn't call to chat. She called to recruit her. It wasn't the first time that she'd asked Phaedra to take a more active role in the foundation.

"I was thinking, dear, that you might consider yourself for the vacant position. I've always wanted you at my side, Phaedra. We work so well together. Don't you remember how successful our last pledge drive was? We raised over three hundred thousand dollars for that women's shelter."

"We have had some good times, haven't we?" Phaedra truly enjoyed working with her mother. Phillipa Burke-Carter was driven and committed, much like her daughter.

"We've worked together well on so many other projects," Phillipa continued. "And I know you get just as much satisfaction of working hard for others. All of your volunteer work, the fundraisers you've organized. Your involvement in the church. Don't tell me that you get more satisfaction from getting some silly contract signed than you do from serving others."

"I don't deny that. It's just…working on your projects takes up so much of my time and I have my own business to run."

"How long have you and Logan been working out there?"

"About six weeks now."

"And they're considering extending the contract?"

"How did you know that?"

"I have my sources," Phillipa said coyly.

"You mean Darryl."

"Yes," she admitted. "He told me how you managed to get the owner to commit to a full six months across all of his branch offices."

"How does Darryl know G-Paw Thibeadaux?"

"Oh, it was some years ago. Darryl saw a golden opportunity in that inspection company. He offered to buy Mr. Thibeadaux out back then."

"No!" Phaedra exclaimed. "I never knew. I wish I had been

armed with that information before I made my first presentation to them. Was it a hostile buyout? Darryl can be very aggressive when he comes across something he wants."

"I wouldn't say aggressive," Phillipa hedged. "Persistent. You know how Darryl is. He put together quite an impressive proposal. He even got as far as presenting to Mr. Thibeadaux. What was it you called him? Hee-haw?"

"G-Paw," Phaedra corrected.

"Yes. G-Paw. That man took the meeting, made Darryl jump through hoops amending the contract and dickering with numbers. Darryl even promised to keep the name of the company and the staff. But that cantankerous old man was just toying with him, making himself and his company look attractive to potential buyers so that he could go off and get an expansion loan. I've never trusted that man after that. He and his entire family are a pack of two-faced double dealers concerned only with making money."

"Mother, that's harsh. They're not all like that. Bastien isn't like that. You've met him. You've seen for yourself."

"Yes, he was very polite and attentive and said all the right things. But he's a Thibeadaux, too, Phaedra. There's no getting around that. That grandfather has a terribly powerful hold over that family. He's not a nice person at all."

"You don't have to tell me that, Mother."

"Darryl told me that when he was doing his research on that G-Paw, he turned up more than one assault charge on his record. Never prosecuted. I think he has connections. The shady kind. He's a liar and a bully and a money-hungry tyrant. I wouldn't believe a word that came out of that entire family's mouths if my life depended on it. A word of caution from your mother, if you're going to continue to deal with those Thibeadauxs, Phaedra. Be very, very careful. Keep your guard up."

"I will," Phaedra promised her.

"And, when you get sick of working with those in the corporate world, you can always come and work with me." She ended brightly. "Consider it, won't you?"

"I'll consider it," Phaedra agreed. "No promises, though."

"Consider it enough to try to make the board meeting today at twelve o'clock?"

"You're pushing it, Mother."

"Simply a gentle nudge in the right direction, dear."

"Being right is a matter of perspective."

"And your mother's perspective is always right."

"Spoken like a true mother."

"Speaking of which, you and that Bastien have gotten very close lately. Any plans of your own for marrying and having—"

"Mother, I've got to go," Phaedra immediately interrupted her. "I have so much to catch up on. Thanks for calling and love you much!"

"But, Phaedra—"

"Bye, Mother. Talk to you sometime before twelve today. Kisses!" Phaedra hung up the phone, not giving her yet another chance to argue. After she hung up the phone, she sat staring at it for several moments, doing something she seldom did— chew her nails.

It didn't surprise her that G-Paw was a dangerous man. His body was ravaged, but his inner rage toward the world was still fierce. Phaedra could see it blazing behind his eyes. It didn't surprise her that he would try to use whoever he could to keep his company solid. He played favorites with his family members, put his foot on the neck of his employees and was openly contemptuous of the contributions of women to his little empire. He was a menace.

At the same time, he inspired fierce loyalty in his relatives. Phaedra could understand that. And she could work with that, no matter how unpleasant G-Paw was. If she could handle managing a full scale evacuation of an oil rig during hurricane season, she was pretty sure that she could handle G-Paw. With Bastien's support, she could handle anything.

By eight-thirty, Phaedra's office was starting to show signs of life. She'd kept her head buried in paperwork but lifted it when the smell of freshly brewed gourmet coffee tickled her nostrils.

"Well, hello stranger!" her administrative assistant, Summer

Davis, said as she flounced into her office, oversized coffee mug in one hand and another stack of mail in the other. "Do my eyes deceive me? Have you really managed to find your way back?"

"Oh, come on now, Summer. I haven't been gone that long."

"No, but even when you were here, your mind was somewhere else. Tell me, how are things going out at Inspectorate? When does Mr. Guillory start phase two?"

"Not sure. He asked me to review his proposal. That's what I'm doing now. He's still on the schedule to be out at Inspectorate until Monday."

"That reminds me about your scheduling, Ms. Burke-Carter. You've been a hard woman to keep track of."

"You may want sync up my schedule with yours." Phaedra handed her the PDA. "I just made some adjustments so I can meet with my mother at lunch today."

"Oh, and don't be late for your meeting this evening with your pastor. He accidentally dialed the wrong extension and got my voice mail instead of yours yesterday. I forwarded the message to you."

"Yes, I heard the message," Phaedra said, marking the meeting on her desk calendar and circling it.

Summer raised an eyebrow at Phaedra. "I'm surprised that you are getting your messages. Your cell phone has been rolling over a lot these past few weeks. Is there something wrong with it? Is that battery not holding its charge? Do I need to have it serviced?"

"No," Phaedra said, folding her hands on top of the desk. "There's nothing wrong with the phone." She used a tone that she hoped said that she didn't want to discuss her activities any further.

"So, if there's nothing wrong with the phone, why haven't you been answering it?"

"I can't hear it ring if it's turned off, Summer."

"Turned off?"

"That's right. I've been turning it off. I didn't want to be disturbed."

"Even if it's potential business?" Summer's eyes widened with disbelief.

"Even if," Phaedra echoed. Another rule tossed out the window. There was more to life than making money.

Summer stuck out her lower lip and dipped her head once in acceptance of her explanation. "Oh, okay then."

Phaedra opened up a file drawer, averting her eyes. "Let me know when you've finished transferring my calendar notices to yours," she said. It was clearly a dismissal.

"Yes, ma'am."

By her tone, Phaedra sensed that she'd hurt her feelings.

Summer turned her back, head lowered as she retrieved the PDA stylus and started to tap the screen to access Phaedra's calendar. She turned around suddenly, holding out the PDA in front of her. "B.T. is trying to reach you."

She waggled the PDA in front of her. "You've got a message coming in right now, and it's got smiley face emoticons and flashing purple hearts all around it."

Phaedra sprang up from her seat and held out her hand. "Never mind about the calendar now, Summer. We can sync up later."

The last time Bastien sent her a text message, she'd started blushing even before she could get to the last line. By the time Phaedra had finished reading it, she was dreaming up excuses for why she needed to make yet another unscheduled visit out to CT Inspectorate, despite her associate Logan handling the training as well as she could.

Summer laughed openly at her; and for a moment, Phaedra thought she was considering playing "keep away" with her and the PDA. The look Phaedra gave her in return immediately killed that playful spirit in her. That message from Bastien was for her eyes only.

"Yes, ma'am," she said placing the PDA in the palm of Phaedra's hand. "Tell Bastien Thibeadaux I said he shouldn't make himself such a stranger, either."

It wasn't hard for Summer to make the connection. She'd been on hand to retrieve the faxed signature page authorizing us to start work at Bastien's company. Sometimes, when he couldn't get her by cell, he called the office and left messages.

"I'll return this to you when I've finished reviewing my messages."

"You mean when you've finished purging or encrypting them," Summer muttered on her way out of the office. She gave Phaedra one last head shake then pulled the door closed behind her.

Okay. She had a point. Phaedra conceded. She couldn't help but smile. Her eyes lowered as she read the message. Only a few short lines. Bastien had been traveling the past few weeks, visiting the owners of grain silos throughout Texas, Louisiana and Oklahoma to touch base with clients. He'd be back in a couple days and had something he needed to tell her. That's all Bastien gave her in the text message, but it was enough to keep him on her mind.

Phaedra settled back at her desk and turned on her computer. She stared at the screen, not really seeing it. She kept thinking about how complicated this situation with Bastien had become. She never mixed business and her personal life. *Never.* She'd seen too many horror stories of how relationships like that had gone astray. Yet, even as she told herself that she should completely extricate herself from CT Inspectorate, she couldn't silence the little voice of hope in the back of her head told her she could make a living and find love in the same place.

Hadn't her own parents built the Burke-Carter Foundation by working side by side for the past thirty years? Hadn't Bastien's cousin Chas found financial and familial stability when he offered his wife, Jacie, a job at CT Inspectorate? These were obvious examples of how work life and wedded bliss were feasible.

Phaedra blew out a shaky breath, wondering how the word *wedding* worked its way into her vocabulary. Bastien's feelings for her, though undeniably potent, still seemed primarily physical. His touch was like a drug. A little taste had her hooked and now she was wide open, craving more. When she was with him she shook, screamed and soared. He left her free to explore and to experiment, never turning her down.

As Phaedra sat there at her desk, recalling the last time Bastien and she had made love, the quiet voice of guilt crept in and tainted the joy she felt when she was with him. They'd made love, but they'd never professed it. She thought he *could* be in love with her. Wished he would be. She'd hoped that infatuation would blossom. She wanted more from Bastien than release from sexual tension. She wanted a deep, committed relationship.

"That's why wedding popped into my head," Phaedra murmured. Aside from her mother's blatant hints, it was the voice that told her she needed something more than that from him. She was willing to commit herself to building something that could withstand their passion's fire and come out tempered and strong. If he gave her the slightest inkling that building a permanent life with her was what he wanted, as well, she would be willing to do whatever it took, whatever she needed to do to build that life. Five-year plan. Fifty-year plan. As long as being together was in their future.

"Phaedra?"

It was Summer again, buzzing her on the intercom.

"Yes, Summer? What is it?" Phaedra responded, rubbing her eyes to erase the visions swimming before her.

"You have a visitor in the reception area."

By habit, Phaedra checked her calendar. She wasn't expecting anyone. "I'll be right out, Summer."

Her suit jacket hung on the back of the chair. Phaedra tossed it around her shoulders, slipping her arms into the sleeves as she headed for the reception area. She didn't know who would be coming to see her unannounced. A referral, perhaps.

She came around the corner, hiding the secret hope that it was Bastien coming home early from his travels. Phaedra tried not to show disappointment when she found another Thibeadaux.

"Mr. Thibeadaux," she greeted Bastien's cousin Remy by holding out her hand to him. She couldn't imagine why Remy had come out to see her. In the times their paths had crossed at CT Inspectorate, he'd never given her any indication that he was concerned with anything she was doing out there.

"Phaedra." He stood up, smiling broadly, with arms outstretched. "Call me Remy. After all, as close as you and Bastien are, we're practically kissing cousins."

For a moment, Phaedra had the impression that he was going

to try to hug her. She couldn't control her reaction. Her back stiffened as he grasped her shoulders and yanked her to him.

"Sorry to come by unannounced, darlin'. But I was in the area so I thought I'd stop by. Do you have a few minutes to meet with me?"

Phillipa's board meeting wasn't until twelve. Phaedra still had plenty of time before she had to leave. "I'm sorry, Remy. This isn't a convenient time. I was just about to head out the door. I have another meeting I need to make," she lied.

"It'll only take a moment, and it's very important."

"Well…um…okay…a few minutes. Can I offer you anything? Coffee?"

"No, thanks. I'm good."

Phaedra doubted that. She withheld further judgment until he told her why he was there. "Right this way, Remy." She gestured, showing the way to her office.

"You have quite a setup here, Phaedra," Remy said, glancing around as they walked. "Love the decor. The light wood tones. Plush pile carpet. The tasteful, eclectic art. You and Jacie would have a field day redecorating Inspectorate."

"You came out all this way to chat about my decorating?"

"Is there a better way to get to know you?"

"Stick to business," Phaedra said sharply. All of her instincts warned her not to trust this man.

"Okay, then. Skipping the pleasantries and starting over. How many folks do you have on staff here?"

"Five permanent employees, a couple of interns and partnerships with several contractors depending on the need and the specialization."

"I guess I'd know that if I paid more attention during your visits to my office, wouldn't I, darlin'? I have to apologize for not giving you the attention…that is, support, that my cousins Chas and Bastien have been giving you. I've been under a lot of stress lately, Phaedra. Working a lot of long hours."

"Everyone at your company has been pulling long hours," she reminded him.

"Agreed," he said. "But we don't all have the same methods

of stress relief that my cousins seem to have. You're a hard-working woman."

"What is that supposed to mean?" Phaedra didn't like his tone or the implications hidden within it.

"What do you think I mean?" he countered, shrugging his shoulders and smiling at her.

She didn't trust his smile any more than she trusted those wrecker truck drivers who'd cornered her. He didn't mean her well.

"Can't a man compliment you?"

Not you, Remy. Phaedra didn't want anything from him. Not even worthless, pretty words.

"How can I help you, Remy?" She pressed him. Let him say what he had to say and get out. She didn't need to humor him anymore.

Remy lifted his hand, thoughtfully stroking his mustache before he answered. "I can see why Bastien's impressed by you. You don't mess around, do you? You get straight to the point."

"Excuse me if I'm abrupt. I am on a tight schedule this morning. I've already told you that."

"You can make time for me," Remy said with the kind of assurance that set her teeth on edge. Remy's eyes raked over her, pausing deliberately at the top button of her blouse as if staring at it could force it to come undone.

"What is it you want, Mr. Thibeadaux?" Phaedra snapped. "I won't ask you again."

"All right. I'll give it to you straight. I want you out of Inspectorate's business."

"Excuse me?"

"You heard me, darlin'. I want you gone. If you think you can come up in Inspectorate and usurp my authority, you've got another think coming."

"Your what?" Laughter bubbled up and came out before Phaedra could control her reaction. "Your authority? Trust me, there's nothing you have that I want."

"That's where you're wrong. I do have something you want. I've got Bastien. All I have to do is say the word and he's out of there. G-Paw won't tolerate another screwup from him."

The speed in which his personality shifted took Phaedra by surprise. She leaned back in her chair, gathering her emotions so that they would not escalate. "Bastien's not messing up," she said quietly. "Not anymore."

"You think not? Because you've come up in there and held a couple of funky little classes? Passed out a few kudos to his trifling, no good gold bricks and think that's going to fix it all?"

"What do you want from me, sir?"

"I want you to leave Bastien alone and go back to wherever it is you came from. Go screw with somebody else's head…or somebody else's cousin, as the case may be."

"I'm not leaving until the person or persons who signed that contract ask me and my associates to leave."

"You mean the contract you got by sleeping with Bastien?"

"That's a lie!"

"Which part is the lie, the part about you sleeping with him or the part about you getting the contract?"

"You're twisting it all to suit yourself. Manipulating events."

"And how is this different from what you've done? Your name isn't on the contract but you're calling the shots just the same. Davis is just your puppet. You're still getting your cut."

It didn't matter what she said to Remy. He was going to think what he wanted. Phaedra would never be able to change his mind. The mysterious "they" she had been so concerned about had finally sought her out.

"You'd do us all a favor if you took the money we've already given you, count it all good and take off. There's nothing more for you there. You've milked out of us all you're going to get."

Phaedra stared him down. It wasn't about the money. "I'm making a difference at CT Inspectorate. The numbers prove it. Accidents are down by thirty percent. Employee morale is up. Production is up. Bastien's area hasn't had a lost time accident in weeks."

"Well, maybe that's because he's stopped cutting corners. Afraid you'd catch him and cut off his supply of easy sex. Duh!" He slapped his head as if the idea just occurred to him.

Remy's words hit her hard.

"What did you say?" she gasped, feeling as if he'd just delivered a debilitating blow to her stomach. She couldn't breathe.

"You heard me every word I said. Although I can't say I blame Bastien though…mercy, mercy, mercy! Woman, you need to be ashamed of yourself!"

"Get out of my office." Phaedra didn't yell. She wanted him to know in no uncertain terms that she meant what she said. "Get out or I'll throw you out."

"What's the matter, sweetness? Truth a little too hard to take?"

"You're a liar." Phaedra confronted him.

"It's obvious you don't believe me. Maybe you'll believe him. From his own hands."

Remy reached inside of his jacket pocket and withdrew several folded sheets of yellow paper. He placed them on her desk, stabbing his index finger at them.

"You recognize these?"

She didn't pick them up but could tell by the color that they were duplicates of requisition forms. A two-part form. One color was the original. The other was submitted to Jacie for processing.

"Every one of them signed and submitted by Bastien himself. Every one of them requests for cheap, low-cost replacements for equipment and supplies. Cutting corners, honey. Just so you'll know…that employee with the cut on his hand? What was his name? Ah, yes. Eduardo! He might not ever have full use of it again. Never would have happened if Bastien had just authorized spending for gloves rated for poor Eduardo's job."

Phaedra didn't move. She wasn't going to let Remy see how upset she really was. She didn't believe him. Bastien wouldn't do that. He cared for his employees. She'd seen it in the way he spoke to them and spoke up for them.

"Go on, Ms. Burke-Carter. Take a look. Check the signature. I know you know it. Bastien's signed enough checks for you to recognize his handwriting."

Phaedra reached out, picked up the requisitions and scanned the line items. On the surface, the list seemed appropriate. But every now and then, an item jumped out at her. Equipment from companies who were under investigation for supplying faulty goods. Ear protection that wasn't adequate for the noise levels in his work environment. Eye protection without side shields. Fall arrest equipment known to snap and break loose.

All of those infractions she was made aware of at CT Inspectorate weren't a series of unrelated incidents but deliberate attempts to cut costs. According to those forms, all of these infractions were sanctioned by Bastien. How could he do something like this if he cared for his employees? Why would he bring her in as a consultant, knowing that she would eventually find out what he'd been doing? Did he think she was stupid? Or did he think she'd be so caught up with him that she would just let these gross violations slide?

The papers fell from her hands back to the desk. Dizzying nausea caused her stomach to roll. "These are direct violations."

"I see you know your regulations," Remy said quietly. "I'll bet you can cite, word for word, what the Occupational Safety and Health Administration says about what we, as a company, are required by law to provide. What Bastien failed to provide. Lover boy slipped up while he was slippin' it to you, darlin'! He was so preoccupied that he forgot to cover his tracks, and look what I found!"

"There has to be a logical explanation for this." Phaedra made the mistake of letting Remy see her falter. Tears rose to her eyes. They were tears of anger. Boiling anger because Remy was low enough to turn on his cousin. His family. Anger fanned by her moments of doubt and insecurity as she thought Bastien might have used her, just as her mother claimed all of those Thibeadauxs would eventually do. She didn't trust Remy, but she did trust her mother. The fact that both of them had come to the same conclusion and she could not made her feel foolish.

"Bastien hired you to keep himself out of hot water with G-Paw and with the Department of Labor. Even if the DOL did find these requisitions, he could turn around and point to you, a respected consultant, and parade you around in front of them. I guess he figured that if he did get caught, the fines wouldn't be so high since he had you to vouch for him."

Phaedra didn't believe Remy. Yet, the evidence lay in front of her. Those were Bastien's requisition forms and his signature. He must have known what he was purchasing and how it would affect his employees. If that were so, then her mother was right. Remy was right. It was all about money for those damned Thibeadauxs.

"So, now you know the truth," he continued. "What are you going to do about this?" Remy demanded. "You're obligated to report him."

"I should report you all," Phaedra snapped.

"Hey, I'm the one who brought this to your attention. You should pin a medal on my chest."

"Snitched on your own cousin, you mean."

"Better him under investigation than me. I'm not going down for his mistakes. He deliberately tried to get over to save a lousy dollar or two. Tsk-tsk. That's a damn shame what little value he puts on human life."

Rubbing her temples, the beginning twinges of a headache crept up Phaedra's neck and settled as throbbing points in her head.

"I don't believe this," Phaedra said.

"Believe it, darlin'. That's the real Bastien for you. Given some more time, you would have eventually figured it out. He's not worth your time." Remy leaned forward across the desk to place his palm against her forehead. "Poor, poor Phaedra. I'm so sorry that you're just one in a chain of fools for him. I would never treat you that way. I know how to treat a lady better than Bastien ever could."

"Don't you touch me!" Phaedra grabbed his hand, twisting his wrist in an automatic reflex that made him wince and pull back to relieve the pain.

Remy rocked back in his seat. "I didn't know you were so particular about who puts their hands on you."

"I've asked you once to leave. I'm not going to ask you again. Get out of my office."

"The same goes for you, Ms. Burke-Carter. If I see you sniffing around CT Inspectorate again—you or your associates—I'll report Bastien myself...and tell our friendly, understanding government watchdogs that you instructed him."

"No one will believe that!"

"Maybe not. But someone might. All it takes is one to get the rumor mill going. Who knows what that'll do to your reputation."

"Why are you doing this? What do you want from me?"

"I told you. I want you out of there. Leave CT Inspectorate alone. Let us handle our own affairs."

"So you can run to your grandfather with these lies? So he can put you over Bastien."

"I'm already over him. I'm the COO, the number two man around that camp. And that's the way it's going to stay."

"No," Phaedra denied, walking to the door and holding it open for him. "You might have the title at CT Inspectorate. You might even have G-Paw's ear. But you'll never, ever be over Bastien. You'll never have G-Paw's respect. Bastien's twice the man you are, Remy."

"He's breaking the law," Remy said. "And you're not turning him in. That makes you an accessory. You could go down, too."

"I could," she admitted. "But not because of you. Not for you…and not on you…and that's what's really getting to you, isn't it?"

"I pegged you as easy the moment I saw you," he sneered, sauntering past her.

"And I know exactly what you are. Now that we have that understanding, get out of my office. Go back to the hole you slithered out of, snake." Phaedra had never felt such malice toward anyone in her life. But Remy had roused up every protective instinct within her. She was not going to let him hurt Bastien.

It took everything Phaedra had in her, every ounce of restraint, to keep from slamming the door after Remy. She was glad that she didn't have her Taser handy. She would have used it and done so with vengeful gusto.

Phaedra looked around her office, turning her nose up in disgust. She imagined that he'd left a slime trail from her desk to the door. He deliberately left the papers on the desk, knowing that she would go through them, pore over them and try to find a logical explanation of how Bastien could have authorized such gross negligence. She was even willing to grasp at illogical ones.

Phaedra sat at her desk, and she read through each and every one of those requisitions. Remy was right about one thing. She did know Bastien's handwriting. She did recognize his signature. Could Remy have forged it? She'd grasped at that faint straw, hoping that, if she could prove an obvious forgery, Remy would be the one she could report. Not Bastien.

"What am I going to do?" Phaedra whispered aloud, rubbing her throbbing temples. What could she do?

Chapter 22

All Bastien wanted to do was duck into the office, file his paperwork and cut out again before anybody knew he was there. He didn't want to talk to anybody. He didn't want to have to deal with anybody else's issues. Just get in and do what he had to do and leave. He had other, more pressing, matters on his mind. It was Friday evening, just before shift change. If he timed it just right, he could get in, get out and nobody would even have to know that he was back in town.

While he was traveling, he made sure to call Phaedra every day. He didn't want a day to go by without letting her know that she was on his mind.

"Hey, Mr. B. I didn't expect to see you back so soon!"

Silvie, the receptionist, was shutting down her computer and gathering her purse as he came through the front door.

Bastien almost cursed. Silvie usually left early on Fridays. He put a fingertip against his lips.

"Shh!" he warned her. "You don't see me."

She grinned back. "It's only a quarter 'til five. You didn't see me tipping out a few minutes early, either."

He gave her a little wave and pushed on the double doors behind her, heading for his office.

"Oh…wait a minute, Mr. B, you should know that—"

"Later, Silvie," Bastien cut her off as the doors swung behind him. He could almost hear her calling him a rude son-of-a-something-or-other, but he wasn't in the mood for it today. If she had something about work for him, it would keep until Monday. He was gonna get out of his button-down shirt, necktie and starched khakis that had been his uniform while he was on the road. Then he would throw on some jeans and a spare shirt that he kept stashed in the office and head right over to Phaedra's. She wasn't expecting him until Sunday, but he couldn't wait that long to see her. He'd called her last night, and everything was fine. More than fine. But the last time he'd called to check on her around lunchtime, there was something different about her tone.

"Hello." When she'd answered, her voice was muffled and low. There was more conversation in the background that he couldn't quite make out.

"Did I catch you at a bad time, *cher?*"

"I was about to go into a meeting," she confessed.

That didn't surprise him. Phaedra was always either leaving a meeting or about to go into another. That woman spent half her life in the company of other people. He supposed he couldn't complain. The reason why he was with her now was because she'd agreed to take the meeting with him.

"Okay, I won't keep you. I just called to tell you that I was thinking about you."

"I understand," she responded in that neutral voice that let him know she wasn't free to talk. But it was more than just neutral. There was a different quality about her voice. She was positively frosty.

"Phaedra, is everything all right?"

Silence greeted him on the other end of the line, so he continued, trying to draw her out.

"You sound a little distracted, *cher.*"

"I'm having one of those days, Bastien."

"Sorry to hear that. I hope it gets better for you."

"So do I, Bastien. So do I."

"Call me later, if you get freed up," he urged her.

"I will," she said. "I have to go now."

"Phaedra?"

"Yes?"

"I miss you, *cher*. When I get back, there's something I want to talk to you about. Something really important. Okay?"

"Okay, bye."

She hung up, and he was left listening to a dial tone. She didn't even ask him what he wanted to talk to her about. That's when Bastien *knew* something was wrong. Something that was more than her being distracted with work.

He loved her. Truly loved her. Beyond what his flesh, his physical senses said he should. Being without her gave him a new perspective about their relationship. He didn't want anyone to question, doubt or criticize the fact that they were together. He wanted them to be solid, secure and sanctioned. And there was only one way to do that.

So he burned up the highway connecting Oklahoma and Texas. He'd called Phaedra only once more while he was on the road and he got her voice mail. Bastien didn't leave a message, hoping that his showing up on her doorstep would be a surprise. As he pushed open the door to his office, he patted his pants pocket and thought about what tiny packages big surprises come in. Tiny. Marquis cut. White gold. Simple. Classic. Elegant. Just like Phaedra.

"Remy?"

Bastien walked into his office and found his cousin standing behind his desk, rummaging through it.

"Bastien. Yo, man. When did you get back?"

"I just got back," Bastien said, dropping his duffel on the floor. "What're you doing in here, Remy? Can I help you with something?"

"Uh, yeah. I was just…um…you know…"

Remy was stuttering. Beads of sweat popped out on his forehead. Bastien knew when he started sweating and stuttering that the next thing to come out of his mouth was a lie. It was his giveaway. His tell.

"I was looking for some extra requisition forms." He finally managed to come up with something.

"Requisition forms?" That didn't even sound right to Bastien. If Remy needed extra forms, he could have gone to Jacie or Silvie or even Chas. Bastien didn't like him rifling through his stuff. He didn't have anything to hide. It was the principle of the matter. This was his office. His sanctuary. Even Chas didn't come in without Bastien's permission.

"Yeah…I need to put in an order for some…uh…you know, some things…and I was all out of forms. All I have are those old ones…and I thought that you might have kept some."

"Jacie usually keeps those," Bastien said. His eyes cut to his desk, with one of the drawers halfway pulled out. A couple of sheets of those two-part yellow-and-white forms were sticking out.

"Are those what you're lookin' for, Remy?" Bastien asked, pointing to the drawer.

"Yeah, but those aren't blank ones," he said.

"Don't see why not. There shouldn't be anything on them. I haven't put in any orders in weeks."

"You sure about that, B?" he asked, smiling at Bastien. Not so much a smile. A self-satisfied, smug grin on his face. Bastien was suspicious. Remy was the one who'd sat on Bastien's reqs for weeks, keeping him from getting what he needed for his people. It took Jacie doing an end-run around him and going straight to Chas to get Bastien's orders approved and processed.

"Positive. G-Paw froze my budget. I'm not spending any money."

"It wasn't all frozen. You got that woman up in here, spending money like crazy."

"All of it necessary, Remy," Bastien said tiredly. Damn! He didn't want to get into another pissing contest with him. Exactly why he wanted to come in quietly and not talk to anybody. He didn't want to have to deal with this mess. Not today.

"Uh-huh," Remy said in a tone that let him know he didn't believe a word he said. Bastien didn't care. He didn't have to. G-Paw and Chas had already approved the budget that would allow the consultants to continue their training. They were making a positive change in his workers. He'd pay out of his own pocket twice what Phaedra and her team were charging for those kinds of results. Not a single accident had occurred since she sent Logan out there to begin working with his employees.

Remy gave Bastien a cool nod then moved around the far side of the desk. Bastien walked around the opposite side, eyeing him as he sat down in his chair. Out of habit, he straightened the papers that Remy left scattered over his desk.

Bastien pulled out one of the requisition forms that Remy had said he couldn't use. The same careless clerical error that he'd corrected long before he went on this road trip was back again. Bastien recalled telling Jacie to make those changes. The safety glasses that were on this list weren't adequate for working around the chemicals in the lab. He'd made this change. How did it get back on the list?

Bastien reached for the phone, thinking that he'd give Jacie a call to talk about it, then stopped. He couldn't get sidetracked. He was supposed be getting cleaned up and then hurrying over to Phaedra's. This conversation could wait.

No. No, it couldn't wait. There was something more going on here than Jacie's slipup.

"Remy," Bastien called out to him. His cousin's hand was already on the door pulling it open.

"What do you want, Bastien?"

"I'm asking you the same question. What do *you* want?"

"What do you mean?"

"These reqs aren't mine, man."

"What are you talking about?"

"I said," he spoke slowly, distinctly, "these aren't mine. They couldn't be. Check the date. How am I gonna sign for something dated five days ago when I was on the road? This isn't a fax. This isn't an e-mail. It's an original. And it didn't come from me."

"I don't know what you're talking about."

"Don't play dumb with me, Remy!" Bastien snapped, balling up one of the bogus requisitions and hurling it at him. "I know my guys, know what they need. I have that catalog practically memorized. This crap that's on here is exactly that. Cheap, knockoff crap. I didn't order it. You did this!"

Remy knelt down, picked up the paper and smoothed it out. He folded it in half and shoved it in his pocket.

"Huh? Really?" He didn't look nearly as surprised as he pretended to sound. "Phaedra thinks that you did."

"What did you say?"

"I said…"

"No, I heard you. I just can't believe something that stupid would come out of your mouth."

"She found out that you've been deliberately shaving costs and putting your people at risk. I told her what you've been doing, and she's gonna make a report to the feds. She doesn't have a choice. She's obligated, Bastien. She's gonna make you go away."

The block of ice Bastien heard in Phaedra's voice the last time he spoke to her settled around his heart. It all made sense to him now. Her attitude. Her abruptness. Phaedra and her family were all about integrity in all business dealings. If she had seen these reqs, she *would* have been obligated to report them.

"Remy, what have you done?" Bastien's voice croaked, hoarse and unsteady.

"I told G-Paw that I wasn't gonna let you take my job, Bastien. You don't belong here. You haven't earned the right to be here."

"You're a lyin' bastard! You've been messing around with my employees. Putting them at risk. Ordering crap instead of the supplies that could have helped them. And for what? Money? You let them get hurt because you're worried I was gonna take something from you?"

"And you've just lost your job and your woman. Don't you worry none about it, pretty boy. I promise you. I'm gonna take real good care of both."

Bastien must've stared at Remy like he had a third eye growing in the middle of his forehead. He couldn't believe he was standing there and talking to him like he was a nothing that he could say and do anything to. Who did he think he was talking to?

Remy had pulled some low down dirty acts since Bastien had

been there. Some of them morally bankrupt but nothing illegal. Remy was sneaky, petty, vindictive and weak. But as long as he had G-Paw's ear, he was in charge.

Fine. Bastien could deal with that. As long as all of his energy was directed at him, he could handle it. He was a big boy and wouldn't go crying on anybody's shoulder. But this…this Bastien couldn't let go. Remy had crossed that line, turning his petty insecurities against Bastien's employees. The ones who only wanted to show that they would work and work hard. All they asked for was a chance to stand up and provide for their families.

What about Phaedra? How had he dragged her into this mess? What had Remy said to her to make her doubt him?

Naw. Hell, naw.

Bastien wasn't going to let him do that to him. To them!

Road weariness fell from him like water beading on a newly waxed car as a surge of adrenaline rushed through him. Bastien shot up from his chair, shoving the huge mahogany desk aside. Papers fluttered in the air like wing-clipped birds.

"You think you bad enough? Come on! Bring it!" Remy stood his ground, thumping his chest, taunting him as Bastien approached. He made the perfect target as Bastien dipped his shoulder and caught him right in the middle of his breastbone.

Remy and Bastien hit the wall so hard the drywall crunched, then cratered, as they collided. Hands clenched, Bastien grabbed two fistfuls of Remy's shirt and slung him around, through the open door, taking the scuffle from the privacy of his office out into the hallway.

Five o'clock. Shift change. Employees were there to witness his complete loss of control. All he could think was that if he let go of that bastard's shirt, the next step would be to wrap his hands around his scrawny neck and squeeze until his eyes bugged.

Remy had Bastien by his shirt, too, but Bastien had the height advantage and the longer reach. He lifted Remy up, slamming him against the wall, ignoring his curses. Bastien's right hand drew back, tightly coiled and primed to strike.

"Bastien!"

Two sets of hands grabbed him before he could do it. One on Bastien's right, one on his left. Chas was on the one on his right, had his hand on Bastien's forearm tugging, holding him back. "Come on, Bastien. Step off. Let him go!"

"Don't do it, boss."

Dennis Keagon stood at Bastien's left. He was the voice of reason in his ear, talking calmly to him to get through the fury that wasn't allowing him to think clearly.

"You can't do it, boss. You know what'll happen if you do, huh? That old man's gonna ship you out of here. If that old man fires you, I'm up next for the promotion. And I'm not ready for that yet."

"Five minutes," Bastien said through clenched teeth. "Look away for five minutes, Chas. That's all I'm asking. Give me five more minutes alone with Remy."

"And I'm telling you that you don't want to do this."

"Three minutes," Bastien bargained. "If you knew what he'd done, Chas, you wouldn't be sayin' that. You don't know what you're asking me to do."

"Yes. Yes, I do, Bastien. Believe me. I've been down that road you're going. You don't want to go there."

He could believe Chas. He knew exactly what Bastien was feeling. He'd put Remy in the hospital once before when he'd discovered for himself just how low he could be. Bastien's head turned, trying to catch Chas's eye. "Chas, he tried to—"

"I know," Chas interrupted him. He nodded once, emphasizing that he wasn't just placating his cousin. There was more to be said, but now wasn't the place or the time.

"You know? You heard us talking from Jacie's office?"

Chas shook his head no, applying pressure on his arm, encouraging him to lower it. "I wasn't in Jacie's office, Bastien. We were all in G-Paw's."

"All?"

"Yeah. Me, Jacie, G-Paw…and Phaedra."

Phaedra?

"Yes, Bastien. She's here. I think you'd better come back to G-Paw's office with me. We've got some things to talk about, and I don't want to do it out in the hall. All right? Can we do that? Take a walk with me?"

Chas kept talking, similar to the way a crisis intervention counselor talks a high-strung jumper down from a rooftop. Bastien took a deep breath, relaxing his arm, so that Chas would see he was getting through to him.

"Good." Chas didn't try hiding the relief in his voice as he patted Bastien on the back.

When Bastien stepped away from him, Remy scuttled away, tugging on his clothes. "You just saved his life, cuz."

"Remy, if you've got a lick of sense, you'll go and wait for us in G-Paw's office."

"Look, Chas, don't you—"

"Now, Remy! Move your narrow ass," Chas barked, looking for a moment like he was seriously considering turning Bastien loose on Remy again.

Chas stood there, waiting with Bastien in the hall until Remy passed them. Remy stared at Bastien, and Bastien glared back. All he needed was for Remy to give him the slightest excuse to go after him again.

As Remy continued on to G-Paw's office, Bastien leaned against the wall, his hands behind his back to keep from reaching out and punching Remy in the back of his head as he moved by. He wanted to. Oh, how badly he wanted to.

Chas then turned to Dennis. "What are you standing around here for? Get your crew together and get them out on the main line, Dennis. The yard's backed up with trains. Another one is due to push into the yard in less than an hour."

"Right away, boss. See you in a minute, Bastien," Dennis said backpedaling, pointing at him. He gave Bastien the look that warned him to keep his cool. Dennis then left through the swinging doors. Chas didn't say anything to Bastien until the doors stopped their back-and-forth motion and closed completely. "You all right now, Bastien? You cool?"

"I've had better days."

"Didn't we talk about this, Bastien? Didn't I warn you not to let Remy push your buttons?"

Bastien paced in the hall, rubbing his hand over his head in resentment. "I couldn't help it this time, Chas. This time, he stepped over the line. He—"

"I know what he did. What he's been doing."

"If you didn't overhear us in the office, how'd you find out?"

"Phaedra told us. That's one helluva lady you've got there, Bastien."

"Yeah, I know." Bastien stopped pacing, turning to Chas with a proud smile on his face.

"She really cares for you, Bastien," he continued.

"Does she?" He wasn't so sure. "I couldn't tell the last time I talked to her."

"What did she say?"

"It's not what she said but how she said it. I can't explain it. Made me think that she was slipping away from me. Like I was losing her."

"Is that why you've broken speed records getting back here to Houston?"

"When I talked to her, Chas, I just had this feeling, right here." Bastien slapped his hand against his stomach. "Had this feeling that something was wrong. That I had to come back. If I've lost us some business because of it, I'm sorry. But I'm not going to risk losing her over profit."

Chas said with confidence. "You're not losing her, Bastien. Whatever else was going on with her when you talked to her, she cares for you very much. That you can believe."

"Remy must have said something to her. Got to her. That's why she was acting like she did. Chas, we've got a good thing, but I know she still has her doubts about us. This happened kinda fast for us."

"Mind if I give you another piece of advice?"

"Go ahead."

"If what you two have is real, if you really care for her and she cares for you, then there isn't anything anyone can say to take that away from you. I don't care how long you've known her or how short a time. Love is love, and it's bigger than any lie Remy can concoct. If you love her and she loves you, then you'll work through it. Believe me, I know. Remy's pulled this crap before. He ran his best game, and she didn't go for it. She's too smart for that."

"You talking about Phaedra or Jacie?"

"Both," Chas admitted. "Remy has this bad habit of thinkin' every woman in the world belongs to him. He tried it with Jacie before we were married. It doesn't surprise me that he'd try it with Phaedra. He knows quality when he sees it. You've got some doubts about Phaedra? Don't. She wouldn't be here if that were the case."

"I didn't know she was here."

"We didn't know you were here, either, until I heard you bustin' up the place. If you're up to it, Bastien, why don't you come with me to G-Paw's office and see if we can't figure all of this out."

"All right," Bastien conceded. "But I'm warning you, Chas. If Remy says one more word to me, just one more word, not you, G-Paw or the whole second shift is gonna stop me from putting my foot so far up Remy's behind, he'll be flossing his teeth with my bootlaces."

"He probably needs a good whuppin'," Chas admitted. "I'm of a mind to hold him down for you. But get a grip on yourself, Bastien. Trust me. You don't want your lady to see you like this."

"I'm cool, Chas. I'm cool," Bastien assured him.

"Good man. Now, come on and let's get this straightened out so we can all get outta here."

Chapter 23

Chas had told them to wait in the office while he went to figure out what the commotion was all about. They all heard the unintelligible shouts in the hall. The raw, unfettered swearing. The thumps. The crashes. The thuds. Phaedra heard it and she instinctively knew. She knew Bastien was involved though she didn't expect him back in Houston until Sunday.

She got out of her chair, started for the door, but Jacie rested her small, soft hand on Phaedra's shoulder and gently guided her back to her seat.

"Wait," she cautioned. "We should wait."

"Let 'em work it out, missy," G-Paw advised. "Let the boys work it out."

"Haven't you been listening to anything I've told you?" Phaedra twisted in her chair and snapped at the old man. She'd just spent the past hour telling them how Remy had come to her office with that stack of lies, trying to convince her that Bastien was responsible for endangering his own employees. She told him how he'd threatened her and harassed her. This was more than boys-will-be-boys behavior. Remy was a menace.

Phaedra tried to remain calm and dispassionate as she impressed on them the seriousness of Remy's actions. She couldn't do it. She just couldn't stay calm. The more she thought of how he tried to poison what she'd found in Bastien, the more furious she became.

"I heard you, gal," G-Paw said. He stood up, leaning heavily on his cane. His face twisted in pain. G-Paw grimaced and gave a soft grunt as he stood and came over to her. He stopped beside Phaedra's chair, staring down at her. For a moment, she thought she saw something she never imagined she would ever see in his rheumy hazel eyes. Concern.

"I heard you," he repeated.

"Then do something about this," Phaedra insisted. "You can stop it."

G-Paw continued toward the door and stepped into the hall. With a strength that belied his frail body, he shouted in the hall. "Remy! Bastien! Chas! In my office. Now!"

Jacie looked over at Phaedra and winked. "Ooh, they're gonna get it now."

"You think this is funny?" Phaedra snapped at her. She didn't mean to turn on Jacie. Since she'd met her, she'd been helpful and kind to her. "I'm sorry." Phaedra immediately apologized.

"It's going to be all right, Phaedra," Jacie assured Phaedra. "We Thibeadauxs know how to handle our business."

"I'm starting to think that too much of handling your own problems is what causes these problems in the first place. You're all so busy trying to handle it yourselves and covering up your deficiencies that you don't realize how destructive your behavior is."

"Phaedra, perhaps you should calm down." Her tone lost some of its warmth. She was talking about the family she'd married into. Her husband. She wasn't going to let Phaedra, an outsider, malign her husband.

"Trust me, this is about as calm as I get when someone threatens me," Phaedra informed her.

Jacie pressed her lips together. "I see your point. Remy does tend to make you want to lose your sense of humor. I wasn't trying to make light of your situation. I just wish I'd had someone to help me when I was going through with those Thibeadaux men. It is a—" she looked toward the ceiling, searching her mind for the right word "—a challenge dealing with them. A challenge and a serious commitment. You're probably wondering right now if it's even worth putting up with the aggravation."

"You should take that mind reading act on the road."

"I'm not reading your mind." Jacie tapped her temple with her index finger. "Those thoughts have been rattling around in there for years. I can't make the decision for you. I can only tell you what I decided to do. The benefits of hanging in there with my Chas are beyond compare. If you want to know a secret," she leaned close and whispered, "Chas and Bastien are so much alike. They're cast from the same mold, Phaedra. They're both incredibly good men. As loyal and as loving as you'd ever hope to find." She winked again. "Their mamas raised them right. I guess two good Thibeadauxs out of three aren't bad odds."

"I'm not normally a gambling woman," Phaedra confessed.

"What changed your mind?" Jacie asked.

"Feeling in my heart as if I'd found a sure thing." Phaedra turned grateful eyes to Jacie and reached out to take her hand. She wasn't her enemy. She shouldn't have taken her anger out on her. Even Remy wasn't her enemy. Phaedra knew the kind of man he was and should have prepared herself better for it.

Phaedra was her own worst enemy for doubting her instincts, for doubting her ability to decide whether she wanted to be in a committed relationship with Bastien. She had hurt herself by second-guessing her heart.

Hands clasped and the beginning of self-conscious laughter was how Bastien found her and Jacie when he entered G-Paw Thibeadaux's office.

"How long have you been here?" he said as he started toward her.

"Have a seat, Bastien." G-Paw stopped him, pointing with his cane across the room to another chair. "You can belly up to your gal later. You, Chas, over there." He directed. "Remy, sit down right there."

G-Paw waited until they were all seated, not saying another word as he laboriously made his way back to his own chair. No one spoke. It was tensely quiet. They could hear every shuffle of G-Paw's feet across the floor. Every creak of his aching joints. Every wheeze from his fluid-filled lungs.

He sat down, pinning each of his "boys" with a hard stare before he asked, "What I want to know is, which one of you chuckle-headed pea brains has been givin' this lady here fits?"

Phaedra blinked, not sure if she'd heard him correctly. G-Paw never had a kind word for her. All of a sudden he had concern for her state of mind? Phaedra exchanged confounded glances with Jacie.

"Well now, don't everybody speak up at once. Remy?" G-Paw shone the spotlight of his displeasure on him.

"I don't know what the hell she's talking about. That bitch has lost her mind. Whatever she's told you is a lie."

Out of the corner of her eye, Phaedra saw Bastien rise from his chair, muttering under his breath. But she didn't need him defending her. Not from verbal assaults like that.

"Don't you ever, ever call me out of my name again, Remy. You came to my office looking for trouble? Well, you've got it now. More than you can stomach, I promise you." No idle threat. She meant it. Everyone in that room knew that she meant it, too.

"Did you go to Phaedra's office today, Remy?" Chas asked him. "And don't you lie to me. I know when you're lying."

"Yeah…yeah, I went to see her at her office," Remy confessed. He made a show of trying to look everyone in the eye to impress them with his sincerity. "I did it because I was worried about her."

"Oh, please. You are so full of it!" Phaedra exclaimed.

G-Paw held up his hand. "Hold on a minute. You've had your chance to say your piece, gal. Let him talk."

"Why would you have reason to be worried for her, Remy?"

Bastien interjected. "Why would you have reason to be even thinking about her?" There was more than animosity in Bastien's tone. It was raw with possessive jealousy.

"Because of you. And what you've been doing," Remy replied.

"And that would be what?"

"You know what. Don't play dumb. Or maybe that isn't an act. You are an idiot."

"This is getting us nowhere." Phaedra grew impatient with Remy's stalling. "Why don't you tell them how you brought me those requisitions, claiming they were Bastien's? Tell them how you told me he was responsible for his employees' accidents? How you insulted my integrity."

This time, Bastien couldn't be kept in his chair. He jumped up, the chair sliding back across the floor with an awful screeching noise that made Phaedra cringe.

"Wait a minute. Wait just a minute now! You misunderstood me!" Remy said, scrambling to get out of Bastien's way. "Phaedra, it was all a misunderstanding. Tell him," he suddenly pleaded as Bastien advanced on him.

"Sit down, Bastien!" G-Paw ordered. "You hear me, boy? I said take your seat. Damn it! I'm not gonna let you turn my company into a free-for-all!"

Bastien was past hearing or caring. In another second, he would be all over Remy. And Phaedra didn't think even his grandfather's viselike control of this family would stop him. As furious as she was at Remy, she didn't want Bastien to be charged with assault if he got to him.

"Bastien," she called his name softly, leaning forward and hoping that a change in pitch would get his attention.

He stopped in mid-stride, looking down at her. Jaw clenched so tightly, she thought he'd crack a molar.

"He's a liar, but not worth fighting," Phaedra offered her.

"He brought you requisitions from Inspectorate?" Bastien asked.

"I gave them to your grandfather. They're signed by you. But the items on the list are questionable."

"Let me see them."

G-Paw picked up the stack that Remy had left in Phaedra's office and passed them to Bastien.

"No…no, this is all wrong," Bastien said, tapping his hand against the paper as he read through them. "I changed these. I know I did. Remember, Jacie? You had me sign these the night that tanker exploded at the port."

Jacie stood up and read over his shoulder. "Not these," she said. "I initialed all the ones that you looked at, Bastien. This must be from that stack that I didn't get a chance to let you review. You told me to bring you all the ones that Remy had been sitting on because of the budget freeze. I didn't bring them to you because G-Paw said no more spending. There was no point."

"But these did come from Remy?" Bastien insisted. "He was the one who brought them to you to process?"

"You signed them," Remy pointed his accusing finger at Bastien. "Not my fault if you're too careless or too lazy to check them before they go out."

"You say one more word to me and I'm gonna knock your teeth down your throat, Remy," Bastien warned. "That's the last time I'm gonna tell you."

"What does it matter who signed what and when?" G-Paw asked. "What's all this fuss about?"

"What's the fuss all about? Mr. Thibeadaux, Remy told me that the employee who was injured…the one who sliced his hand…was wearing gloves that Bastien ordered. Cheap knockoffs that wouldn't protect him. That's what the fuss is all about. The disregard for your own employees' safety." Phaedra stated.

"Remy's a liar," Jacie said stoutly. "Everybody knows that. Whatever he told you about what Bastien did…or didn't do…was a lie, too. Possibly to get to you. Eduardo wasn't wearing gloves the day he sliced his hand with that box cutter," Jacie said specifically to Phaedra. "I should know. I was the one who rushed him to the emergency room to get stitches. That's what prompted Bastien to check into our PPE gear in the first place. That's when he first started the extra spending. He was trying to make sure that his folks had what they needed to do their jobs. I guess Remy didn't like what he was doing and decided to make a few adjustments to his purchases."

"Is that true, Remy?" G-Paw looked up at his nephew, his lower jaw working.

"I…I was only doing what you told me to, G-Paw. I was only handling my business. And now y'all want to gang up on me because I made this company a little money."

"Money? I'm so sick of hearing about you grubbing for another damned dollar!" Bastien turned his back on his grandfather, starting for the door.

"Bastien, where are you going?" Chas tried to intercept him.

Bastien pushed his cousin aside. "Don't know. Don't care. As long as it's out of here." Bastien swept up Remy and G-Paw in his indictment.

"Bastien," Phaedra began, reaching out to him.

But the look he turned on her was so frigid she couldn't believe that this was the same man. How could this be the same man who disregarded his own safety and shielded her from flying glass the night of the tanker explosion? Who was this man who turned away from her now?

Bastien looked back over his shoulder once, then flung open the door to G-Paw's office and retreated down the hall.

Phaedra sat there, physically and emotionally drained, gripping the chair's armrests until she couldn't hear his footsteps echoing in the hall anymore.

Jacie turned to her. "What are you sitting there for, Phaedra? Go after him," she urged.

"I don't think Bastien wants my company right now," Phaedra said, choking on tears that she didn't dare shed in front of them.

"Trust me," Jacie continued, "he doesn't want to be alone. He just doesn't want to be around us." She gave a fleeting look at Chas. A silent, secret moment passed between them, giving Phaedra the impression that there was a way of dealing with these Thibeadaux men that she hadn't quite gotten the hang of yet.

"Go on," Chas reinforced his wife's urging. "We'll handle this."

"Mr. Thibeadaux, if you please." Phaedra needed to address

G-Paw to impress upon him that he couldn't allow a greedy, un-scrupulous person like Remy to remain at the head of the company while Bastien, the essence of caring and commitment, walked out the door.

"Don't waste your breath on me." G-Paw waved Phaedra out the door, his manner no less gruff than all the other times he'd spoken to her, but his eyes gave her another message. Maybe she was starting to figure it out. His eyes told her clearly what she should be saving herself for. For what…and for who.

Chapter 24

Bastien was having second thoughts about his hasty exit, especially when the agonized look on Phaedra's face came to his mind. Still, how could he go back there after that? What was he going to do now? Pick up his job like nothing ever happened? Like his own blood kin didn't try to frame him? Put his employees in harm's way? Steal his woman? Why would he subject himself to something like that for another day?

"Bastien! Bastien, wait!"

Phaedra was calling him, but Bastien didn't stop walking or turn around to acknowledge that he'd heard her.

He stopped by his office long enough to pick up his duffel bag and cram in a few personal effects. He didn't have a plan now. His five-year plan was shot to hell.

All he knew was that he had to get out of there. Get out now and go where the pursuit of money wasn't an excuse for any type of lowdown behavior.

For years, he'd turned a blind eye to what was going on. He told himself that if he worked hard enough, kept his head down and earned his top-dog position, he could change the system. Chas and Jacie were good people; but they weren't interested in reining in Remy. Didn't care if G-Paw went around spouting off his poison. They were as happy as honeymooners, content to put in their day's work and hurry home to their private haven.

No...no, this isn't the place for me anymore. Bastien resigned himself. It was time to go.

Phaedra paused in the doorway, arms tightly clasped, gazing at him with those sad, dark eyes.

"Bastien," she called to him again. This time Bastien looked up at her but didn't stop his packing.

"What do you want?" He didn't care if he sounded ungracious. He needed distance. And it was going to start with her.

"I want to talk to you."

"Oh yeah?" he said, hard and sarcastic. Now she wanted to talk? After practically hanging up on him? What could she possibly have to say to him now? She was as bothered that Remy didn't care about the employees at Inspectorate as he was. Still, she'd let him get to her. She'd let him convince her that he was a part of it. The plain truth was, she didn't trust him.

"Yeah," she said, imitating his harsh tone. Bastien felt himself sinking further into despair. They didn't talk to, or at, each other like that. Even on their worst days, they tried to remain thoughtful, respectful.

"Give me a minute, Bastien. A minute of your time to listen to me." Her pleading tone got his attention. He stopped packing.

He sat in his chair, spread his arms and said, "Fine. Talk. Sixty seconds. The clock's ticking. Go!"

"I'll talk only if you promise to listen to me. Really listen to what I have to say."

"I'm listening."

"No," she contradicted. "You aren't. Not with this." She pointed to her heart. "Otherwise you wouldn't be so angry with me."

"I'm not angry," Bastien lied.

Phaedra stepped into the office, stepped over the mess left on the floor by his tantrum. She came in, ignoring the guest chairs and instead perched on the corner of the desk, where she could be close to him. She crossed her legs and clasped her fingers over her knee.

Bastien couldn't help it. His eyes were immediately drawn to her long, stocking covered legs. He forced himself to raise his eyes, keep them trained on her face. She wasn't going to get him distracted so easily. Not this time.

Keep your eyes on her face, Bastien. He warned himself. But he was already starting to feel the familiar tug on his groin that told him even in his anger, he wanted to hold her.

"You didn't know Remy was changing your requisitions, did you?" It wasn't really a question from her. There was certainty in her tone.

"You had the chance to ask me that this morning when I called you," Bastien pointed out for her. "When you knew what Remy was trying to do. Why are you asking me now?"

"I'm performing due diligence and confirming what I already knew," she insisted. "I'm asking you to make sure that you know that I knew that you didn't know." After making that statement, she smiled and sort of shook her head, as if she couldn't follow that convoluted sentence herself.

"God, this makes my head hurt," Bastien said, rubbing his temples. "No, Phaedra. I had no idea. Not really. Jacie brought some of those reqs to me. I caught the errors and corrected them. I thought they were clerical errors. I know what my employees need and how to get it for them. I wouldn't do that."

"I believe you, Bastien," she said, releasing her legs and leaning forward to clasp his hands in her hers. She gave him a reassuring squeeze.

"You believe me? No, you don't, Phaedra! You don't believe me."

Bastien jerked his hands out of hers, even though her touch immediately started his heart racing. At that moment, he wished she didn't affect him so. Wished that he had an immunity to her touch. That woman got to him. She always could. And as he looked into her dark eyes, he feared—and hoped—that she always would.

"How could you say that, Bastien? I wouldn't have come

here, bringing this matter to your family's attention, if I didn't believe you. I came here to defend you…to stand up for you! Why would I do that if I didn't believe you? I didn't know if the others were all aware of what Remy was doing. I didn't know if they'd sanctioned it or turned a blind eye. I came here not knowing what I'd walked into. I did it anyway. I did it for you."

Shadows of doubt crossed his face.

"Then why wouldn't you talk to me the last time I called you. You sounded so cold. Something was wrong. I could feel it. You'd never sounded like that before. When I found out what Remy was doing and he told me how you were going to report me, I thought he'd turned you against me."

"Bastien, when you called me, I was just about to go into another meeting. I told you that."

"Something about this was different. You were different. You hung up on me, *cher*."

"Of course I was upset, Bastien! I'd just learned that a longtime friend of the family had terminal cancer. She was stepping down from a cabinet position in the Burke-Carter Foundation. Yes, I was angry that Remy had come to my office with those lies. But I'd put that behind me to focus on my family. Whatever it was you thought I was thinking or feeling when we last spoke had nothing to do with you or your family. You just caught me at a bad time. If I hurt you, I apologize. But as I recall, you've had one or two of those bad moments yourself. I didn't take it personally when you had to rush me off the phone…or cut our visits short. I didn't assume that your feelings for me…whatever they are…had changed."

"But Remy—" Bastien began his protest.

"Oh, Remy can go take a flying leap! I'm talking about us. You and me. Do you remember how powerful our first meeting was? How instantly we connected? When I came to Inspectorate, I went in with my eyes and my heart wide open. I didn't listen to my head. I followed you with my heart, because I believed in you, I trusted you…I love you, Bastien!"

She lowered her eyes, biting her lip as if she couldn't believe that she'd let the words slip.

Bastien reached out, lifted her chin, scrutinizing her face. Phaedra had a perfect poker face. Not this time. This time her emotion was fully out there for Bastien to see.

"You love me?"

"Yes." She nodded. As he held her chin between her finger-tips, he watched her eyes form dark pools. Eyelids fluttered, sending two glistening tears streaking toward his hand. "Yes, Bastien. I love you…I've been in love with you since I was a silly college girl."

"Oh, *cher*…" Slipping out of his chair, and falling to his knees in front of her, he buried his head in her lap. "I thought I'd lost you."

"The only one who's lost is Remy," she said sadly. Phaedra stroked his hair, soothing him. "I almost feel sorry for him."

Bastien lifted his head to look at her. "Don't waste your pity on him."

"I won't," Phaedra said. "If you tell me that you love me, too, Bastien."

Planning wasn't Bastien's strongest character trait. He was the first to admit that he was headstrong and often went off half-cocked. And if he'd thought about it more, planned it better, he probably wouldn't have proposed to Phaedra like that. Not in the middle of his office. Not in the middle of that mess. Not in the aftermath of all that turmoil. He would have done it at the beach house. Back where he realized that she was the woman he wanted.

But where Phaedra was all logic and practicality, he was impulse and instinct. He couldn't have picked a more perfect moment to show her that he wanted nothing less from her than total commitment.

Reaching into his pocket, Bastien pulled out the gift box that he'd purchased before leaving Houston for his road trip.

"What this?" she asked as he placed the box in her hand. Phaedra stared at it as if she were too afraid to open it.

"You gonna stand there looking at it all day?"

"Bastien…I…." Phaedra hesitated.

"Fine. I'll do it myself." Bastien took the initiative and lifted the lid off the purple velvet ring box. Nestled against a backdrop of gold silk, the engagement ring that he had custom-designed caught the light and sparkled. As enticing as the ice was, it couldn't compare to the light in Phaedra's eyes as he slipped it on her finger.

"This isn't how I was gonna originally propose to you, Phaedra. Not without flowers. Or romantic music. Not even a bottle of champagne to toast," he whispered to her. "But I'm asking you anyway. Will you marry me?"

"I don't need all of that!" she cried out, flinging her arms around his neck. "All I need to know is that you love me, Bastien. If you love me, really love me, then the answer is yes! Of course it's yes!"

Bastien hugged Phaedra. Holding tightly to her and thanking his blessings for second chances.

"Hrrrumph! Such a tender moment."

G-Paw stood in the open doorway. Bastien didn't know for how long. He didn't care. Nothing he could say to him would get to him now.

"I guess that means I need to get used to seeing you around here more often now, don't I, gal?"

G-Paw didn't address Bastien, but directed his comments at Phaedra. "That makes sense. Bastien will be spending a lot more time up here since I've cut Remy loose. What about it, boy? You think you're ready to take the helm as my chief operations officer?"

"Bastien!" Phaedra gasped in surprise. "You—"

Bastien interrupted her, standing to position himself between her and G-Paw.

"No, G-Paw, I'm not."

"It's a really big promotion. You should think about it."

"She's agreed to be my wife," Bastien confessed, glancing at Phaedra for confirmation. "But she won't have to be around here. Not around you or Remy. There won't be any reason for her to be…because I won't be here."

"Bastien," Phaedra murmured. "What are you talking about?" She squeezed his hand. A nonverbal question. Did he know what he was doing? Was he sure about this?

"I've had it, Phaedra. I'm through. I'm done. Done with this job. Done with those people."

"Those people?" G-Paw rasped, incredulous. "Your people. Your kinfolk. Your flesh and blood."

"People who cared anything about me wouldn't do anything to hurt me…or the people I care about. My employees. My woman. No, G-Paw. Remy was right about one thing. I don't belong here."

"Bastien, you can't walk out on your employees. They need you." G-Paw pressed the one tender spot that would have made him reconsider.

Stubbornly, Bastien shook his head. "They don't need me, G-Paw. If you won't go back on your word, with Remy out of the way, they won't have to worry about being held back. And if there's anything you've shown me, it's that you are a man of your word. You do exactly what you say you're going to do."

"I need somebody to work this division, Bastien. Chas can't do it all."

"I've already got somebody in mind for the job. Dennis Keagon's a good man. He's up for a promotion. He's ready for running the second shift crew. And you've already seen what Alonzo Benavidez can do to keep the first shift running tight. I won't go before I've given both the benefit of everything I know. But know this, old man, I'm not hanging around here any longer than I have to."

"I don't want anybody running this company but a Thibea-daux," G-Paw declared. "That's the way it is. That's the way it's always gonna be. Where will you go, Bastien?" G-Paw actually sounded concerned. Bastien didn't trust him. That old man was crafty and manipulative. He'd taught Remy all that he knew as well.

Bastien shrugged. He hadn't thought that far ahead. At the moment, he was running full speed on instinct and intuition.

"I have the perfect job for you." Phaedra stood next to him. "A seat on my family's board of directors at the Burke-Carter Foundation." She smiled at him. "I'll just have to tell my mother that we're a package deal."

G-Paw made his way into Bastien's office. "I'm gonna be sorry to see you go, son," he said.

"Don't you worry none, G-Paw. Dennis and Alonzo will keep

the contracts and the money flowing in. You won't lose any profit."

"That ain't exactly what I mean, boy," he said. "I wanna be the first to congratulate you two. Maybe, if I can't have you here, I'll wait for Chas's boys…or, maybe you need to start having babies early, gal."

"Thank you, Mr. Thibeadaux." Phaedra graciously accepted his offer of peace. "I'll give your offer serious consideration." She held her hand out to him; but G-Paw stepped closer, awkwardly embracing her. Bastien wasn't ready to go there with him yet. He dipped his head in a curt nod, acknowledging him and dismissing him at the same time.

"He's so sad," she whispered, her heart going out to him, as he shuffled out the door. "Such a lonely old man."

"More like pathetic," Bastien retorted.

"I don't think he has long for this world, Bastien. Maybe you should reconsider leaving. At least go reconcile with him. Make peace with your grandfather before it's too late. You'll regret it if you don't."

"That old man will not only be around to dance at our wedding but he's mean enough to be around to dance on our graves!"

"Bastien." She chastised him.

"I'm going, I'm going. Tell me, *cher,* is this the way you're going to boss me around after we're married?"

"And you'll love every minute of it, too," she declared, rising on tiptoe to kiss him. She disengaged, sending him with a gentle shove in G-Paw's direction. "Go, on! Handle your business."

Epilogue

Right in the middle of the lane, the ball switched directions, cutting sharply to the left, on an unstoppable collision course with the lead pin. Bastien didn't even watch it fall. He knew it was a strike the moment it left his fingertips.

"Whoo-whee! That boy's hot tonight!" Solly shot up out of his seat, raising his hand for a high five. In mid-slap, he drew his hand back, pretending to shy away from his friend's sizzling hand.

Bastien looked over at Phaedra and winked. She pretended to ignore him, nudging Jacie with her elbow.

"Oh, I bet he thinks he's the stuff because he's made three strikes in a row," Jacie grumbled, turning up her nose and sticking her tongue out at Bastien.

"Now, now, Jacie. Be nice. It's all for a good cause," Chas reminded her. "What does that make now? Five thousand you've raised for the food pantry, Bastien?"

He wasn't really keeping score but Phaedra was. This charity bowl-a-thon was Bastien's first big event as part of the Burke-

Carter Foundation. He'd been planning it for months after she learned that there was such a passion in his old stomping grounds for the game. Up and down the bowling alley at Solly's Fast Lanz, almost every lane was occupied by participants in the charity event. Not bad for his first time out of the gate. Bastien couldn't resist bragging just a little bit. Still, he knew he couldn't have pulled it off completely without Phaedra's support. She knew how to work her contacts for pledges, organize transportation to the event and get local media coverage.

"You're up, Jacie. Bowl a strike for me," Phaedra said, shifting uncomfortably in her chair with an audible groan.

"You all right, Phaedra?" Jacie turned a concerned look to her sister-in-law.

"I'm fine…I'm fine," she said, grimacing, then smiling when Bastien started toward her. "No, you stay over there, Bastien! Guys against the girls, remember?"

"Maybe if I came over there, *cher,* some of my luck will rub off on you." Proudly, possessively he placed his hand against her swollen stomach and rubbed in small, circular motions to soothe the child squirming impatiently inside her.

So much for his five-year plan. Bastien was happy to adjust his goals. Within the second year of being married to Phaedra, they were already expecting their first child.

"Seems to me that there's been too much rubbing around here already." G-Paw observed from his seat at a nearby table. "I'm up to my ears in you good-for-nothin' Thibeadauxs and you keep poppin' out more like it's goin' out of style."

Bastien looked back at the old man and could do nothing but laugh. His prediction had come true. That stubborn old man had not only danced at his wedding but argued Bastien down when he wanted to cut in on that old man's monopolizing of Phaedra. He had a new kidney and a new lease on life. He would be around for many years yet.

Maybe that isn't so bad, after all, Bastien mused. That mean old man had taught him many lessons. Not all of them he wanted to learn, but learn from him Bastien did. And, if he really thought about it, he had to grudgingly thank that old man. If it weren't for G-Paw guiding him, shaping him, even at times manipulating him, Bastien might still be in New Orleans, living a life that was never meant for him. Never having the chance to find Phaedra again. Helluva roundabout way to get to that point in his life. But there he was. There they *all* were.

Bastien hadn't completely cut all ties to Inspectorate. He kept checking in on Dennis and Alonzo. Checking in with family. Chas. Jacie. G-Paw. Making sure that Remy stayed in check. After all, he was a Thibeadaux. And like it or not, CT Inspectorate was his legacy, too. He had just as much responsibility to see that it remained strong. With the coming of his own child, he had both responsibility and reason.

Leaning down, he placed a tender kiss on Phaedra's stomach and grinned when Phaedra grimaced again. Her stomach shifted and rolled.

"I think she knows you're here," Phaedra said, placing her hand on either side of her stomach. "She won't stop squirming."

"She?" Bastien repeated. "No, I think that's a boy. Another bad-assed little Thibeadaux boy."

"Heaven help us if that's true," Phaedra replied.

They'd deliberately avoided learning the sex of the baby, wanting to keep it a joyous surprise until the end. Not knowing was all right with Bastien. Either way, it would be a Thibeadaux—destined for this legacy of loyalty and love.

* * * * *

Lesson #2:
Passion is sweeter the second time around…

Sweet Deception

National Bestselling Author

ROCHELLE ALERS

For Myles Eaton, forgiving Zebrina Cooper for marrying another man has been easier than forgetting their passion. Now she's back, carrying secrets. And she has one summer to convince Myles he's the only man she's ever loved.

For generations, the Eaton family has been dedicated to teaching others. Now siblings Belinda, Myles and Chandra are about to get some sexy, surprising lessons in love.

Coming the first week of December 2009 wherever books are sold.

KIMANI™
ROMANCE

www.kimanipress.com
www.myspace.com/kimanipress

KPRA1401209

Ten years.
Eight grads.
One weekend.
The homecoming
of a lifetime.

TENDER TO HIS TOUCH

Essence
bestselling author
ADRIANNE BYRD

The final book in the
Hollington Homecoming series.

Beverly and Lucius are each looking for a hot hookup at their
ten-year college reunion. They've both been burned by love, but a
"no strings" affair sounds just right. *Until* Beverly starts arousing
feelings that make Lucius long to turn their sizzling affair into a
lifetime of passion. Can he prove to this unforgettable woman
that there is life—and love—after college?

Hollington Homecoming:
Where old friends reunite…
and new passions take flight.

HOLLINGTON
HOMECOMING

KIMANI™
ROMANCE

Coming the first week of December 2009
wherever books are sold.

www.kimanipress.com
www.myspace.com/kimanipress

KPAB1411209

Once, she belonged to him—body and soul.

His PERFECT MATCH

Fan-Favorite author

Elaine Overton

Years ago Elizabeth Donovan made the biggest mistake of her life—leaving Darius North standing at the altar. Now she's desperate, and only Darius can help. Darius has never forgiven her for her cruel behavior, but he agrees to help... for a price. He wants the honeymoon they never had!

"Very entertaining and thought-provoking."
—*RT Book Reviews* on *Sugar Rush*

Coming the first week of December 2009 wherever books are sold.

KIMANI™ ROMANCE

www.kimanipress.com
www.myspace.com/kimanipress

KPEO1431209

REQUEST YOUR FREE BOOKS!

2 FREE NOVELS PLUS 2 FREE GIFTS!

KIMANI ROMANCE ™

Love's ultimate destination!

YES! Please send me 2 FREE Kimani™ Romance novels and my 2 FREE gifts (gifts are worth about $10). After receiving them, if I don't wish to receive any more books, I can return the shipping statement marked "cancel." If I don't cancel, I will receive 4 brand-new novels every month and be billed just $4.69 per book in the U.S. or $5.24 per book in Canada. That's a savings of over 20% off the cover price. It's quite a bargain! Shipping and handling is just 50¢ per book.* I understand that accepting the 2 free books and gifts places me under no obligation to buy anything. I can always return a shipment and cancel at any time. Even if I never buy another book from Kimani Press, the two free books and gifts are mine to keep forever.

168 XDN EYQG   368 XDN EYQS

Name	(PLEASE PRINT)	
Address		Apt. #
City	State/Prov.	Zip/Postal Code

Signature (if under 18, a parent or guardian must sign)

Mail to The Reader Service:
IN U.S.A.: P.O. Box 1867, Buffalo, NY 14240-1867
IN CANADA: P.O. Box 609, Fort Erie, Ontario L2A 5X3

Not valid to current subscribers of Kimani Romance books.

Want to try two free books from another line?
Call 1-800-873-8635 or visit www.morefreebooks.com.

* Terms and prices subject to change without notice. Prices do not include applicable taxes. Sales tax applicable in N.Y. Canadian residents will be charged applicable provincial taxes and GST. Offer not valid in Quebec. This offer is limited to one order per household. All orders subject to approval. Credit or debit balances in a customer's account(s) may be offset by any other outstanding balance owed by or to the customer. Please allow 4 to 6 weeks for delivery. Offer available while quantities last.

Your Privacy: Kimani Press is committed to protecting your privacy. Our Privacy Policy is available online at www.eHarlequin.com or upon request from the Reader Service. From time to time we make our lists of customers available to reputable third parties who may have a product or service of interest to you. If you would prefer we not share your name and address, please check here. ☐

KROM09

Essence **Bestselling Author**

GWYNNE FORSTER

Out of affection and
loneliness, Melinda Rodgers
married a wealthy older man.
Now a widow at twenty-nine,
she must remarry within the
year or lose her inheritance.

As executor, handsome
Blake Hunter insists Melinda
carry out the will's terms. And
judging by the dangerous,
unfulfilled yearning that's
simmered between them
for years, Blake may be the
man to bring her the most
passionate kind of love…
or the most heartbreaking
betrayal.

SCARLET WOMAN

"A delightful book romance lovers will enjoy."
—*RT Book Reviews* on *Once in a Lifetime*

*Coming the first week of December 2009
wherever books are sold.*

www.kimanipress.com
www.myspace.com/kimanipress

KPGF1691209

Have you discovered the Westmoreland family?

NEW YORK TIMES AND *USA TODAY*
BESTSELLING AUTHOR

BRENDA JACKSON

*Find out where it all started
with these fabulous 2-in-1 novels.*

On Sale December 29, 2009
Contains: *Delaney's Desert Sheikh*
and *Seduced by a Stranger* (brand-new)

On Sale January 26, 2010
Contains: *A Little Dare*
and *Thorn's Challenge*

www.kimanipress.com
www.myspace.com/kimanipress

KPBJW10SP

HELP CELEBRATE
ARABESQUE'S
15TH ANNIVERSARY!

2009 marks Arabesque's 15th anniversary!

Help us celebrate by telling us about your most special memories and moments with Arabesque books. Entries will be judged by the Arabesque Anniversary Committee based on which are the most touching and well written. Fifteen lucky winners will receive as a prize a full-grain leather duffel bag with the Arabesque anniversary logo.

How to Enter: To enter, hand-print (or type) on an 8 ½" x 11" plain piece of paper your full name, mailing address, telephone number and a description of your most special memories and moments with Arabesque books (in two hundred [200] words or less) and send it to "Arabesque 15th Anniversary Contest 20901"—in the U.S.: Kimani Press, 233 Broadway, Suite 1001, New York, NY 10279, or in Canada: 225 Duncan Mill Road, Don Mills, ON M3B 3K9. No other method of entry will be accepted. The contest begins on July 1, 2009, and ends on December 31, 2009. Entries must be postmarked by December 31, 2009, and received by January 8, 2010. A copy of these Official Rules is available online at www.myspace.com/kimanipress, or to obtain a copy of these Official Rules (prior to November 30, 2009), send a self-addressed, stamped envelope (postage not required from residents of VT) to "Arabesque 15th Anniversary Contest 20901 Rules," 225 Duncan Mill Road, Don Mills, ON M3B 3K9. Limit one (1) entry per person. If more than one (1) entry is received from the same person, only the first eligible entry submitted will be considered. By entering the contest, entrants agree to be bound by these Official Rules and the decisions of Harlequin Enterprises Limited (the "Sponsor"), which are final and binding.

NO PURCHASE NECESSARY. Open to legal residents of U.S. and Canada (except Quebec) who have reached the age of majority at time of entry. Void where prohibited by law. Approximate retail value of each prize: $131.00 (USD).

VISIT **WWW.MYSPACE.COM/KIMANIPRESS**
FOR THE COMPLETE OFFICIAL RULES

KP15ARACONTEST